Two Trees

Publisher's Press

Printed and bound in the United States of America.

This book is dedicated to my wife, Sheryl, who sold her home so I could buy violin wood.

Chapter 1: Richard

$\mathcal{T}$he applause engulfed the concert hall and it surged to an almost deafening level when Richard Gaspar returned to the stage for his third, and final encore.

'Almost deafening' was the determining factor for Richard as he took his long, sweeping strides back across the glowing, hand-rubbed hardwood floor with his violin under his arm and his bow in his hand. Many great virtuosi had performed upon this stage over the past hundred and fifty years and this was not Richard Gaspar's first time.

"No more than three encores tonight," Richard told himself. "More than three this evening would come across as arrogance. I must wait until the audience unanimously decides it and 'all' the critics say the right words."

Richard Gaspar had plenty of arrogance, but his training and many years of performing in the public spotlight had enabled him to use it to obtain his goals, without tarnishing his image.

"Someday it will be four encores, then five," he mused as he smiled and squinted his eyes against the glaring lights so he could see the vast, cheering crowd.

Richard's smile grew larger as he briskly drew to a stop at center stage by the conductor, in front of all the other talented musicians that had accompanied him that evening. There he faced his admirers head-on in the middle of the spotlight and took his bows.

He looked magnificent in his black, French-cut tails. A tall, distinguished gentleman of thirty-four with an obvious European pedigree, complete with olive skin and wavy, jet-black hair.

His eyes were dark and captivating, while his sparkling white teeth could be seen from the back row. His smile came across as a mischievous grin to some in the audience, but to most, especially his loyal female admirers, it was daring and exciting.

His entire image was striking and his features could be considered almost perfect, except for two large scars that ran across his left cheek. But the deep scars only seemed to give him an aura of danger and mystique; adding even more to the intrigue and his popularity with the women.

Richard was exhilarated. He was in his element, standing in the blinding spotlight, bowing to the large, cheering crowd that filled the old, classic-style concert hall to capacity. He knew that some in the audience had paid very dearly to hear him perform tonight and he mouthed the words, "Thank you," for many different reasons as he lowered himself and closed his eyes.

Richard took in a full, deep breath as he raised back up. He seemed to take in the applause along with the air he breathed. Then he paused just long enough to wink at the governor's enthralled, fourteen-year-old daughter sitting in the front row. She smiled back up at Richard with a blush, then she closed her eyes and fell back into her seat with a sigh.

Richard knew the games to play and the fine lines to walk as a seasoned, veteran performer, and he loved to play them and walk them to their very limits.

Richard constantly monitored the music and art world reviews and he knew right where he was on the ladder of success, though he placed himself just a few rungs higher than most of the critics put him. But, by either standard, he was near the top and still moving up.

He also knew that he had to keep climbing so he could continue to draw the large crowds and receive all the financial benefits that came with them.

As Richard held his violin and looked into the crowd, he remembered the words, "Never go back, always go forward, then just keep on going."

They were the words of Carl Reber, his last violin teacher. Carl was responsible for most of Richard's success as a solo artist and Richard now lived by every word Carl had told him over the years.

He had motivated Richard far more than any other teacher could have. Carl was possessed with an unbelievably, relentless driving force and he had successfully passed it on to Richard before he died.

Carl had also told Richard, "The audience needs to feel more than just satisfied when you take your last bow, but you must do it in a way that leaves them wanting more. Then someday, when they least expect it, give them 'more'."

When Carl said the words, he would hold up his right hand in a tight fist and shake it in front of Richard. He would always finish with his eyes gleaming and his voice deepening with determination, "Then you will 'own' them."

"One of my best performances," Richard thought to himself as he raised up again to face the sold-out crowd whose applause was finally starting to dwindle.

Richard looked out into the faces of the audience, and he couldn't help himself. He swung his long, outstretched arm around to the symphony and conductor one more time, prompting yet another surge in the applause; which of course, he took for himself.

The violinists all looked up when he turned their way. Some of them looked at him with forced smiles, while others perceptibly rolled their eyes, but they still politely applauded him for a third time.

"They wish they were me," Richard told himself as he reminisced about the almost impossible passages he had played flawlessly that night.

Richard knew that the musicians didn't 'really' wish they were him, but he also knew that every one of them wished they could 'play' as well as he, and to Richard that was just as good.

"The violists played flat tonight," he thought to himself as his eyes followed his outstretched arm around the stage from section to section.

Then his smile got bigger and he almost laughed out loud when he looked at them and thought of his favorite viola joke...

"An ambitious young man was determined to learn the mysterious secret of the greatest living violist. He followed the old virtuoso from concert to concert, listening to the old master play. He even secretly followed him from hotel to hotel and restaurant to restaurant, trying to find out what no other violist had ever been able to learn from him.

"While watching the old man backstage, he discovered that before every performance the virtuoso would pull the left lapel of his jacket away from his body and look inside. Then he would instantly beam with confidence, pick up his viola, walk out on stage and play better than any of his contemporaries believed possible.

"The young man followed him even more desperately now, trying to get a peek inside the jacket. Performance after performance he would sneak backstage, but the jacket was always in the old man's possession as though it were his life's blood.

"Then it happened; on a very hot evening during intermission, the virtuoso removed his jacket and set it on his case just before he was called away with an emergency phone call. The young man instantly ran over with his hands trembling as he picked up the jacket and looked inside.

"It was then that he learned the great secret. An old, tattered card stapled to the lapel had the words written upon it...

"VIOLA, left hand. BOW, right hand."

Richard suppressed another chuckle when he finished thinking about the joke. Then he eyed the huge 17-1/4" Gaspar Da Salo in the principal violist's hands and he knew very well that none of the viola jokes were true.

Richard had learned to play both the viola and the cello as part of his training. He remembered well how his left hand and fingers had to stretch to reach the notes. It still amazed him what a difference just a few extra millimeters in the length of a string really made when performing difficult pieces.

No, he knew they were good. But the jokes were still funny anyway, and he smiled as his arm continued to swing around the symphony toward the cellos.

"The cellos were too loud," Richard thought to himself, and his expression turned a little stern.

He had played with his bow almost on top of his violin's bridge most of the night trying to get more volume out of it. Then, when the cellos came in during the third movement, he pushed down so hard that the stick was in the middle of the horse hair and rubbing against the strings just so his violin could compete with their large, booming voices.

But Richard's face softened a little as he thought about how wonderful their 'booming voices' really were.

He looked at the rows of dedicated musicians holding their large, majestic instruments in front of them and he remembered just how much he loved cellos. He 'could' forgive them, if he only had a violin with a voice that could carry above theirs to the back of the hall.

"Soon," he thought to himself, "very soon."

Still, tonight was good and 'he' was good, so Richard Gaspar switched his violin and bow to his left hand and he congratulated the conductor one last time.

Then, after a smile and a small bow to the conductor, he briskly turned back toward the audience to take in one more round of applause before he waved good-bye and exited stage left.

Chapter 2: Michelle

The press and many of Richard's fans began to gather in the hall before he reached the dressing room where he had warmed up before the concert. He gave them a quick glance and paused just long enough with his best photographic smile for a few flashes to go off, then continued over to the table where his smooth, black leather case lay waiting for him.

If there had been anything other than his precious violin in his hand, Richard may well have dropped it when he flinched.

"Is it really her?" Richard asked himself, as he looked back toward the crowd again.

"It can't be!"

But there she was, standing and talking with the critics and reporters, just as excited and energetic as ever. She was faced the other way, but he could still tell that it was her. She was even wearing the same summer dress with her shoulder length, light-brown hair done in the same hair style, complete with the small puff of curls at the end. The dress and hairstyle were now outdated and that combination was unmistakably 'hers'.

Just as her name was forming in Richard's mouth, she turned around.

Totally out of form and character for Richard Gaspar, he anxiously blurted out, "Michelle...," as she squarely faced him.

"Who is Michelle?" came a very different voice from the young woman than he had expected to hear.

Richard stopped dead in his tracks and it took him a few seconds to recover. She looked like Michelle, but her eyes and mouth were those of a stranger.

Richard had been caught off guard and now it was necessary for a quick recovery before he had to answer any questions from the reporters who had seen him hedge.

In an apologetic tone he lied, "Michelle is my cousin from Greece. I haven't seen her in over five years and you look just like her." With his captivating smile he added, "She is a beautiful, striking woman. I thought you...she had come to surprise me at the end of my tour."

It only took a moment for the inquisitive 'attack mode' expression of a true reporter to leave the young woman's face and it was quickly replaced by a smile in response to Richard's flattering words.

Julia Rice, a critic that Richard knew from the Herald Newspaper was standing right next to the young woman and following Richard's last comment she offered, "Let me introduce Janice Perry to you, Richard. She is the youngest music critic ever to work for the Herald. I'm breaking her in and showing her the ropes."

"Breaking her in?" asked Richard as he raised his eyebrows and looked at Julia.

"So, how will the Herald's most distinguished ladies of culture respond to my performance tonight?" he asked, now that he had fully regained his composure.

Julia turned to Janice with a nod and an expression that looked rehearsed.

Janice then turned toward Richard and spoke in an exaggerated, matter-of-fact tone, "We don't usually discuss our opinions before going to print at the Herald, but for you Mr. Gaspar, we will make an exception."

She looked down at the notepad in her hand and declared, "A fitting performance to end the latest tour of Gaspar."

"Fitting?!" Richard burst out. First, he looked back at Janice with a look of disbelief, then he looked over to Julia, who he knew had really penned the words.

"What do you mean by 'fitting'?" Richard asked, finding

himself almost unable to keep at a proper level of composure.

"Would you prefer, predictable?" Julia responded.

Janice jumped right back in as she read the next line written on her notepad, "An air of virtuosity, yet lacking full expression."

Julia and Janice both turned to each other as evil little smiles and winks exchanged between them.

"What more do you want?" Richard asked with a sincerely hurt tone in his voice.

Julia lifted up her right arm and with a relaxed, circular, outgoing motion of her hand and fingers she responded, "Technically perfect, but 'I've' had better."

Then Julia and Janice both lifted their noses in the air, turned and walked away laughing.

By the time Richard could lift his jaw up, and by the time he could come up with a response, the two critics had disappeared into the noisy crowd.

Richard was stunned and the words 'Technically perfect, but I've had better!' grated over and over in his mind while he walked back to his violin case and hastily raised the lid so he could put his violin away.

Julia loved to tease Richard that way, and he knew that the review would be a little kinder than her words tonight had indicated. Yet he still knew that the review would lack the high praise and enthusiastic adjectives and adverbs that he desperately desired from her.

He stopped for a moment and looked down at the violin he held in his hand.

It was a fine instrument, made in Cremona, Italy by Carlo Bergonzi in 1720. It was one of Bergonzi's finest works and Richard considered his violin a great concert instrument, though at the same time he also realized it was slightly below the famed Stradivari and Guarneri master instruments he had always dreamed of owning.

The violin had become available when he was thirteen years old. His parents had spent their life savings and mortgaged their large home to pay the $60,000 for it. It was now worth many times that amount and it had served him well for all these years, but lately he found that it no longer totally satisfied his needs.

Richard had continued playing on the violin longer than his disciplined, professional savvy should have allowed him to, but he had his reasons; they were sentimental reasons, and Richard Gaspar did not have many sentimental reasons in his life.

Julia's words weighed heavily on his professional mind now and he realized that it was time in his career to get an instrument that could deliver more.

"Is that what she meant?" Richard wondered, as he thought about Julia's comments again.

Then, as he looked back down at his violin, he clenched his jaw and said, "What does she know anyway?"

Julia was just one of many critics. Richard knew that most of the other critics adored him and they wrote the words that he wanted to read in the papers the mornings after his performances.

Yet, he was torn. Was there 'more' that he or his violin could give? Not just intonation and volume, but something more?

While these thoughts ran through Richard's mind his eyes wandered across the Bergonzi again. He stopped moving when he looked at an old scratch in its belly.

It all came rushing back to him now. "Michelle!" the girl he thought he had seen tonight.

The noise of the crowd went quiet while her name lingered in his mind and his right hand slowly opened the small compartment inside his violin case. He instinctively pulled out a soft cotton cloth and began to lovingly wipe the rosin off of his instrument while his devoted fans waited for him to return.

Richard was normally considered anything but an over-emotional person, but he had a hard time seeing clearly while he removed the rosin that clung to the violin's strings.

Even after all these years he could not forget Michelle, and her memory still kept him from ever loving anyone else.

He thought about Janice, the young, new critic from the Herald as she stood in front of him just moments ago. He realized that she was a fine-looking woman and she seemed very nice, in spite of the words that Julia had told her to say.

Then Richard shook his head and thought to himself, "No. Women may look right, even more importantly they may act and talk right, but they simply are not right. They are not Michelle and they never will be."

Next he passed the cloth between the strings and the fingerboard to remove the rosin that had been deposited there during the performance.

There was much more rosin than usual on his violin tonight. He added more to his bow during the intermission than ever before in order to get every bit of volume out of his violin that he could.

With Michelle there was simply more, much more, and Richard knew that less would never do.

As he wiped the cloth across the scar in his violin's belly he remembered the day that the injury had been inflicted.

It was the afternoon he met Michelle Ross.

Richard was practicing on his newly acquired Bergonzi in the large, elegantly furnished study of his parent's home. They had bought him the Bergonzi about a month previous because he needed a violin that could be used for a solo career.

Richard was ambitious to live the life of a professional musician and he was excited that he finally owned a violin made in Cremona, Italy by one of the 'great makers'. He was deeply engrossed in his studies and he was still trying to fully adapt and adjust to the full-size Bergonzi after playing upon his three-quarter-size violin for the past three years.

Richard was only thirteen, but he was already aspiring to be a great virtuoso someday. He was dedicated to a life of music and he practiced between four and five hours every day.

Richard was practicing his arpeggios, trying to keep up

with his closest friend, his large black metronome.

His fingers were flying up and down the silver wound, gut strings against the mirror smooth, ebony fingerboard with his serious and relentless style. He would never go on to the next piece of music or exercise until the previous one had been played flawlessly from memory.

It was early in the afternoon. He had heard the front doorbell ring a few minutes ago and he could now hear his mother talking to someone in the large, front entry of the house. But, as usual, he ignored her and kept on practicing. Usually his mother would close the study door so she could carry on a conversation while Richard practiced, but this time it remained open.

"Interesting," he thought to himself when he noticed that his mother was talking in the voice that she only used when she was addressing small children.

Finally the front door closed and he put his mind fully back into his studies with the metronome constantly clicking away at 120 beats per minute.

Just for an instant, before his music stand came flying at him, Richard could hear the scamper of clawed feet on the hardwood floor and see the furry face of a long-haired puppy coming toward him at full speed out of the corner of his eye.

He instinctively turned away and pulled the violin protectively under his arm. But he was not fast enough to keep the edge of the music stand from biting into the belly of his precious Bergonzi as it continued to the floor, leaving the largest mark on the violin in its 250 year existence.

First he looked down at his precious violin in shock. Then he angrily turned and looked up from the damage and into the eyes of an eleven-year-old girl with light-brown hair who was now holding the small, hairy dog in her arms.

Even though Richard was only thirteen years old he could instantly tell by her plain clothes and simple smile that she was not from a wealthy family. He could also tell by the look on her face that she had no idea what her dog had just done to his valuable violin.

It only took Richard a second to fill his lungs and yell at the top of his angry voice, "Look what you've done!"

"Look at my violin!" he continued in a rage, "MY BERGONZI! Do you have any idea what this violin cost?"

Not even giving her a chance to reply, Richard glared at the little girl and grit his teeth while she just looked up at him with an apologetic, hurt look on her face.

"Are you going to pay for this?" he asked as he held his violin out for her to see the damage.

"Who are you anyway?" he viciously barked out, before finally giving her a chance to respond.

His face was right up to hers now with as much hate in his eyes as a thirteen-year-old boy could possibly muster.

She backed away a few inches while looking at him with large, innocent, chestnut eyes. Her soft, white face lowered a little and turned even more pale as her eyes slowly looked down at the violin that Richard held in his clenched fist. Then she slowly looked back up at Richard and backed away another step.

She was small and delicate for her age and Richard stood a good foot taller than she did as he glared down at her and waited for a reply.

She just stood silently, without uttering a word, looking meekly up into Richard's red, angry face. Then her eyes saddened and she pulled her puppy up a little higher and closer in front of her. Next she began trembling, and her lips pursed together as large tears welled up in her big, soft eyes.

The tears finally burst out and ran down her cheeks in waves. Then she lifted her puppy up even higher and tried to cover her face with it while she stood in front of Richard in fear.

When Richard shook the violin and began to yell again, she turned and ran toward the front door with her small, black shoes and white socks scurrying across the hardwood floor.

She passed Richard's mother at full speed in the entry. She only hesitated long enough to turn the large, brass handle of the front door and throw it open so she could run out as fast as she possibly could. Richard, not wanting the little girl to get away so easily, quickly followed after her with his violin and bow still in his hand.

He stepped into the large, open doorway just in time to watch the little girl stumble and fall down the last three stairs and onto the walkway, where her tender, bare knees dug into the rough, unforgiving, concrete.

Her momentum threw her down onto her left elbow that protected the puppy, then onto her other flailing arm as she tried unsuccessfully to keep her head up. The puppy in her arm yapped as she sprawled out, face down on the ground.

She lay motionless for a few seconds with her left cheek lying on the concrete and her short pleated skirt up over her back.

After a moment of silence, she painfully lifted herself up to a sitting position and pulled her skirt back down while letting out a soft whimper and a short, pathetic cry.

Richard's mother came walking up from behind him while he watched the little girl fall down the steps. She glanced out the door just as the little girl looked up at Richard. Richard glared back down at her with a mean look on his face and shook his violin.

The little girl frantically struggled to her feet, leaving small spots of blood on the concrete where she had landed. Her legs shook and she could barely stand, but she turned around and without saying a word she started to hobble away.

She never let go of her puppy and she held him even tighter while she took one step after another, even though the arm that held him was badly hurt and bleeding.

Then the little girl painfully shuffled away as fast as she could, down the sidewalk and out of sight.

Chapter 3: Sam

Richard placed the soft silk cover over his Bergonzi and closed the lid. He fastened the latches and resolutely zippered the cover closed.

"I am in control," he thought to himself as he firmly gripped the leather handle of the case and picked it up. Then he turned to the crowd and forced a smile.

Normally Richard 'was' in control, but when it came to Michelle he became another person; a weaker person in some ways, but a much better person in others.

Richard quickly pushed everything from his mind as he approached his admirers and then sat down to sign autographs.

It took over an hour for the crowd to fade away. Richard wanted each and every eager fan that pushed their program or autograph book forward to have the opportunity of relishing the moment that they received it back, embellished with his precious signature.

As he signed the last program with his nearly perfect handwriting, he looked up to see if there were any more fans waiting, or if indeed he was done.

The crowd was gone now, and as the last fan disappeared from sight, an older gentleman came down the hall and walked up to the small table with a smile on his face. It was immediately apparent that Richard was pleasantly surprised.

"Sam, it's good to see you. How are you?"

"Ricky!" was his only reply, before giving Richard a big hug when he stood up. Richard hadn't been called Ricky for many years but he didn't mind it from Sam.

"What brings you here, Sam? Not just my performance?" asked Richard.

"In a way, yes," replied Samuel.

"Oh really? And how is that?" he asked, unable to hide his surprise.

"I flew here tonight so I could hear you play again, Richard. I have also attended all of your other performances over the last few weeks without you knowing, for a reason."

Samuel knew that he now had Richard's full attention as he continued, "I've read all of the reviews and I've seen you evolve into one of the best musicians alive. But I believe you have gone as far as you can go..."

Samuel hesitated just long enough for Richard's eyebrows to raise before he added, "without help".

These were the exact same words that Samuel had used many years ago when Richard was struggling to make his mark in the world.

It was the year after Richard left home, while he was struggling to launch his solo career. He was twenty-two years old, single, and alone with only his violin and metronome to keep him company. He was working his way up to the first chair in the local symphony but he was having no success breaking into the world of a professional, solo artist.

Samuel had walked into his life just when Richard seemed to be having the most difficult time moving forward in his career, and it was then that Samuel had said those words to him for the first time.

It was just moments after Richard performed the 'Beethoven Violin Concerto' with the community symphony. Samuel had greeted Richard before he had even fully exited the stage after his performance.

He had come up to Richard, smiling and holding out his hand as he said, "I believe you have gone as far as you can go..." then after a slight pause, he added, "without help."

Before Richard could respond, Samuel had continued, "Hello, let me introduce myself. My name is Samuel Jackson and I would like to be your sponsor."

Richard's first impulse was to scoff and say, "And who are you? What do you mean as far as I can go?"

But he hesitated just enough to realize how long he had been trying with no real success and how many doors had been shut to him for unknown reasons. Richard decided to go against his normal instincts and he responded instead with, "Go on."

Samuel spent the next five years as Richard's sponsor. He opened many doors that Richard didn't even know existed, one after the other. He introduced Richard to the finest teachers around the world, including Carl Reber, and he paid for everything.

They traveled the world together from competition to competition and from performance to performance, taking each one in stride and building upon each victory. All that Samuel had asked in return was to be remembered someday.

Samuel had informed Richard soon after they started traveling together, "All I ask from you is that some day, probably when I am dead and gone and my money and I are long forgotten, when you stand on stage after giving the greatest performance of your life, as you take that fifth and final bow, hesitate at the bottom for just a moment and remember Sam."

Samuel was still standing and waiting for Richard's response, just as he had twelve years ago.

"What kind of help?" asked Richard, remembering their first meeting. "Are you going to sponsor me all over again? And are you sure you're up to it, old man?"

"You must realize that I'm getting pretty set in my ways to start learning new tricks from an old dodger like you."

Richard smiled while he spoke, then he gave Samuel another hug.

A solemn look came over Samuel's face when Richard stepped back.

"You need another violin," Samuel told him, before looking down at Richard's violin case.

Richard placed his hand on top of the case and responded, 'This one has a lot of sentimental value to me, Sam, and I don't get much of that any more."

"I know," replied Samuel. "Keep it. You should never sell it, but you still need another violin."

Richard looked at his old sponsor's face for a minute and finally admitted, "I was thinking the same thing tonight when I was standing on stage taking my bows.

"If I only had an instrument that could boom over the top of the loudest symphony and penetrate to the back row, no matter how large the concert hall. Then I could impress the critics that are still holding out."

"All that is true," confirmed Samuel, "but the critics don't need another violin, you do. 'YOU' need another instrument."

"Go on," Richard responded. He purposely used the exact same words he had used twelve years ago.

Samuel continued, "I understand that you have been visiting violin dealers during this past tour. I figure with the amount of time you have spent looking and saving for an instrument, along with your recent earnings, you must be getting pretty close to taking the plunge."

Richard nodded his head. He had been looking seriously for a violin during the past few months and now he was getting very close to deciding what he really wanted.

Samuel nodded back at Richard and said, "My friends in London, New York and Chicago still call me upon occasion and they speak highly of you. I know we had some differences of opinion when we parted, but rest assured, I only want the best for you."

Then Samuel stopped for a moment before changing his voice to a very coarse whisper, "Though I still hold you to our agreement, Ricky."

Samuel smiled and looked Richard straight in the eyes while he continued with his funny old imitation of the pirate Long John Silver. He even squinted his left eye like he would when Richard was young. "You haven't forgot our agreement have ye, Ricky?"

Richard shook his head.

"Arrh, that's good, Matey, don't go backing out on a deal with old Sam, will ye?"

"No, of course not old man," was Richard's sincere reply as he remembered Samuel's simple request in exchange for all he had done.

"Good. Then let's get on with it, Matey."

After that, Samuel continued in his normal voice again, "What do you think? What have you found? Does anything out there interest you?"

Richard took in a deep breath and replied, "I was considering both of the Stradivaris available in London. Each instrument has its strong points and its drawbacks.

"The 1713 is in the best condition. It is an elegant instrument, well balanced, open and free with a lot going for it, though it is just a little hollow on the D string.

"The 1721, on the other hand, has a richer, fuller sound, but I worry about all the repair work and I wonder how stable it would be, travelling as much as I do.

"I am considering the Joseph Guarneri in New York. It is a more powerful instrument than the other two, but it still lacks the sparkle on the E string that I have gotten so used to with my Bergonzi. Who knows? Maybe with a sound post adjustment it would fit the bill."

Then Richard stopped talking and started shaking his head as he continued, "Four million dollars though! Unless I could dig up Paganini as a duet partner I'd be paying for it the rest of my life. I don't suppose you have two million extra dollars in your wallet?"

Samuel only smiled and shook his head. But both of them realized that if that's what it would take, Samuel would have sold all that he still owned and bought it for Richard.

After a moment of silence Samuel looked at Richard and tried to sense the right moment to risk what he was going to say next.

When Richard gave Samuel a curious look, then a smile, Samuel carefully delivered the words, "I know of a man who makes violins."

"A new violin?! Are you kidding, Sam?"

Richard paused just long enough after his exclamations to realize that Samuel was serious.

"I'm through trying new violins, Sam. You know what it's like. I had makers hounding me before and after concerts trying to get me to try their homemade violins, or at best, their 'copies' of old instruments. They would almost throw them at me and beat me over the head with them. When I hesitated, they would offer them to me for almost free. In fact some of them 'were' free if I would just endorse the maker's instruments.

"I finally tried a couple of the very nicest ones with the promise that they would get better with age and playing, only to find out that with time, they either became harsh or the sound simply faded away, regardless of how they were readjusted.

"One violin's belly developed so many cracks in it that at the end of six months it was more like wood holding glue together, and the sound that it once had died off with each new repair."

Samuel was prepared for this kind of reaction. Slowly and resolutely he answered, "This man hounds no one, he makes no copies, and he does not give his violins away."

"What is his name?" asked Richard, shaking his head.

"Jonathan Dewey," Samuel replied, still very cautiously.

"What kind of name is Dewey for a luthier?" Richard's patience was starting to wear thin.

"What kind of name is Richard Gaspar for a virtuoso?" Samuel snapped back.

Richard had debated biting his tongue before making his last comment as he remembered their conversations about changing his name for more audience appeal. Richard had refused to even consider it because he felt it would dishonor his family name.

Richard slowly settled down a little and in a calmer voice admitted, "I have heard his name, and I've heard some impressive comments about his instruments from other people, but I have never seen one."

Richard's harsh-toned voice softened just a little as he asked, "So, who is Jonathan Dewey? And if he makes the instruments you and others allude to why isn't he more famous?"

Samuel smiled now that Richard was at least willing to listen.

"Time has always told who the true masters are, Richard, but the world does not judge very well until the great artists are long dead and gone."

Then Samuel sat down on the edge of the table and relaxed a little, now that Richard was listening.

"If you had wandered along a dusty road late at night in 1889 and found a poor, beggarly-looking man painting a picture of the night sky by candlelight would you have offered him fifty dollars for the painting or would you have walked on by, shaking your head like all the others did?

"If you had walked past Stradivari's famous violin shop and down the street just a couple of blocks in 1743 and noticed a rather rundown shop with a weather-beaten man looking 20 years older than he really was, dressed in loose, tattered clothing, resembling a drunk more than a luthier, would you have stopped and bought the heavy violin with the bulky scroll in the window for a mere pittance? Or would you have wondered why he even bothered to try and then pitied him as you walked away?"

Richard knew that Samuel was referring to Nicolo Paganini's violin, made by Joseph Guarneri Del Gesu, which is valued at over forty million dollars; easily the most valuable musical instrument in the world.

Samuel continued, "I don't know too much about Jonathan Dewey Luthier, but I visited with him a little when I was ordering instruments for two of my prodigies. All of us are 'much more' than satisfied with those instruments."

Richard was surprised at the way Samuel talked about the violins. Samuel was as harsh of critic as anyone when it came to fine violins.

Samuel nodded his head when he saw the startled look on Richard's face, "He is different though, and he lives in a different world. But rest assured, his instruments are for real."

With a sound of both curiosity and doubt in his voice, Richard asked, "Can his instruments 'really' compare with a Stradivari or Guarneri?"

Samuel looked Richard in the eyes and replied, "No living maker can compare with Stradivari or Guarneri. You know that. It's like comparing yourself with Columbus and trying to cross the ocean and discover America again for the first time.

"It's like trying to compare your new painting of the "Last Supper" with DaVinci's old one, then expecting the curators to pull his down and put yours on display instead.

"This violinmaker is different from the rest, Richard. He is a "living" maker. He is alive now, and he makes master instruments for 'living' performers just like was done over 250 years ago in Cremona."

Samuel put his hand on Richard's shoulder, "His instruments cannot compare with the old masters."

Then with a slight raise of his eyebrows Samuel added, "You might also say that the old masters cannot compare with his instruments, either."

Richard was amazed at Samuel, and shocked at his last statement.

Samuel lowered his hand and took a step back, "If you question their quality, Richard, the answer is, yes. They are made at the highest level of craftsmanship and with the finest ingredients that have ever been used. But more than that, he will make the instrument you 'need'."

Richard finally responded to Samuel's unbelievable comments, "Even if this luthier could make a better violin than I have now, what about my reputation? What about its effect on my career? What about the people who come to the concerts simply to hear a fine Stradivari or Guarneri worth millions of dollars?

"Do you really think that I am in a position to challenge

the stand of all the virtuosi of the last 250 years? If you thought I was against a brick wall when you first met me, imagine the brick wall I would beat my head against if I were to walk onto stage with one of his 'new' violins.

"I've also heard that he will not make copies or artificially wear his instruments."

Samuel nodded his head in reply.

With Samuel's confirmation, Richard continued with renewed anger, "At least the other new violins I tried were beat up and looked like old master instruments so most of the audience didn't even know that they were new. Did you hear those two critics tonight?"

Richard's temper was starting to flare as he remembered the words again and repeated them to Samuel, "'An air of virtuosity, yet lacking full expression.' Could you imagine their response to a shiny new violin?!"

Samuel calmly responded, "They were talking about 'you' tonight, not your violin."

"I don't care, I'm not taking that chance, Sam. I 'need' the extra respect that comes to those who play upon one of the old, great masters."

"You need to learn to respect the great masters for what they are, whether living or dead, Richard. Don't forget, you hoped to become a master yourself someday. I assumed it was while you were still alive."

Richard just got more frustrated. "I don't have time for this and I am not the one to buck the system. I am part of the system and I like it.

"In six weeks I have to play an entirely new program at Carnegie Hall and I have a lot of work to do."

As Richard finished speaking he picked up his violin, shook his head and walked away.

"Wait," Samuel called out.

When he caught back up to Richard, he said, "I thought you might feel this way and I know that you have spent a lot of time trying out instruments. I also know how much time and money you've wasted on new instruments in the past."

Richard stopped and turned as Samuel pulled Richard's

empty hand open and said, "Here. Take this."

Samuel firmly placed two airline tickets and a check with a business card stapled to it into Richard's hand.

Richard reluctantly put his violin case over his shoulder using its strap and he opened the tickets.

"What's this?" he asked, while he opened the first airline ticket and started reading.

It was to LaGuardia Airport, New York, New York, with the words 'Carnegie Hall' written across it. The next ticket was to St. George, Utah, via Las Vegas, and the check read:

Pay to the order of:
          Jonathan Dewey Luthier
          $35,000.00
    Thirty-Five Thousand Dollars with no 'sense'
For: a violin   Samuel J. Jackson

Samuel replied with a smile, "There are two of his instruments in the violin shop at Carnegie Hall right now. You know where Carnegie Hall is, don't you?"

Richard responded, "I thought the shop in Carnegie Hall only dealt in fine, old master instruments."

In a serious tone, Samuel replied, "They also carry his; call Mr. Singer and specifically ask for them."

In a lighter tone Samuel continued, "Since you will be performing there in six weeks anyway, fly out at my expense. Play on the stage a little, set your goals, focus your mind on the music and invite Mark and Cercie to listen and also have them play the two violins for you.

Samuel could tell that Richard was still not convinced, and he almost begged as he continued, "Try them out, compare them with your Bergonzi and the Guarneri you talk so highly about. If you like them, do yourself a favor and use the other ticket, and the check.

"The change of atmosphere will be good for you while you practice for the concert, and after six weeks you just might have the violin that you 'need'."

Richard wasn't convinced, "I still don't like the idea of

performing on a new violin, Sam."

"Don't think of it as a new violin, Richard, think of it as an original work of art being made by a living master for a living master, and allow a foolish old man with no sense to sponsor you this one last time."

After finishing, Samuel grabbed Richard's hand and shook it.

Samuel smiled as he crumpled the check and tickets firmly between their hands, then he turned and left Richard standing alone in the hall.

Chapter 4: The Violins

Richard approached from the left entrance at Carnegie Hall and saw his two best friends, Mark and Cercie Copala, standing in the middle of the stage talking to each other. He looked at them for a moment and thought of the many lonely months that had passed since he had visited with them. Even though the tour had been very satisfying professionally, he smiled and felt the hollow, empty feeling inside disappear.

Other than Samuel and the Copalas, there were no others that Richard could call true friends during the past fifteen years. All of the other people in his life, including Carl, were merely business associates or acquaintances.

Mark and Cercie were great people in Richard's mind, as well as great musicians. To top it off, they both played first chair in the Philharmonic; Mark on his violin and Cercie on her viola.

They had become close friends the first day they met, while touring an old vineyard in Italy. Mark and Cercie were on their honeymoon, while Richard was taking a much needed vacation.

They were the only visitors in the vineyard's wine cellar that day and were listening to the tour guide talk about the large wooden casks and rows of barrels that surrounded them. Richard was ardently discussing the different vintages with the guide when the power went off. Then the guide told them to remain calm while he went for a flashlight.

Mark, Cercie and Richard sat down and began to talk together in the dark; first about fine wines, then about music and their lives. By the time the guide finally returned with the flashlight they were all friends, laughing and joking together. They even told him to go away and quit bothering them when he offered to show them the way out.

Richard visited with Mark and Cercie every time he went to Europe and they took many trips together over the years. When Mark and Cercie decided to move to the United States, Richard loaned them his apartment in New York for a few months so they could get settled into their new positions without the normal hassles of finding a place to live.

Cercie was the first to look over and notice Richard coming toward them on the stage. She lightly tapped Mark on the shoulder and headed toward Richard with a smile. She walked up to him in her cool, flowing style with her long, black, steely hair waving behind her, while her hips swayed back and forth. Richard wondered if she was exaggerating her movements just a little more than usual so he would notice that her hair was now past her waist.

She gave him an energetic hug as her aromatic hair swung around him, delivering a potpourri of scents. Each fragrance that exuded from her hair seemed to sweep by him in its own turn, tantalizing his senses as her face came up next to his.

Richard had always admired Cercie, it was as if 'she' were the essence of old Italy. She smelled of fine wine, oil paintings, roses, rare spices and much more.

It always amazed him how he could smell each fragrance in its turn, sweet and distinct, and yet they never seemed to mix together in the air or detract from each other.

It was always a wonderful experience getting a hug from her and he felt bad for not making arrangements during his tour to visit them.

Cercie stepped back and looked at Richard, and he at her.

Richard had never considered her outrageously beautiful yet there was always that thrill and mystery that lingered around her as well as her aura of elegance. As they exchanged kisses on the cheek Richard thought to himself, "Mark is a lucky man."

He marvelled how Mark and Cercie seemed to have been made for each other. They were such a perfect match, personally and professionally.

Each of them was top notch on their own instrument, but when they played duets it was unbelievable; absolutely impeccable and deeply passionate at the same time.

While they received mixed reviews for their individual performances, the audiences and critics all loved them when they performed together. Each one's music added and complemented the other's until they crescendoed to a much higher level than each of them could ever achieve separately.

Richard turned and gave Mark a firm, genuine hug with his free arm and then they exchanged greetings.

Next Cercie put a hand on each of their shoulders and said, "I understand we are finally helping you do some serious shopping, Richard."

Richard was still a little hesitant about trying out the new instruments but he smiled and nodded his head.

"It's about time!" Cercie exclaimed. "She never was quite right for you, Richard."

Then her long, slender fingers eased their way around the handle of Richard's violin case and lifted it away from him. Normally his reaction would be to hold on tight, but Cercie was his dearest friend and he trusted her implicitly. She turned and gently placed his violin case on the large, wooden table sitting at center stage. The table had a padded silk covering on it for the instruments to rest upon so it would be easier to compare them that morning.

Cercie turned her head back toward Richard while she unfastened the latches of his violin case and told him, "She is much too serious for you, Richard. You need to loosen up a little and have some fun."

Then Cercie paused and looked at the black case while she brought her hand up to her chin, as if pondering something, "And there's something else about her..."

"Who?" asked Richard. He thought that Cercie was referring to some woman now by the way she talked.

"Your Bergonzi, of course!" responded Cercie, a little surprised at Richard.

She turned back around and opened the case. "You've had her all these years and you act as though you don't even know her!

"You're like the little Jewish boy whose match was made for him when he was a teenager. He marries the girl, lives with her, eats with her, sleeps with her and then even has children with her."

Cercie pulled the Bergonzi out of its case and lifted it up to her chest as she turned back toward Richard.

"Then he rolls over in bed one morning, throws down the covers, stares at her and asks, "Who are you?"

Cercie finished talking at the same time she lifted his Bergonzi up and looked at it with bulging eyes.

Richard looked at Cercie with a puzzled look on his face, then he turned and looked over at Mark who was unsuccessfully trying to suppress a laugh. Tears were forming in Mark's eyes as he tried to look at Richard with a straight face.

Richard did not enjoy being the brunt of jokes, even from his best friends.

Mark knew how sensitive he was about jokes and apologized, "We're sorry Richard. Everyone looks at music differently. Cercie and I just get more emotionally involved when it comes to the instruments we play. She didn't mean any offense."

Then Mark glanced back over at Cercie with a look of reprimand for her joke. Cercie returned with a look in her eyes of innocence that could melt the hardest of hearts until Mark's face softened.

Richard stood and stared while Mark and Cercie looked at each other. Each of their expressions quickly changed until they both looked at each other with looks of wanton desire.

By the look on their faces, Richard was afraid they would passionately fall into each others arms and roll around on the hardwood floor.

After composing themselves, Cercie turned to Richard and spoke for them both, "We are here to help you Richard. We can give you our advice and opinions, but you are the only one that can choose the instrument that is right for you."

As soon as Cercie finished speaking, the two violin dealers Richard had called the day before stepped forward. They had each been waiting patiently for their cue at the other side of the stage.

The dealers greeted Richard and his friends with large smiles, then with handshakes after they had placed their valuable merchandise on the large table.

"These are the two instruments you requested, Mr. Gaspar," offered Mr. Singer, the first dealer, who was referring to the instruments of Jonathan Dewey Luthier. "Realize that we also have many fine, old Italian instruments to choose from."

Richard understood the dealer's reluctance to bring only these two violins. Any player of Richard's caliber would usually be offended at the prospect of trying a new violin, as indeed, deep down inside, Richard still was.

"And this is the fine Joseph Guarneri you played upon in 'our' shop," announced the second dealer as he bowed politely and turned back toward the table. He opened the case and turned it toward Richard. "We have made a slight soundpost adjustment and have put the same kind of E string on it that you have on your Bergonzi. We hope it will now answer to 'all' your needs."

Richard instinctively reached for the Guarneri and picked it up with reverence.

"Four million dollars," he thought as he turned it over in his hands.

After admiring it silently for a few minutes, he softly laid it on the padded silk cloth that covered the table.

Richard pulled his favorite bow out of his own case and tightened the hair until it was just right before applying a small amount of fresh rosin to it.

He picked up the Guarneri and tuned the strings as he walked over to where he would be performing on stage in six weeks.

"Hear how it rings!" Richard exclaimed after he finished adjusting the strings.

Without waiting for a response his bow came down and music instantly burst forth from the two-hundred-and-fifty-year-old master violin.

His fingers flew up and down each string, one after the other, testing its full range of tone in all of the positions. Then he played arpeggios across all four strings with his fingers flying effortlessly and free.

Each note was pure and sweet when he played soft, and yet when he pushed a little harder it became full and powerful, reaching easily to the back of the large hall with power to spare.

Without even hesitating between songs, Richard played a magnificent cadenza and finished with his bow flying off the strings.

"You have done it!" Richard exclaimed as he turned to the second dealer, who responded with a large smile.

Mr. Singer reacted with a noticeable sigh as he stood by the two, yet unopened, violin cases. Richard looked down at the Guarneri and a smile spread across his face while he walked back to the others who were still standing by the table.

He held the violin out so the stage lights would shine fully upon it and admired it more. Then he rocked it back and forth while the colors glowed under the lights.

"And so much of the original varnish left! Look how the colors change and dance in the flames of the maple. No new instrument could ever look like this!"

He held it out for Mark and Cercie to see.

"What do you think? Do I really need to look any further?"

"It is wonderful," they both quickly replied.

"I knew it! I knew this violin was mine the first time I picked it up. Then it's settled, I will take it!" Richard declared as he turned and faced the second dealer.

The dealer's face beamed and he nodded his head as Richard made the declaration.

"What about the others?" Cercie inquired, almost hesitant to interrupt Richard's euphoria.

"What about them?" was Richard's reply. "Nothing else could ever compare to this." He held the Guarneri up for a moment and admired it again. After a minute, he gently placed it back into its soft, velvet-lined case and closed the lid.

When the latches were fastened, Richard grabbed the second dealer's arm and sauntered around the stage with him discussing money down, insurance and interest.

Cercie smiled when she saw that Richard was so happy, then she slowly turned to the first dealer and asked, "Mr. Singer, do you mind if I try one of 'your' violins while we let Richard take care of his business?"

Mark and Cercie were each accomplished on both the violin and viola and they enjoyed playing upon each other's instruments from time to time.

"Certainly, Madame," he replied, with a slow, polite bow. "You may prefer to try this one first," he added as he motioned to the light-blue case on her right.

"And perhaps the gentleman may wish to bow a few notes upon this one?" inquired Mr. Singer, while he looked at Mark and motioned toward the dark, red and brown leather case covered with hand-forged steel rivets sitting on the table.

Mark responded to his offer with a short, "Yes, please."

Cercie had already unfastened the latches on the light-blue case when Mark answered Mr. Singer, and after she lifted up the lid she let out a startled gasp.

It was audible enough that Richard turned his head to see what had happened. But, seeing no movement or anything unusual going on, he continued talking with the second dealer, who now had papers spread out on a folding table at the side of the stage and was punching numbers into his calculator.

Mark had just started to unfasten one of the latches on the case in front of him when Cercie gasped. He quickly turned and looked over at her, wondering if she had somehow hurt herself on the latches.

Mark stopped moving as he watched Cercie stand motionless, staring down into the case with a shocked look on her face. He couldn't tell if it was horror or sorrow.

Then Mark felt a twinge of deja vu that went back through the years. It only took him a moment to realize that Cercie's expression was identical to one ten years ago in Italy as he watched her gaze down at his seven-year-old niece Tiana, at her funeral.

The pointless tragedy and deep emotions had burned the images of that day into both of their minds forever.

Mark then looked down into the case that lay in front of Cercie. There was an elegant light-brown violin nestled in a satiny, sky-blue fabric that was sewn into a fine pattern of tucks and folds, just like Tiana's coffin.

He could not help thinking of the sorrow and the feeling of disbelief they both felt as they stared down at Tiana when she lay in her small coffin. Her delicate, tiny face was so pitifully sweet and her pure white dress made her look like an angel. Mark closed his eyes and he could still clearly see her light-brown hair with the two small butterflies pinned in it.

He had loved Tiana so much, everyone did.

Mark looked back up at Cercie and he noticed that her eyes were fixed upon the violin bow. In the lid of the violin case hung a delicately carved pernambuco bow with two small mother-of-pearl butterflies inlaid in its ebony frog.

Cercie could not move her eyes from the bow and after a few minutes she began to quietly cry. Mark watched in understanding and sympathy as tears dropped from her cheeks and stained the soft, silk fabric lining of the case.

Mr. Singer and Cercie both stood motionless on opposite sides of the table for a minute. Cercie was so overcome that she couldn't even lift her arms to wipe the tears from her eyes.

Finally she looked up at Mr. Singer with a questioning look on her face. He responded with a silent look of understanding and compassion, then he offered his handkerchief and gave her a gentle, reassuring nod and a smile.

After she had wiped her eyes, he motioned for her to play the violin. She hesitated, but Mr. Singer gently persuaded her with an expression that seemed to say, "Trust me, it will be all right."

Cercie slowly lifted the violin out of its case with trembling hands and admired how its color changed when the stage lights shone directly upon its surface. It was as though the lights had brought the violin to life.

She now held the glowing violin and looked at it as though it were the most precious gift in the world.

Cercie smiled at its elegance and form, then softly touched the cheeks of the violin's top with her fingers. After gently placing it on the large, silk cloth she tightened the elegantly inlaid butterfly bow with both of her hands, then she lifted the violin under her chin and began to play.

Richard, who was still at the side of the stage talking with the second dealer stopped in the middle of a sentence when the softly dancing, elegant notes came floating over to him.

A tingling sensation floated up Richard's spine that left his head swimming as if he were in a dream by the time Cercie had played only a dozen notes. He quickly turned, though every move he made felt like it was being performed in slow motion, while the notes danced back and forth in his head.

The crisp spiccato notes Cercie played on the G string sounded like church bells, while those she played on the E string sounded like the tinkling of small wind chimes. When Cercie played smooth, flowing passages, they were so indescribably sweet that Richard could taste them in his mouth.

Richard had never heard words ever spoken by critics

that could possibly describe the elegant sounds that he was listening to now.

The music seemed to dance and float effortlessly across the stage. It sang out over the empty chairs. It laughed up to the ceiling and floated effortlessly away. The violin cried to itself and to everyone there as the bow and Cercie's fingers played upon its strings. And all of the sounds were in the purest, sweetest voice of a child.

They all stood spellbound the entire time. Everyone was gazing toward Cercie as though they were looking through a morning mist while she played. The notes floated on and on, happy and free, never seeming to ever die away.

They just floated out forever, then they would linger in the air, filling it with a sweetness.

No one moved from where they stood while Cercie played for fear of disturbing the feeling in the air, and they remained perfectly still until after she had played the last note. They even wondered to themselves if they 'could' move while Cercie played, the sounds were so entrancing. The voice of the violin never really did die away, everyone just noticed that it was no longer in the air after a few minutes.

Mark's hand, which had remained motionless the entire time, slowly reached out and grabbed the center latch. He became anxious and felt almost afraid of what might be waiting for him inside.

Each of the large, hand-forged steel latches that held the case closed had two separate sets of bars, so Mark had to use both of his hands to open each of them.

The large hinges on the back of the case moaned and creaked as they rotated, sending a shiver that ran down Mark's spine and into his legs.

Inside the leather case lay a dark-brown, almost black, violin. Its form seemed large and strong; almost crude, but not. The case was lined with thick, dark, heavily beaded leather that reminded him of an old gladiator's uniform or a blacksmith's apron.

Mark lifted the violin out of the case and noticed it had

a 'heft' to it. Then as he held it in his hand he realized that it wasn't much heavier than his own violin, it just 'seemed' to have a presence of weight. The scroll was somewhat squarish and bold, with large eyes deeply set amongst the fluting and the edges of the instrument were thick and substantial.

He pulled the large bow out of the lid of the case. It was very plain and strung heavy with a pepper-colored horse hair. As he tightened the bow Mark could feel the strength of the pernambuco stick and he instinctively knew how this violin was meant to be played. He drew the bow up high in the air, then he immediately laid it aggressively into the strings.

A loud, deep, gruff voice boomed through the concert hall. It crashed against the back wall and bounced back with so much force that it felt as though everyone on the stage had been slapped in the face with the echo.

Mark paused for a moment and let the sound die away while each person there felt the hair on the back of their neck prick up with a feeling of fear and intimidation.

'Boom!' The sound bellowed out again with the same effect.

'Boom!' Again and again, as Mark bore down hard on the strings, filling the hall with its large bellowing voice.

Mark continued playing and the bold passages of music echoed through the large hall with unbelievable strength. The massive sounds even bolted out the doors and echoed further down the halls and into the foyer.

Mark himself seemed to change character as he played. He began digging into the violin harder and harder, lower and lower into the notes until he was digging into the G string with all his might. The sounds crashed through the air with unbelievable deafening force as he played relentlessly on and on.

Sweat was pouring from his face and Mark stood exhausted when he finished the last note and laid the violin back into its heavy leather case. He loosened the bow and hung it back on its rack in the lid without saying a word.

The lid came down with a firm thud and clank that echoed like a dungeon door across the stage. Then Mark fastened the large, steel latches that held the lid securely closed.

Chapter 5: The Desert

$\mathcal{R}$eality slapped Richard in the face and he finally seemed to wake up when he walked off the jet at the Las Vegas airport and looked around.

"What am I doing here?" he asked himself as he walked up the ramp toward the bright lights, then on through the jingling, colorfully-lit slot machines.

Richard had packed his bags and taken the earliest flight available the next morning. He was still used to traveling day or night from his long tour and he didn't think anything of climbing onto a jet in the middle of the night and sleeping on the way. Richard had learned to put up with many things while touring different parts of the world over the years.

"But I've never been a gambler," he told himself while he looked at the slot machines and waited for his luggage, "Yet here I am travelling across the country to the middle of the desert where I plan on blindly ordering a violin from someone I've never met. All in the hopes that this new violin will be better than one of the greatest Guarneris in the world!"

Richard actually put his head in his hands and shook it back and forth while he waited in the lounge for the next shuttle that would drive him to St. George, Utah.

He looked over to the slot machines again and thought, "My odds would be much better pulling the handle of that million-dollar slot machine over there than betting on this violinmaker succeeding!"

"And that would only take a minute of my time and cost

me one dollar."

"I've never been a gambler," Richard told himself once more.

"It's your turn, Richard," George Gaspar Sr.'s husky voice announced from the open doorway of the parlor where his cousin Tony had just exited.

When Richard saw the big grin on Tony's face he knew things would be good this year. Richard's eyes lit up and he slowly walked into his grandfather's parlor even though he wanted to run.

The rest of the house was clean and proper, but his grandfather's parlor was different. It was lit with old snarly-shaped candles and it had many strange things hanging upon its walls and from the ceiling. It was eerie and haunting, just the way his grandfather liked it.

While Richard's grandmother was raised a sophisticated, 'well to do' woman of social position, his grandfather had lived the life of a gypsy and a fortune teller until he married her. He had 'repented of his ways', as his grandmother put it, except for the fortune telling he performed for his grandchildren every few years when they came to visit during the holiday season.

This was the one and only thing that his grandmother was willing to put up with from his grandfather's past, and it had turned into a great family tradition over the years.

The fortune telling was always done in different ways each time Richard visited with him and it was also different for each of the other grandchildren. Most of them liked visiting grandfather in the parlor better than Christmas day itself, and sometimes the presents received in the parlor were the best and most cherished of all.

Richard's eyes scanned the walls and he looked at every square inch while he slowly worked his way over to where his grandfather was sitting. Gold tassels and colored silks hung from the walls in regular intervals and there were strange paintings and statues between each one.

There were also curiosities that boggled the mind sitting

on dozens of shelves that were scattered up and down the walls below the paintings, including a set of shrunken heads with bones through their noses and their eyelids sewn shut.

His grandfather had told Richard that the heads were two explorers he knew when he was young and that he had read their fortunes and warned them not to go on their last journey.

Richard had nightmares about them and many other things that were in his grandfather's parlor, but he also had many wonderful dreams about the other things his grandfather showed him and told him about.

But best of all, there was an original oil painting of Nicolo Paganini playing the violin for a woman, and below the painting on a shelf was a small box. Richard knew that the box contained the old silver ring, set with a large oval ruby, that Paganini was wearing in the painting.

There were many other things on the tables and shelves that the other grandchildren loved best, including tarot cards, crystal balls and ancient vases full of wonderful things but Paganini was always Richard's favorite.

Richard walked over and sat down on a chair that was placed in front of a small, ornate table. The top and edges were engraved and embellished with colorful symbols and writings, while the carved legs were covered in gold. The table was hundreds of years old and Richard had heard many stories about it from his grandfather. Richard loved to look all around it each time he came to visit his grandfather's parlor.

Instead of the large crystal ball sitting on the table like the last time Richard came to visit, there were five silver goblets lined up and turned upside down in front of him.

He looked up from the cups, into his grandfather's face and smiled. No one's fortune had ever been bad and he knew great things could come in very small packages.

"This is not a game this time Richard," his grandfather said with a solemn look on his face.

Richard got the funny feeling that his fortune this year was going to be a grown-up one, and very different from the last time he came to visit when he was only seven years old. Now he was eleven.

"And this is not necessarily your future," his grandfather added, "These cups, and what lies underneath them will tell you who you are."

"I know who I am, grandpa. I'm Richard Gaspar," answered Richard in a matter of fact tone. "And I'm going to be the greatest violin player who ever lived."

His grandfather smiled. After all, he was the one responsible for Richard playing the violin and also for him starting at such a young age. He had given Richard a special present the very first time they sat across from each other at this table when Richard was only four years old.

It was a violin. A very small violin, and when Richard found out that his grandfather had carved it himself he prized it above everything else he owned and begged his parents for lessons so he could play it.

"I know that you will," responded his grandfather with a proud smile on his face. "But this will tell you what kind of person you are."

Then his grandfather pointed to each of the cups with his index finger, put both of his hands on his knees and looked at Richard.

"Choose a cup."

Richard smiled again, then he looked at the five silver cups lined up across the table. They were all exactly the same, except they were old and worn just a little differently.

Richard pointed to the third cup from his left and waited for his grandfather to pick it up. His grandfather shook his head and told him, "So you never question whether this is real or not, you pick it up."

Richard eagerly picked up the silver cup and looked down at the table. There were three shiny buffalo nickels sitting next to each other.

Richard's eyes grew wide as he looked at them. He loved old coins but he had not started a collection of his own yet.

His grandfather smiled when he saw the look on Richard's face and said, "Only touch their edges when you pick them up. They are the rarest three coins of their kind and they are very valuable."

Richard carefully picked up each nickel by its edge, one at a time, and looked at them with awe. Even though Richard was young, his father had taught him how to carefully handle valuable things.

"Thank you, grandfather," Richard said, knowing that if his grandfather said something was valuable, it really was.

"Now, would you like to risk them and try for something more valuable?" asked his grandfather with his eyes narrowing a little.

Richard looked at the nickels, then he looked over to the box that sat below the picture of Paganini and asked, "Is Paganini's ring still in that box over there Grandpa?"

His grandfather's face beamed as he answered, "It is."

"Then I'll keep the nickels, no matter what Grandfather," Richard declared.

"Your father has taught you well," commented his grandfather. "Go ahead and see what you would have gotten."

Richard reached over and picked up the first silver cup and turned it over. There were five large gold coins sitting on the table underneath it.

"Now pick up the others," offered his grandfather after seeing that Richard was unphased at the sight of the gold coins.

When Richard lifted up each of the other three silver cups, there was nothing underneath them.

Even though the gold coins were from his grandfather's country and worth nearly twice as much as the buffalo nickels, Richard was never sorry for taking the sure thing and he treasured the three nickels next to his violin that his grandfather had made him.

"What am I doing here?" Richard asked himself again, as the shuttle merged onto the interstate freeway and headed north.

Richard was quickly carried out of the heart of Las Vegas and toward the edge of town where his surroundings abruptly changed from casinos and the city into a barren, windswept desert.

Richard questioned if what had happened yesterday at Carnegie Hall was real or just a dream. He questioned it even more while he looked out across the hot, dry sand toward the barren, seemingly burnt mountains beyond.

He had been rational and reserved enough to leave a deposit with the second dealer for the Guarneri before he left New York. He made sure in writing that he had the first rights of refusal for it until the six weeks were over.

He knew the Guarneri was a magnificent instrument, one of the finest in existence with an impeccable history and provenance. It was everything he wanted in a violin with the prestige and status to go along with it. Now, here he was travelling through the desert in search of the perfect violin.

Yet the sounds he heard at Carnegie Hall still haunted him. The feelings he felt as his two most loved and trusted friends played upon those other two instruments were nothing like he had ever experienced before.

He looked out the window of the van, cleared his mind and tried to relax.

It didn't take long for the sun and the desert to infuse Richard with a dreamy melancholy as he looked out across the hot dry sand. It was only sparsely dotted, here and there, with a few lonely sagebrush and cactus. As the large van travelled across the desert basin his eyes wandered over to the distant rocks and mountains.

His mind drifted and Richard now imagined himself marooned out here with no water, left alone, with only snakes and scorpions to keep him company. He thought of himself outside on his hands and knees with the sun beating down on him as he desperately tried to find shade, and he wondered how anyone could possibly survive.

"The only hope," he thought to himself, "would be to reach those mountains ahead where there may be shade and water."

The van made its way across the hot valley floor and up to the rocky, shadeless incline where Richard looked around and now imagined his dry, sunbleached bones sitting against one of the boulders they passed.

Then he turned around and looked back to the valley floor. Even though it was engulfed in mirages and heat waves it looked pretty good compared to the rocky, barren slopes that now surrounded him.

Mark and Cercie had discussed the two instruments with Richard and they had all agreed together that neither of the two violins was right for him. But Mark and Cercie also believed that if this luthier could make both of those instruments he could make the instrument Richard needed.

It was strange though. Who was this maker? Where did he come from? Was he for real?

"And yet," Richard thought to himself as he stared out of the window, "he must be real enough."

Before Richard left the concert hall yesterday Cercie had written out a check to Mr. Singer and the violin shop at Carnegie Hall. She now owned the golden-brown violin with the butterfly bow in the light-blue case.

Richard remembered back when Mark and Cercie had scraped every penny together that they possibly could and how they begged loans from their closest friends so they could buy her old Bresian viola. Then yesterday, out of the blue, she paid almost the same amount for this new violin as she had for her viola.

Mark had not even flinched at the price. He just nodded his approval as Cercie wrote out the check and balanced their savings book. The Copalas weren't poor, but Richard knew it must have taken most of their savings to purchase it.

When Richard asked why she was buying the violin and where she would play it, and then when he reminded her that she was a violist, she only answered, "It's just what I need, and it's very special to me. I'll tell you sometime; perhaps when you get back from your trip with your violin."

"My trip," he thought, "my violin." He still had a hard time picturing the violin of his dreams in this hot, dusty desert.

Richard had visited Las Vegas before, but this trip was much different. Instead of being shuttled directly to and from the concert hall in a limousine he was travelling across the desert in a van with people who didn't even know who he was. Even the shuttle driver had asked him how to spell his last name.

The shuttle was nice enough, but no matter how nice it was he just seemed out of place in the sands of Nevada and Southern Utah with his Bergonzi at his side.

If he were to imagine himself buying a violin from a living master it would have been in one of the shops in Cremona, Italy.

Richard had visited Cremona during one of his many tours of Europe and visited many of the makers there.

He had wanted to see the 'City of Masters' with its buildings, centuries old, standing just as they had at the time of Stradivari. He loved the old, musty smell of a classic Italian town with arched doorways and peaceful inner gardens surrounded by tall, private walls full of windows and terraces.

He visited the home and shop where Stradivari lived with his first wife and where he developed his own style of instrument after leaving the shop of Nicolo Amati. Richard had even seen the nails in the rafters where Stradivari had hung his wood for making his instruments over 300 years ago.

Richard looked in awe at the tools and molds of Stradivari in the museum, realizing that they were the very tools and templates which had created some of the greatest instruments in the history of the world.

It amazed him how simple and crude the tools were that shaped and finished the most elegant violins, violas and cellos known to man.

Richard had also visited the house where Joseph Guarneri had struggled to make a living down the street a few blocks from Stradivari. Joseph was finally forced into selling the home which had been in the family for generations to pay his debts, then he rented it back from the new owner for the last few years of his life.

Richard now sat and wondered about Samuel's words.

If he had walked down that street in 1743 and noticed a violin in 'that' window would he have bought it? Or, would he have said to himself, "No, I need a fine, old Nicolo Amati or a Jacob Stainer. If this Joseph Guarneri is a great maker he should be more famous and everyone knows that it takes fifty to a hundred years for a fine violin to mature."

Until yesterday Richard knew what his answer would have been to that question.

Richard looked down at the black leather case sitting by his side which contained his 1720 Carlo Bergonzi. Bergonzi was the greatest apprentice of Antonio Stradivari. It was Carlo, not Stradivari's children, who inherited the great master's best tools and templates when he died.

This violin was made during the prime of Cremona. Antonio Stradivari was on one corner, Joseph Guarneri was down the street, Carlo Bergonzi just a few blocks away and a dozen other makers surrounded them trying to be worthy of the title of "Master Luthier."

He thought of the Bergonzi with its nick in the belly and his mind floated back to that day again.

"How could you do that to her, Ricky?" demanded his mother as she looked down at Richard with her hands on her hips.

"What did I do? Did you see what she and her dog did to my Bergonzi?" defended Richard as he held up the violin with the fresh scar on its belly.

"That's no excuse for destroying a well-meaning little girl's feelings and hurting her like that," she said.

His mother loved to use passionate words like 'destroy' on occasions like this.

"If you ever hope to become any kind of gentleman, you

will go to her home and ask her to forgive you."

"I don't even know who she is," defiantly replied Richard.

"Her name is Michelle Ross. She just moved into the old Pritchard house down the street with her parents. She came by to say 'hello' and to see if we had any girls her age she could play with. She seemed so friendly and commented on how well you were playing in the study that I thought you may want to meet her."

"I hope they plan on cleaning that old dump up," was all Richard could come up with.

"Didn't you hear me, young man?" his mother's voice raised a pitch.

"Yes, I heard you. You want me to go say I'm sorry for her almost ruining my new violin."

His mother hadn't spanked him since he was five years old, but he knew he was walking the fine line now by the look on her face. Backing away quickly, before he even gave her the chance, Richard exclaimed, "I'm sorry! I'll do it!"

"And you'll mean it, young man! Sincerely! Or else!"

Richard slowly walked back into the study and over to the mantle where the metronome was still clicking away. He switched it off and stared at it for a minute.

"I didn't even get to finish my practice time," he thought.

He looked down again at the scratch on his prized violin before he took much more than the usual amount of time to put it away in its case. Next he picked up his music one piece at a time and slowly slid them in the top pocket of his zippered violin case cover, one by one.

He zippered it closed so slow that it sounded more like his metronome than a zipper. Then he slowly and carefully tilted back up the old, ornate music stand and set it against the wall where it belonged. He rotated the music stand and adjusted the legs more than once before he finally left it alone.

"Now!" his mother yelled, though she said she never yelled.

Her voice prompted him, though it did not speed up the pace of his feet as he walked out of the parlor and into the entry. He meandered across the large Persian rug, while he gazed around at everything in the entry he had seen a thousand times before.

His mother opened the door for him and he slowly walked out onto the porch. He looked around before continuing on down the stairs. There was no one in sight and he hung his head down and looked at his feet. Richard did not like to apologize to anyone, ever.

He walked down the stairs where Michelle had tripped and he stopped and looked at the small, red patches on the cement where she had landed.

"Dumb girl!" he thought to himself. Then he walked on past after scuffing one of the red spots with his shoe. "She should have stayed and taken the consequences instead of crying and running away."

And yet, as he remembered the look in her eyes, he knew he had hurt her. Her face had turned instantly from happiness to despair, right in front of him, and he had done it.

"Good," he said out loud, trying to convince himself that she deserved what she got, but not loud enough for his mother to hear.

He continued on, still scuffing the sidewalk with his feet as he walked. When he reached the gate and lifted the latch he turned around just to make sure.

"Yep, there she is, still standing in the doorway making sure I keep on going, with 'that' look on her face," he silently thought to himself.

"Yep, girls grow up to be women," he thought, even though he didn't really know what he meant by it.

Walking from his house to the old Pritchett home was like walking slowly from the penthouse down to the laundry room in a fine hotel. Even the sidewalk became a little rougher and there seemed to be more and more cracks in it the farther he travelled from his house and the closer he got to hers. He even noticed a couple small drops of blood by one of the cracks along the way.

Richard noticed the blood and the sidewalk so much because he was still looking down and scuffing his shoes while he tried to think of what he was going to say, or how to say it so he would look good but still get the job done.

When he reached the corner of the street where the old Pritchard home was he stopped and looked around. He looked at the old house down the street, then he turned and looked down the street on his left and started walking that way instead.

Richard walked around the other block three times before he finally headed down the street that the Pritchard house was on.

Eventually Richard arrived at one of the rattiest yards in town. There was no fence so he walked across the patchy, brown grass toward the small front door with paint peeling off of it. There were cardboard moving boxes piled everywhere and a washing machine sitting in the middle of the lawn. He had seen the U-haul truck and trailer parked here two days ago and had wondered what kind of people would buy this dump.

He stood on the doorstep a minute before he rang the doorbell. He was still trying to figure out what he was going to say. He had narrowed it down to a couple of different options by the time he pushed the button and figured he would just play it by ear.

When he heard footsteps coming toward the door he considered bailing out and running, but he thought to himself, "Then I wouldn't be any different than her."

The door swung open and a thin, tired looking woman with mousy-brown hair opened the door.

"Well, hello. May I help you?" Margie Ross asked with a small smile.

"Does a Michelle Ross live here?" Richard answered in a slightly reluctant tone.

Her eyebrows lifted with understanding while she looked him over from head to toe. She had expected a little larger sized 'monster boy'.

"You must be Richard. I'm Michelle's mother," she replied.

"This lady already knows," Richard thought to himself, "I better be careful what I say."

"I came to apologize for how I acted," Richard said in a slow, solemn tone.

"You may want to come back a little later, Richard. Michelle's still pretty upset," Margie replied.

Richard knew his mother would never leave him alone until the deed was done.

"Please," using the most pathetic voice he could, "could I just talk to her for one minute?"

Margie hesitated while Richard looked at her with pleading eyes.

"Come on in, and we'll see," was her reluctant reply.

Richard walked in the front door and he instantly sensed there was more going on here than met the eye. He had the feeling he was walking into an ambush or over the top of a pit covered with branches, complete with wild tigers circling in the bottom. He didn't know why he felt that way; after all, what could an eleven-year-old girl and her mother do to him anyway?

As they walked down the hall together, Richard lingered just far enough behind to tuck and run if panthers leapt out at him from behind a door or around the corner. When they got closer to the door on the left, he could hear something.

"Oh great," he thought, "it's probably been over forty-five minutes and she's still crying."

As Margie slowly opened the door, Richard could hear Michelle's low, moaning sobs and quick, uneven breaths more clearly.

Richard slowly moved his head around the doorjamb until he could see cardboard boxes lining the far wall, then as he continued into the room he saw 'her'.

She was half lying, half sitting on her bed and both knees were propped up with pillows under them. On each knee was a large cotton bandage about four inches square with white medical tape crossed over each one.

Both bandages had small blotches of bright crimson showing between the tape and there was fresh blood running down her right leg. She had another large bandage taped onto the palm of her right hand with scrapes running up her forearm. Another, wider bandage was wrapped around her left elbow and she was holding her arm straight out in front of her. Richard knew that it was the arm that had been holding and protecting her puppy.

Then, to top it all off, there was a large, white gauze wrapping around her forehead. It was holding an ice pack tightly against a large purple lump that had formed there.

The gauze was holding her hair straight up around the edges, with the ends of it curling over and hanging down in front of her scraped up face and red, swollen eyes.

"Michelle, honey," her mother spoke softly as she walked up to her bed. Richard was following cautiously behind, almost in shock.

"Michelle?" she repeated.

After a few labored, jerky breaths between long, labored sobs, Michelle slowly looked up. Upon seeing Richard, she immediately flinched and cowered against her headboard like a trapped, wounded animal. She even covered her head as though she thought he would reach out and strike her.

Her little dog left her side to stand on the edge of the bed facing Richard and he started snarling and barking at Richard with his sharp, little teeth showing.

Richard stood paralyzed with his mouth wide open, while Michelle quivered and sobbed and the little dog barked at him.

"I think you better go," said Michelle's mother as she turned toward Richard.

Richard just stood there, dumbfounded. He simply couldn't move. He knew he was a little stuck up on the scales of life, but he had never purposely hurt anyone, let alone tortured anyone or anything, in his life.

Richard looked down at Michelle quivering and shaking and he thought of the time he was so upset and started crying when the other boys at the baseball field were torturing a grasshopper. They were pulling off its legs and laughing at its pain, and there was nothing he could do to stop them.

Now, right here, right now, in front of his own eyes, lay a

helpless, eleven-year-old girl cowering in fear that he would hit her, torture her, or even worse.

Something inside him broke. Something that felt like a huge giant was grabbing him by the shoulders and legs from behind, putting his knee in the small of Richard's back and then 'snap', right in two.

Richard's lower lip started to quiver and tears welled up in his eyes. He remembered how Michelle's face looked when she stood in front of him in the study and now he knew how it must have felt.

"I'm sorry," he blurted out. His voice cracked when he spoke. "I didn't know you would get hurt. I didn't mean it, I take it back. I take it all back."

Michelle still cowered against the headboard with her face turned away. The little dog was barking even louder now.

"You need to go now." Mrs. Ross was insistent and she put her hand firmly on Richard's shoulder.

"Please, forgive me," Richard asked, not willing to leave yet.

Michelle didn't answer.

Richard became desperate and started shaking.

"I will do anything," he cried.

When Michelle didn't respond, Richard broke free and ran around to her on the other side of the bed. Then he knelt down right beside her. He desperately looked at her, wishing that she would lower her arms and quit shaking. He wished more than anything that she would look at him and forgive him, as he begged and pleaded, "I promise, I'll do anything."

Michelle slowly turned her head toward Richard and looked at him with her wide, innocent eyes full of tears and slowly whispered, "Be my friend."

Richard's mind wandered over the years and it floated out across the hot dry sand of the desert while he watched it go by. From that moment on they were friends.

Chapter 6: The Luthier

Richard drove up the freeway the next morning in his newly rented, four-wheel-drive Blazer. It was the nicest vehicle he could rent in St. George.

"That's all right," he thought, "I just might do a little exploring anyway."

The nicest hotel room in town was about one-third the price of an average room in Manhattan. It was roomy, and since it was summer he didn't have any trouble arranging the empty rooms on each side of him so he could practice unmolested.

Richard was the most relentless disciplinarian when it came to practicing the violin; ten to twelve hours a day, seven days a week when there was a deadline to meet. The six-week deadline was very important so he knew he would be gearing up and digging in as hard as ever while he was here. At the same time, he also realized that there had to be a time for rest and relaxation, so he took a deep breath and tried to unwind a little.

He played with the idea that he might even see some sights and wander a little in the days to come, since he had never been to this part of the country before. As much as he had travelled the world, this was one place he had never been. Of course he had never been to Siberia in the dead of winter either.

Still, he enjoyed the change of pace and he hoped that this trip would be a new experience for him as he headed further out of town. Not just ordering a new violin, but Southern Utah itself.

This whole area was different with its vast open territory, small pioneer towns, huge rock canyons called Zion and St. George.

"Saint George and the dragon," Richard thought to himself.

His grandfather had told him many stories and legends over the years about many great people. And while his grandfather seemed to concentrate on Nicolo Paganini he also covered a lot of other ground and Richard enjoyed them all.

Richard pondered the great knight's deeds that had earned him sainthood. Saint George, the pillar of chastity and bravery; he was almost considered the inventor of chivalry itself. The great protector of women and their virtue.

As Richard drove up the freeway and looked around him he thought, "Looks like the dragon burned the place up before giving in." Then he smiled to himself as he continued north fifteen miles to a small town called Leeds.

Richard just could not imagine a luthier choosing to set up shop out here in the middle of the desert. There were no great concert halls, no large opera houses, no cathedrals, no old world art and culture and most of all, no customers. It didn't make sense to him. Why here? Why not Cremona?

As he pulled off the only exit leading to the small town he slowed down and looked around at the old houses, barns and a couple of pastures. It had been a long time since he had been in a truly small town.

He drove up the quaint street and the feeling that life itself was slowing down came over him. He knew that if he took his pulse right now it would be at least ten beats a minute slower than normal. He remembered that these small towns had a whole different feeling in them and the people were different.

Michelle had come from a small town.

He smiled and waved back at some children playing in the irrigation ditch by the side of the road. It had been a long time since he had been waved at by someone that didn't know who he was.

He glanced down at the directions lying on the seat beside him. He had printed them off the Luthier's internet site and he thought to himself, "At least this violin maker is somewhat up to date."

Then he couldn't help but smile at himself as he remembered how only two days ago he had wished the violin maker had been dead for 250 years.

Richard had not spoken directly with the Luthier yet. He had reached the Luthier's answering machine but did not leave a message until after calling Samuel who assured him that the Luthier was expecting him. Then he left a message telling the Luthier that he would fly out and meet him when he arrived.

He was in this thing now and he dove right in. That was his style, though he was now questioning his decision.

Richard travelled all the way through the small town, which took about three minutes. After that, he continued following Main Street until there were no more signs of civilization and it turned into an old highway. As far as Richard could tell, Main Street was the only street in town other than short dead end roads leading nowhere.

"You're joking," Richard said out loud after driving along the deserted highway when he finally saw the small sign that simply said 'violins'. It was sitting at the end of an old dirt and gravel washboard road almost hidden by the sagebrush.

If he hadn't come this far already and then been put in this relaxed small town mood he may have turned around in disgust right then and there and headed back to New York for the Guarneri.

Yet he had come so far already.

He shook his head and turned onto the old dirt road as rabbits leapt across the path in front of him. After driving close to a mile and dodging four rabbits he passed over a cattle guard.

"I wonder if he makes his own hide glue?" Richard asked himself while he looked around for the cows.

At the next turn he was even more surprised. The arrow on the next sign directed him right through the middle of an orchard. While he reluctantly continued driving forward, he passed every kind of fruit tree that he had ever seen.

The branches of the cherry trees were drooping down with the weight of the bright, juicy, red fruit and the other trees were not very far behind. He noticed pears, apricots, peaches, plums, figs, nectarines, pomegranates and many more.

Then, his interest was really sparked when a vineyard appeared on his left with green grapes under the leaves, just starting to turn colors. Richard found himself wondering if the Luthier had his own label. Richard had always had time for fine wine and now he also had the money.

He smiled as he thought of his moderate, private collection. He enjoyed dabbling with wines, preferring the unusual and extraordinary. He had never heard of Utah wine before and the thought was beginning to intrigue him, at least as an 'unusual' wine.

Just when Richard wondered if this violin shop was for real and if there was a violinmaker out here at all he emerged out of the other side of the orchard and saw it.

There it was. A violin shop, right in the middle of the sand and sagebrush!

It was an enormous violin shop by anyone's standards and Richard's jaw dropped. He was used to seeing small, crowded shops tucked away in the corners or alleys of the large cities, not huge buildings standing all by themselves in the middle of the desert.

"Amazing," he found himself talking out loud to himself again as he pulled up next to a white Mercedes that was parked in front. He paused for a few minutes wondering what to expect next.

"Who is this man? How old is he? What is he like? If he can really make instruments in the quality of the old masters where did he learn?"

Visions of witches hovering over a boiling pot with

cobwebs hanging from the ceiling to the floor started forming in his mind. Bats in the belfry, rats in the cellar, "Who knows?" he thought. With his dreams as a boy and everything that had happened in the last two days, what could he expect? What would this man, this 'luthier' be like? Well, he was about to finally find out.

With all these thoughts running through his mind, Richard opened the door of the air-conditioned Blazer and stepped outside.

He was greeted with a blast of hot, desert air. It hit him with such a powerful force that he imagined it must feel like standing in front of a blast-furnace when the door is opened. The hot sand quickly warmed up the soles of his feet while he stood outside the Blazer and grabbed his violin case. He was concerned about the heat's effect on his violin and he hurried over to the door of the shop where there was some shade.

As he reached for the door handle he could hear cello music coming from inside.

A small sign on the door read, "Come in. You are welcome," but he hesitated so he could listen while a cellist finished off the last two movements of the 'Elgar Cello Concerto'.

"Magnificent!" he thought. "Truly impressive."

These words and others ran through Richard's mind as he stood outside the door. He then thought of Julia and Janice, the music critics from the Herald, as he realized that he was using the very words that he wished they had used!

"Who else has been lured out here to the desert?" he wondered. "Maybe this luthier 'is' for real if he can lure players such as this cellist and myself out to the desert to buy his instruments."

Richard was sure he recognized the style of the cellist. There was a distinct flamboyant flair at the end of each phrase he knew he had heard somewhere before.

He had been introduced to all the top cellists in the world at one time or another and had performed with a good number of them at least once. He was anxious to see which one was sitting on the other side of the door, here in the middle of the desert.

As the music came to an end Richard pushed open the door with a big grin on his face. Looking up at him from the cello chair was a small boy with his mother standing by his side.

"Is it as you wish now?" asked a man sitting on another chair in front of the boy. The man had curly dark hair with a touch of gray on both sides and a beard. His long sleeve shirt and pants were all cotton with solid vibrant colors.

"Yes, Sir," was the boy's only reply, other than a smile, as he turned back toward the Luthier.

"Good, I am as always, your servant," smiled the man.

And with that said, they all turned toward Richard who was still standing in the doorway.

"Richard Gaspar! What a pleasure," the mother of the boy exclaimed.

The little boy held the cello and bow in his left hand and then stood up, "It's a pleasure to meet you, Sir, my name is Christopher." He then offered his hand to Richard.

"The pleasure is all mine," Richard found himself saying as he shook the young boy's hand in disbelief.

"It is not possible!" he thought to himself, recalling the concerto he had heard just moments before while he stood outside the door. But there was the cello, here was the boy, and the music still sat upon the music stand!

He was stunned, though he was still too polite to ask if it was really the boy playing the cello. He was dumbfounded, and now questioned if the music he had heard was really as good as he remembered it after all.

He stood in astonishment as the little boy and his mother packed up their things and walked out the door in silence with the music still ringing in Richard's ears.

After Richard stood and watched them leave he turned to the man and asked, "How is it that I've never heard of Christopher before?"

After he finished speaking, he realized that introductions

had not been made between the Luthier and himself yet.

"He is very young and needs his childhood," was the reply.

Richard thought about the answer. "But still, people should know!"

"People will know of him soon enough," replied the Luthier, acting as though he regretted the thought of it.

Then remembering his faux pas, Richard excused and introduced himself, "Pardon me, I am Richard Gaspar."

"Yes, and I am Jonathan Dewey Luthier," the Luthier replied. He said the word 'luthier' in such a way that Richard couldn't decide if it was a title or his last name.

"How was your journey?"

"Fine," replied Richard. "But that's quite a desert you have out there."

"Yes, it is. Would you like a cool drink of our spring water while you relax a moment?" offered the Luthier as he motioned to a water cooler with an old-fashioned glass bottle sitting on top. Then the Luthier also motioned to a silk-covered table for cases and instruments to be placed upon.

Richard glanced down at a small waste basket full of cups by the water cooler and he realized that a drink of cool water as you walked in the shop door was the rule and not the exception.

"And I will be no exception," Richard thought to himself as he wiped a small bead of perspiration from off his forehead. The shop was cool but he hadn't fully recovered from the time he had spent standing outside the door in the heat.

"Yes, thank you," Richard responded as he placed his Bergonzi on the table and drank a cool, tall glass of water from the cooler.

The Luthier drank from his own cup at the same time and he seemed to savor every drop.

"Do you require anything before we begin?" the Luthier asked when he had finished his drink.

"A violin," was Richard's reply. He had been distracted as he tilted his head back to drink and noticed the hundreds of pieces of fine tonewood hanging from the ceiling of the shop. "Unbelievable," thought Richard, as the Luthier had asked his question. He was not naive about the value of violin wood.

"Yes, I know. Would you like me to make it, or would you like to take it with you now so you can finish it later?" the Luthier asked as he pointed to the wood that hung from the ceiling.

They laughed together a little while they both looked up at the wood and Richard finally realized what was actually asked.

"No thank you, I'm fine."

"Good. Do you have any time constraints or are you free?" asked the Luthier.

"I am as free as a bird," he answered, using the same expression he always responded with when asked if he were married, "...except to prepare for my concert in six weeks."

Richard then patted his hand on top of his violin case where there was a large amount of music in the zippered top flap.

"Very good," the Luthier commented. "I usually start with a small tour of the shop. Would you like that?" he asked as he turned toward the large, open work area.

"Certainly," replied Richard as he followed the Luthier.

"I suppose you have visited a few violin shops over the years?"

"A few," was Richard's reply.

"Very good," the Luthier commented again with a nod of his head. "Take a moment to look around, and then tell me, how does this one strike you?"

Richard took a good look around the shop for the first time. He was standing at the edge of what he would call the entry and he looked back into the shop as far as he could see.

He could tell that it was nothing like any other violin shop he had ever been in. The entrance was lined with a mixture of original oil paintings and prints of Vincent Van Gogh's finest works while the ceiling was high and tapered with most of it covered with hundreds and hundreds of pieces of hanging tonewood. By their size and shape, he knew that they had been specially cut to make violins, violas, and cellos.

But Richard had never seen so much fine wood, even in the largest shops in Europe where many makers worked together and shared the same supply.

He could not see the back wall because the shop itself was one large, open area that wrapped around a center room; something like a hexagon donut with a roof. Richard could only see a portion of the shop from where he stood since it would be necessary to walk in a large circle to see it all. It gave the shop the feeling that it went on forever.

He could see dozens of wooden benches arrayed throughout the shop with thousands of carving tools and fixtures lining the walls. Many of the tools were like those he had seen in other shops around the world, while others were not, and it all seemed laid out so differently than he would have expected.

It was enormous.

"It's the largest violin shop I've ever seen," commented Richard. "Are there other workers here?"

As he thought about his question, he remembered that his was the only vehicle outside now that the white Mercedes had left.

"I need the room to move freely, especially when I make the cellos," responded the Luthier as he looked around.

Then he lifted his head and closed his eyes, "I also need to know how their voices will project in a concert hall and come across to a large audience."

Richard nodded his head. He could appreciate the necessity of playing the instruments in a large room, but then he wondered about the Luthier's 'large audience' comment as he looked at only a dozen chairs scattered throughout the shop.

"I also require a place for each tool and the freedom to perform every task uninhibited," the Luthier continued. "There are no workers or employees here. I have an apprentice, but he is on his odyssey, visiting all the great instruments around the world, just as I did when I was younger."

The Luthier continued with a proud sort of smile, "My son also makes violins, but he is at basic training for the National Guard, otherwise he would be here. Any more questions before we begin?"

"No. I'll just listen," replied Richard.

The Luthier seemed very impressed with Richard's response and he smiled as though to say, "Good answer."

Then he showed Richard through the shop and explained the process of making a violin, viola, or cello and answered his questions.

There were profound differences between this and the other violin shops he had been in...

In the very back was a blacksmithing area that looked as though it had been transported through time. The largest coke-fired forge was located outside the back door while the smaller electric one was inside. There were many antique anvils of all sizes and shapes as well as hammers, tongs, files, clamps and many hand-forged iron fixtures of all descriptions that covered the sheetmetal-covered walls.

Next there was a welding area. Richard was amazed as he went through each area of the shop that every section was fully outfitted; complete in and of itself to do the work necessary there, even if it meant duplicating many of the tools. The welding area had its own forge and anvil as well as torches, welders of all kinds, stacks of different alloys, grinders, files, buffers, and everything else necessary for welding or brazing any kind of metal together.

There was also a casting area with ovens, wax injectors, mold-making equipment, sandblasters and polishing tools.

The gold and silversmithing area even included tools for cutting, faceting and mounting precious and semiprecious stones.

In the middle of this area Richard saw the molds and dies for making violin, viola, and cello cases. There were dozens of different styles and sizes and he couldn't help thinking about the two very special cases that he had seen on the stage in Carnegie Hall.

The machine shop had surprised Richard the most though, with its large metalworking equipment. There were lathes, mills, saws, shears, presses, and grinders. The sheer size of some of the machines was intimidating.

On the other hand, the laboratory appealed to Richard's analytical mind and the technology there was astounding. Microscopes, assay equipment, computer sound analyzers, chemicals, atmospheric chambers and ovens, and more testing and measuring equipment than he had ever seen at the finest universities. From the scanning-electron-microscope and PH meters to the spectrophotometer and the strength-testing equipment.

"It would take many lifetimes to collect the tools here and learn how to use them," Richard declared as he stood back and looked at it all.

"I don't spend much time back here any more, other than when I make the cases for the instruments," answered the Luthier. "Most of this equipment was used to find answers and to make my original tools that will now last for many years."

Richard then glanced over to a large bench covered with black silk and special gem setting tools that caught his attention while the Luthier spoke.

There were two swords lying on the bench; a long one and a short one. Their perfectly polished surfaces glistened and shimmered in the light and a strange wavy pattern that ran along both of their long sharp edges seemed to glow from where Richard stood. Lying between the two swords were two unfinished wooden sheaths or scabbards.

Richard could tell that the scabbards were being intricately carved and inlaid with gold and precious stones. Richard knew very little about swords, but these looked like they were very special.

The Luthier noticed Richard looking at the swords and told him, "When I do need something special or different, all these tools become indispensable." Then the Luthier moved on as though he didn't want to stay and explain the swords.

They continued through the shop together and the Luthier seemed to look at each tool with a longing love that sometimes turned into what Richard could have mistaken for as lust.

When they were leaving the last section in the back of the shop, the Luthier stopped and turned to Richard and admitted with a smile, "I do love tools. My wife has never been jealous of any other woman, only my tools."

Michelle was never jealous. She never had to be. She had an energy and a presence that kept Richard from wanting to spend time with anyone else but her. From the moment he stood at the side of her bed he knew she was different. Not just different from any girl he had ever met, different from anyone.

It struck him on the way back home from her house that day that he had only heard Michelle speak three words.

She went from being a total stranger, to his worst enemy, to his best friend with three words!

Richard soon found out that she was always that way. Michelle would carefully choose her words and she always meant more than she said.

As Richard walked up the front steps of his home he was greeted at the door by his mother. "She must have been watching and waiting for me the whole time!" he told himself. "Boy, does she need a life of her own!"

"Well?" she asked with a stern look on her face and her hands on her hips.

"I apologized and she accepted," Richard smugly replied as he walked back in the house and on into the study.

He left his mother standing in the entry, speechless with a puzzled look on her face, wondering what on earth was going on.

Then Richard didn't even give her a chance to ask any more questions. He just opened his case, pulled out the Bergonzi and its bow, switched on the metronome and began practicing again, as though nothing had ever happened.

He had played the song a hundred times before. But as Richard's mind wandered back down the sidewalk to the old Pritchard house he smiled and now the music seemed different.

As he played this time, his violin had a small scar just noticeable out of the corner of his eye, and he had a friend.

When Richard and the Luthier reached the area of the shop where the violins, violas and cellos were made things became more familiar to him. Yet, there were still many differences from the other shops he had been in before.

The Luthier hung his wood from the ceiling to allow the warm, dry desert air to pass freely between each piece, "To cure it and to allow each piece to fully relax over a period of ten to fifteen years," the Luthier had explained.

Richard recalled that all the other shops he had visited had dried their wood in neat little piles on the floor for only a year or two. When the Luthier pulled down two pieces of wood to show him, Richard also remembered the nails in the roof of Stradivari's shop.

Richard looked at the two pieces of wood very carefully. One was curly maple, while the other was fine-grained spruce. Even though he knew it took two trees to make the body of a violin, it seemed strange to see them side by side and listen to the Luthier talk about the different characteristics of each one.

Richard had always looked at violins as a whole picture and a complete work of art. He knew better, but he still thought of them as though they came from only one tree.

"It takes two trees to make a master violin," the Luthier said. "One can never succeed without the other and I travel the world to find just the right combinations. Most of the maple comes from Canada, Bosnia, and Germany, while most of the spruce comes from France, Italy, and the Tyrolean alps. I have obtained wood from other places, but it is very rare.

It is cut, split and waxed as soon as it is chopped down, then it must be hung from the ceiling until it is ready."

The Luthier talked and talked about his wood and the trees it came from. It was like he was talking about his closest friends and sometimes it sounded like the Luthier felt he had 'saved' them by chopping them down.

Richard could tell that the Luthier loved the trees he had gathered from around the world even more than he 'loved' his tools.

The Luthier designed and made all of his own molds and templates for his instruments and each one was 'original'. The other violinmakers Richard had visited over the years had all bragged how their molds and templates were exact copies of certain Stradivari and Guarneri instruments.

Richard noticed how similar the Luthier's molds were to the ones used by Stradivari, now saved in the museum in Cremona, yet each mold of the Luthier's was a little different and had its own style.

The Luthier then told Richard, "The Master Luthier must determine the final shape, style, sound, and character of the instrument before ever beginning."

Then, straightening up just a little, he continued, "I make no copies; no master ever has. Copies can have no soul of their own."

Richard brightened up a little at this remark. He realized that every new instrument he had seen or played upon was a copy. Almost every instrument made in the past 250 years was a copy! Richard could just imagine the response all the other makers would have to a statement like this, and now he understood a little better why the Luthier lived like a hermit away from everyone else. He didn't pull any punches.

Richard held the large yellow and red pieces of fossilized Baltic amber and dragons blood in his hands and it truly impressed him that the Luthier completely made his own varnish with these and other very rare and ancient raw materials. The Luthier also made a special varnish mixture for each instrument. It reminded Richard of the old master painters that he had learned about in college, who would make and mix their own pigments for their paintings.

"Follow me please," beckoned the Luthier as he finished giving what he called the 'standard tour' to Richard. "I need to take care of some varnish outside while we talk."

They both walked out of the shop and over to an old metal bench outside. It had a canopy over it for shade and there was a thick, dark liquid boiling in a pot.

"Now for your questions," the Luthier offered, as he picked up a dark stick and started stirring the ingredients that Richard assumed would go into violin varnish. There was a large, slow fan blowing the fumes away from them while the pot smoked away. The fan and the shade made the heat outside a little more bearable but it was still very hot.

Richard figured it was time to get to the meat of it. "Can you really do it? Can you make a better instrument than the Guarneri in New York?"

The Luthier slowly turned and gave Richard a discerning look.

"Better?" the Luthier responded. Richard could not tell whether the Luthier was making a statement or asking a question. Then musing and pulling at his beard with the fingers of his left hand, his right hand still stirring the contents of the pot, the Luthier added, "Everyone's definition of 'better' is different when it comes to violins, Mr. Gaspar. What would 'you' call a 'better' instrument?"

"Louder overall," Richard immediately responded, "and if it were possible, even deeper on the G string." Richard knew he was asking for more than any violin could deliver, but his list went on. "More fullness on the D and A strings and even a sweeter E string than my Bergonzi. But, most of all, the ability to sway the crowd."

With Richard's last comment came a noticeable smile and a raise of the eyebrows on the Luthier's face.

"I see," he slowly replied.

"Tell me, was the dark-brown violin in the leather case

'loud' and deep enough for you, Mr. Gaspar?" the Luthier asked quietly, except for sarcastically emphasizing the word 'loud'.

"That instrument is why I am here," Richard replied, with his face becoming animated as he spoke. "It had 'incredible' power. It was unbelievably loud. It could overpower even the largest symphony's fortzando."

As Richard continued describing the dark violin, he spoke enthusiastically, then as he finished, his comments became critical, "The tone was so wonderfully deep, and yet it had a character that was hard and unforgiving. It also didn't seem to want to respond well to light, intricate phrases."

"I will take that as a yes," said the Luthier. "And the light, golden-brown violin in the powder-blue case. Was it sweet enough?"

"Yes," was Richard's simple answer to the question this time as he looked into the Luthier's eyes, remembering how sweet the violin really was.

"Tell me what you mean by fullness," the Luthier prompted Richard to continue.

"Body, what some refer to as 'soul'," Richard said, emphasizing the word the Luthier had used earlier.

The Luthier then spoke in a very matter-of-fact tone, "The Guarneri you speak of is one of the finest instruments in the world, with a truly great soul. Many other performers would choose it over the instrument I will make for you."

The Luthier stopped stirring the ingredients in the pot and set the stirring stick down on a little holder on the bench and turned to face Richard straight on.

"Yes, I can give your instrument volume, Mr. Gaspar. Yes, I can make your instrument sweet, and yes, I believe I can give it the 'soul' you need. But..." the Luthier paused for a moment before finishing, "...'you' must sway the crowd."

With that, the Luthier picked up the stick and started stirring again.

"How long would it take if you start now?" Richard asked

eagerly.

"Including the time to finish 'that' violin," the Luthier answered, while he turned to look up at a violin on the roof of his shop sitting in the sun and then back down into his varnish pot, "it should take a little more than six weeks."

When Richard hesitated and got a worried look on his face, the Luthier stepped back into the blazing heat of the sun and let its rays soak into his skin for a minute. He then smiled at Richard and corrected himself, "Five-and-a-half weeks."

"And how much will it cost?" asked Richard with a smile of his own now that the time frame met his needs.

"Your violin's total cost will be thirty-five thousand dollars, including tax."

"OK, let's do it then," said Richard as he pulled out the check that Samuel had given him with the airline tickets. Then he handed the slightly crumpled check with the business card still stapled to it to the Luthier.

The Luthier slowly lifted his left hand and took the check from Richard. He barely even looked at it before lifting the varnish pot by its handle with his right hand and calmly placing the check under the pot, burning it immediately to ashes.

"What the hell are you doing?"

Richard seldom ever swore, though he thought this was as appropriate of time as any, while he stood there demanding an answer from the Luthier.

He glanced down and realized that both of his fists were clenched tightly while he stared at the Luthier, but he didn't loosen them.

"Hell has nothing to do with your friend's check, what I do here, or with the violin I will make you. 'You' must pay for the violin that I will make for you."

"What does it matter where the money comes from?" yelled Richard.

"For your violin, it matters."

Chapter 7: Two Trees

Richard was startled and just stood there with his fists clenched glaring at the Luthier.

"What did this guy want? Who, or 'what', did he think he was?" He couldn't believe this was happening to 'him', Richard Gaspar, one of the greatest players in the world. He had dropped everything, flown across the country in the middle of the night, driven through two states, handed a man he didn't even know a check for thirty-five thousand dollars and watched him burn it to ashes in front of his face.

"Then that man wants me to give him another check out of my own account for a violin of his?!" Richard was fuming more than the varnish pot sitting on the bench in front of him.

Richard thought of how he could be playing upon the Guarneri right now. In fact, he could be playing on it by tomorrow evening if he just headed out now and flew back to New York tonight and forgot this whole crazy mess.

That would be the safe thing to do, the sure bet. That's who Richard Gaspar really was, just like his grandfather's silver cups had told him. He was not a gambler or one who liked to take risks and he didn't like having to trust other people for anything.

And yet the sweet sounds of the delicate golden-brown violin still haunted him, and the massive volume of the dark-brown violin crashing through the concert hall still rang in his ears.

Could this man really do it? Or was he just going to

waste Richard's time like all the others? Thirty-five thousand dollars of his own money now, then he had to wait six weeks to find out!

He stood motionless and wished, "If I could only ask Michelle this time."

Michelle had come back over to Richard's house the very next morning.

"Can Richard play?" Michelle asked Richard's mother as she stood at the door. Michelle was standing in the doorway with large white bandages still covering all her wounds from the day before, though they had been replaced with slightly smaller, fresh ones.

"Well, I don't know," answered Richard's mother with the most puzzled look on her face Richard had ever seen.

Richard had been putting away his violin when he heard the doorbell ring and had walked stealthily behind the partially open study door to watch his mother and Michelle and so he could listen to what they said.

"I believe he is in the study finishing his lesson. Would you like 'me' to ask him for you?" Apprehension was painted all over his mother's face.

"That's OK, I'll do it," was her dainty reply, accompanied with a small curtsy. She then tenderly hobbled over to the study door, with Richard's mother following closely behind. Richard had quietly backed away from the door and was pretending that he had just closed his violin case as Michelle carefully walked around the door and asked, "Would you like to play?"

Richard looked up and then walked over to her, knowing his mother was just on the other side of the door.

"It would be my pleasure, Miss," he responded with a bow, in his most eloquent tone of voice.

He then escorted Michelle as gently as he could across the entry, right past his mother, and toward the front door.

"Please, after you," he offered, while he reached for the handle and swung the door open for her.

As they walked out together Richard was sure that his mother was standing in the entry, insane with wonder.

Richard wasn't quite sure why he did it. He figured it was worth it, though, just to see the look on his mother's face when he glanced back on his way out the front door.

He really did feel bad about yesterday and he wanted to make it up to Michelle, somehow. When he thought about how badly he had acted and how much it had hurt her, it made him ache inside.

But most of all, for some reason he couldn't explain, he wanted to see what this girl was all about. He didn't have anyone he could call a friend.

Richard had never spent much time with other boys. Maybe it was because his interests seemed so different than theirs. He spent more time playing the violin than the other boys spent watching TV, and most boys his age watched a 'lot' of television. Maybe it was because he was an only child and had never learned to get along very well with other children. He didn't know why, he just knew that that's the way it was.

Richard was expecting Michelle to laugh and say something about how he acted as they walked out the door, but she didn't.

Michelle never did say anything about the act he put on in the study and his opening the door for her like a stately gentleman. In fact, he got the impression that 'that' was how she thought it was supposed to be.

He wondered if it was because he lived in a big house and she thought that's how rich people normally acted. After all, she did live in the old Pritchard home.

"What do you want to do?" asked Richard, as he walked beside her down the sidewalk.

She looked over at him and answered, "Talk."

"Talk? I thought you asked if I could play?"

She stopped and looked from Richard's eyes down to the bandages on her knees, then back to his eyes. It was then that Richard realized how she could talk with her eyes. Michelle didn't need many words.

"I guess you're right," Richard agreed as they walked across Maple Street and toward the city park.

As they walked down the sidewalk in front of the park,

Michelle carefully looked through the fence and across the grass at all the trees. Her eyes and face seemed to be searching for something while she carefully lead the way. As soon as they walked through the large, metal gate, Michelle headed straight toward two trees that stood only about five or six feet apart.

She walked over to one of them and sat down against it with her legs sticking straight out toward the other tree. Richard followed her example and sat down against the other tree and faced her. As he straightened out his legs, the bottoms of their shoes just barely touched each other. Richard had the feeling she had planned it that way and he thought to himself, "She really is different."

Then it struck him that this was something 'real' friends might do.

"Well, what do you want to talk about?" he asked while he looked around the park.

Michelle didn't answer until Richard's gaze had wandered back to her face and he was looking straight into her eyes.

"You."

No one had ever asked him to talk about himself before, other than maybe the first day in school each year. He thought for a minute on how to answer her or what to say.

The whole time he thought about how to answer, he was looking in her eyes. Once she got him looking into them, he couldn't look away.

Finally he started talking with just a touch of pride, "I play the violin. I want to be the greatest violin player who ever lived and perform all over the world."

He waited for her reaction. She just sat there smiling and waited for him to go on. "I'm pretty good at video games. I like to swim, especially diving, and I collect coins.

"I have a complete set of buffalo nickels," he continued with a smile, looking for her reaction.

Michelle just sat against the tree smiling and waiting for him to go on.

"Something is wrong," he thought. "Why is she just sitting there smiling at me?" He waited a minute to see if she would say something, but she didn't.

"OK, what's up?" he finally asked. He was still sitting against his tree with his shoes touching hers, looking into her eyes.

She smiled and said, "A friend and a gentleman would say, 'you first'".

Richard thought, "An etiquette lesson, huh?" Then he turned his head and looked over toward the stream that ran through the park, not far from where they sat. His gaze meandered from it over to some large thorn bushes clear on the other side of the park and started nodding his head as he thought about it, "OK, I can play along. After all, I was the one who started it back at the house."

So he turned and looked back in Michelle's eyes.

Even though Richard was only thirteen years old it didn't take him long to figure out that there was nothing in this world like looking into her eyes. "Not the boy-girl thing," he thought to himself. "This is different."

It was as if, as long as he was looking into her eyes, nothing else mattered, because she was his friend. He also realized as they sat there looking at each other now, that she was giving him that same look she had given him yesterday while he knelt at the side of her bed and she said the words, "Be my friend."

Richard sensed that this friendship would be different from any other. He somehow knew that as they sat there with their backs against the trees and their feet touching they were becoming true friends.

He took a deep breath, he knew this was for keeps. He knew the other boys would give him a bad time for playing with a girl, but as he looked into her eyes nothing else mattered. She wanted a friend and he could tell that she wanted their friendship to be perfect from the start.

Without waiting any longer, realizing this was a road of no return, Richard smiled and said, "No, please, you first."

"Thank you," she said, batting her eyelids.

Her eyes said it with a little twinkle that made Richard

feel like a million dollars. Their friendship was not normally as formal as these first few words exchanged between them, in fact, it turned out to be just the opposite. Polite words were almost never spoken, they didn't need to be, they were shown in their eyes and actions each day, through thick and thin.

"I 'love' the violin," Michelle said with a smile, "and I believe you will become that greatest player in the world." She paused so she could give him a look of confidence. "I've never played a video game, but I will try, if you will show me how."

Then she started taking off her shoes.

When Richard just sat there looking at her she said, "Come on," as though he knew what was going on.

She waited for Richard to start taking off his shoes, then she slowly took hers off so he could finish taking off his second sock at the same time she did.

Then they slowly and ceremoniously put their bare feet together as though it were some kind of ritual. And when that was done they wiggled their toes together and laughed.

"Something like blood brothers," Richard thought to himself as he looked at her, "only this isn't as painful."

Their smiles grew even bigger and they laughed again while their toes wiggled together some more.

Then Michelle said, "You like to swim and dive."

She slowly tilted her head back and looked up into the sky with a dreamy look on her face. Then she closed her eyes and said, "I like to take off all my clothes and swim in the middle of a pond or lake late at night and look up at the stars." Then she waved her arms back as though she were swimming.

Richard blushed. He had never heard anyone talk like that before. He couldn't imagine skinny-dipping out in the open where someone might see him.

Michelle looked back into Richard's eyes without missing a beat. "On my fifth birthday my father gave me a buffalo nickel that he found a long time ago and told me to take care of it because it was very valuable. I keep it hidden in a special box under my mattress. A whole set must be worth a fortune! Will you show it to me sometime?"

"Sure," was his reply, and he realized they were now true friends.

They came back to the park the next day and without even saying a word they both took off their shoes and socks and sat down together under the two trees and put their feet together. They sat a moment and looked at each other, then they wiggled their toes as if to say 'hi' and then they laughed.

Next they looked deep into each other's eyes for a long time as big smiles spread across each of their faces. Then they talked. Michelle first, of course.

That became their ritual each day. Even when it rained or the wind blew, it was the same.

It only took a few days for Michelle's scrapes and bruises to heal enough for her to get around better and soon they were running and playing together everywhere.

Each morning Richard would practice his violin while Michelle helped her mother. Then, in the afternoons when they were both free, they would meet between the two trees and head out from there.

They walked everywhere together and explored the whole town, street by street, but at the end of each day they always ended up between the two trees with their feet together and a wiggle of their toes to say good-bye before they parted and went to their separate homes.

Michelle's first great adventure was to walk through each and every store in town, discovering and learning about everything there was to see. Then if they couldn't figure out what something was between the two of them, Michelle would ask whoever was standing next to them in the aisle.

Most people were happy to help her and they answered her questions if they could. If there weren't any other customers nearby, or if they didn't know the answers, Michelle would then carry the items up to the counter and ask the salesman.

Richard felt a little uncomfortable disturbing the salesmen at first, but the owners and salesclerks were always so cheerful in their responses to Michelle that he began to relax. Soon, he felt at ease and found himself asking questions and joining in the conversations while they worked their way through the town.

Richard had no idea how many different things there were just sitting on the shelves of the stores and how many nice people you could meet and the things you could learn from them by just asking.

The trouble was, Michelle loved to learn about every last item.

After they had visited about half of the stores in town, they visited the drugstore one afternoon. Mrs. Becker, the neighborhood gossip, was standing right beside them at the counter when Michelle walked up and asked what some items were for and how to use them. It only took a moment for Richard and Michelle to find themselves escorted out the front door by a hostile clerk telling them not to come back for at least ten years, with Mrs. Becker gasping for air in the background.

Richard and Michelle looked at each other with a whole mixture of expressions as they straightened themselves up and walked back to the park to sit between the trees before heading home.

Richard thought he knew what the items might have been and he was willing to keep quiet and let it end there. Michelle, on the other hand, was never satisfied unless she knew all the answers. Michelle went home that afternoon and asked her mother what the items were that she had carried up to the counter.

The next afternoon after Richard and Michelle sat down between the two trees, took off their shoes and wiggled their toes together, she told him everything. It didn't embarrass her at all, sitting there with their bare feet and toes together, looking him in the eyes and telling him all about the birds and the bees.

Richard found over the years that between asking everyone

everything and the books they read together under the shade of the two trees, Michelle had the answers to everything he could ever imagine.

It would amaze Richard, as they sat between the two trees month after month, and year after year that no matter how smart he thought he was, and he was an A student in school, that Michelle always seemed to understand everything a little better than he did.

Richard found he could trust Michelle's opinions more than his own, and as time went by, when he needed her each time something important came along, she would always be there, sitting between the two trees with the answer.

Chapter 8: The Officer

*H*e knew he needed her now, while he stood staring at the Luthier with his fists clenched and his jaw set tight. Richard dug his fingernails into the palms of his hands trying to suppress his emotions. He fought as hard as he could to maintain discipline and control himself as he tried to keep them from showing, but it was no use; he choked up and started to lose control as he thought of Michelle.

He needed her, and she wasn't there.

"I'm not putting up with this! And I'm not putting up with you!" Richard yelled at the Luthier.

The Luthier stood motionless over his varnish pot and didn't say a word while Richard stomped back over to the violin shop and threw open the door.

Richard stormed inside, grabbed his Bergonzi and left the door wide open while he jumped back into the Blazer. He revved the engine as soon as it came to life and dropped it into gear, then he roared off through the orchard, sending rocks flying out from underneath the spinning tires as he went.

"Who does this guy think he is?" fumed Richard as he drove back down the gravel road.

"I wonder what Sam will have to say when I tell him the #*! violin maker burned up his check!"

With his jaw set tight and his hands clenched on the steering wheel he pulled back onto the pavement and gave it a little more gas. Richard was tired of this charade and he was ready for the respect and courtesy he knew the dealer in New York would give him when he went back to buy the Guarneri. He smiled at himself as he set his sights for New York, then he drove back down the Main Street of Leeds a bit faster than he had come up it.

He had been able to push Michelle to the back of his mind over the years, until this business of buying a different violin came up. Now he found himself thinking about her almost constantly again. He had been able to manage just fine living alone and taking care of himself all these years. He could put up with his life and his career just the way it was. But he couldn't put up with the grief and torment again! He pounded his fist on the dashboard as tears of rage welled up in his eyes.

No. He was going to New York now, buying the Guarneri, and getting back on with his life just the way he had planned before talking to Samuel.

Just as Richard reached the south end of town flashing blue and red lights caught his eye in the rear view mirror. "#*!, *@!, and *#*&*!" he said out loud as he looked down at the speedometer.

He was going faster, but "sixty in a thirty-five" was how the ticket finally read when the officer handed the copy back to Richard.

It could have been worse, a lot worse, if Richard had not got a grip on himself by the time the officer reached his window. He was at least grateful that his 'practiced skills of control' helped keep the conversation at an 'acceptable level' between the officer and himself.

"Considering my mood," he snapped at himself, "I did rather well."

"Here you go Mr. Gaspar," the officer said as he handed the ticket to Richard.

"That baby will cost you a little," he added, pointing at the ticket in Richard's hand.

"I know this little truck here is a rental and you're from out of town, but if you're still around next Wednesday afternoon and could come up to the town hall between four and five and take our 'Happy Driver Safety Course', it'll save you fifty bucks." The officer now gave Richard a smile as he spoke.

Richard had a hard time forcing out a pleasant looking smile in return, but he answered, "I'll think about it, thank you."

Richard was anxious to leave so he could be back in Las Vegas in time to catch a flight back tonight, but he was waiting for the officer's cue to exit.

"Richard Gaspar. Richard Gaspar. I know I've heard that name before," the officer said while scratching his head. "Are you related to anyone famous?"

Richard closed his eyes and shook his head. "What an idiot!" he thought to himself.

"Have we met somewhere?" The officer lifted up his sunglasses and took a closer look at Richard's face. Richard opened his eyes and sat still while the officer looked him over again. The officer's face was going through all kinds of different skewed and contorted expressions the entire time he examined Richard's features.

"I can't believe this!" Richard thought, and he still looked straight ahead with his hands on the steering wheel. He was even more impatient to leave now.

Then the officer's eyes brightened and he stood back.

"I've got it!" he exclaimed, as he dropped his sunglasses back in place.

"I never forget a face!" the officer exclaimed again.

"You're that violin player! My mother has a copy of your record...uh, well, CD anyway, sitting on her stereo at home, right now, as we speak!" The officer's smile appeared on his face again and he surmised, "You must have just come from Jonathan Dewey's place north of town to buy a 'real' violin."

The officer stood back, drew in his breath and whistled as he looked at the dust and dings that showed around the bottom of the blazer, especially around the back where the tires had spit up the dirt and rocks while Richard spun the tires when he left the violin shop. Then the officer took in another deep breath, "Only, by the look on your face as you drove by, and by the look of your vehicle here, you probably couldn't afford one, huh? Is that it?"

Richard made no reply. He just gave the officer a look of disgust and rolled his eyes while the officer continued, "That happens a lot. That's too bad. How much did he ask? I hear they're getting pretty expensive these days."

Richard didn't even bother answering. His patience was running thin.

"My daughter is learning how to play the cello. She says she would like one of his instruments when she gets good enough. I don't know though, being a police officer doesn't pay too much, though I have heard of him cutting deals if someone is good but can't quite afford it. You must make pretty good money living back East, huh? Did you ask him if he took payments? I heard though, that he wouldn't. Suzy should probably start saving up now. Do you play the cello too? Do you give lessons?"

"That's it!! I can't take any more!" Richard almost blurted out loud.

"He burned up my check!" exclaimed Richard, as his eyes flared at the officer. Then he quickly faced forward again looking down the road in front of him.

"Ooh-wee!", said the officer as he backed away just a little bit. "Got to you, did he?"

Richard thought the officer almost seemed to take joy in Richard's anger and his losing control.

"Wouldn't take your money, huh? What did you do? Insult his wife or step on her cat's tail? You must have really ticked him off if he wouldn't take 'your' money."

Richard didn't even look at the officer while he answered him, "It wasn't 'my' money. The violin was supposed to be a gift from an old friend of mine. It was 'my friend's' money."

Richard was heating up now and his knuckles went white as he gripped the steering wheel of the Blazer even tighter.

"Why am I talking to you about this anyway?!" Richard angrily told the officer. "Am I free to go now or not?"

"Ooh-wee!" the officer exclaimed again. Then he said in a firm tone, "You aren't going anywhere just yet, Mister

Gaspar. You aren't driving down 'my' road until you simmer down a bit.

"You see, I don't want you tearing up the road or plowing into any of these children while you're having this little tizzy fit of yours," then the officer pointed over to the group of young children still playing in the water at the side of the road.

Richard knew he had blown it with the officer, so he just gave in. He pulled his hands off the steering wheel, sat back in his seat, took a deep breath and looked back up at the officer.

"That's a little better now. So, he wouldn't take your friend's money, eh?" A puzzled look appeared on the officer's face.

"I don't know what's up, unless your friend insulted Jonathan's wife or stepped on her cat's tail, but I will tell you something; the people who come from his shop and drive down this street with an instrument of his in their car are never mean or ornery. I've seen them drive up, everyone in the car with scowls on their faces, but if they drive back down with one of his instruments in the car, it's always with a smile.

"Not everyone buys from him, though, and those people drive back down the street with the same o'nery looks on their faces as when they came.

"Tell you what, it looks like you could use about fifteen or twenty more minutes to simmer down and I need a drink. Jump into the back of my car here and I'll buy you a grape soda up at the store."

What could Richard say? He reluctantly stepped out of his Blazer and into the back seat of the police car.

"Regulations, you know," the officer apologized with a smile, referring to his making Richard sit in the back 'cage' of the patrol car. As the door closed behind him, Richard looked around at his surroundings; first at the heavy steel screen that separated him from the officer, then at the blatant lack of door handles and window cranks.

Even though the day was hot and Richard was

perspiring, it sent a chill down his spine. He had only been in the back seat of a police car one other time in his life. It was just before he turned sixteen. Only it was Michelle and he together, sitting in the back seat of the police car looking at each other that late September night.

Chapter 9: The Lake

"*It's your fault*," Richard matter-of-factly whispered over to Michelle, who was sitting on the other side of the seat looking at him.

"I know, I'm sorry," was Michelle's simple, quiet reply.

That was all they said to each other while they rode across town in the back seat of the squad car on their way to the police station. Richard turned his head and silently looked out his window until they pulled in and stopped by the front steps.

"But did you have fun?" Michelle asked with a smile on her face.

Richard turned and just stared at Michelle in disbelief as his door was opened for him and as he awkwardly stood up with both of his hands securely held together with handcuffs behind his back.

While the patrol car drove up the Main Street of Leeds Richard sat in the back seat with his head up against the window and watched the children playing happily together in the water. As he watched the houses go by and looked into each of the children's faces while they played in front of their homes, his mind wandered back through the years and he thought of all the events that led up to that night...

"The phone is for you, Richard," his mother's voice echoed through the entry and into the study where he was practicing.

"OK, mom," he replied. Then he carefully set his violin

down, walked over and took the phone from his mother. Richard hardly ever received any phone calls and he wondered who it could be.

"Wear your swimming suit under your clothes and bring a towel," Michelle's eager voice requested from the receiver.

"Is it OK if I go swimming today?" Richard turned and asked his mother.

"As long as there is someone there who can see you two, just in case something happens," was her reply.

Since there was always someone around the lake in the summer, Richard took her answer as a yes.

"OK," was his reply to Michelle, then he hung up the phone.

They didn't talk on the phone very often and their conversations were all pretty much like that. Short, and to the point.

He knew what the phone call meant. Michelle's scrapes and bruises were now healed enough to go swimming in the lake. Richard loved to swim and dive but he hadn't been in the water since the day he met Michelle over three weeks ago. They had walked down to the docks and talked about it, but they were waiting for her wounds to fully heal. It was still a hot summer and he was really looking forward to diving into the cool water of the lake again.

Richard turned his large black metronome back on and set its speed up another notch, he wondered how well Michelle could swim or if she could keep up with him. "That's all right," he thought, "Even if she can't swim very well Michelle is always a lot of fun, no matter what we do."

He was thinking of the times they rode their bicycles together. Richard could ride a lot faster than Michelle and found that he had to slow down so she could keep up, but when they got where they were going she always had something fun to do and he always had a good time.

"It's always worth waiting for Michelle," Richard realized, while he finished playing his scales and studies flawlessly in record time and went back to his room to change.

Richard's otherwise bleak and sanitary room already showed signs of him having a friend now. A few days ago Michelle and Richard sat between the two trees and drew two pictures of each other with colored pencils that Michelle had asked Richard to bring that day.

When they were done they gave their favorite picture to each other and they both hung them on their bedroom walls. Richard's two pictures were taped side by side above his study desk, the one he drew of Michelle and her favorite one she drew of him, and he smiled as he looked at them both for a minute.

While Richard was changing and getting ready to leave, his mother called to him, "You need to wear a hat. The sun is extra hot today."

Richard never wore a hat. The only hat he owned was a goofy one his father bought when they went fishing together last summer. It was floppy and still too large for him and it seemed to be meant to look funny anyway.

"It's not worth arguing with her though," he realized by the time he walked out of his room. So he reluctantly went back and put the goofy hat on sideways.

He walked by his mother in the kitchen with the hat on and she couldn't hide a small laugh when she remembered how funny it looked on him.

"I guess we need to get you another hat," she said with a smile as she straightened it on Richard's head. But, not willing to change a direct order, she added, "But you still need to wear this one today."

Richard stood, waiting between the trees, wondering what Michelle would think about the hat.

He couldn't believe it when she came walking up with her mother's large, old-fashioned hat on backwards! Michelle pulled off her shoes, then they both sat down at the same time and wiggled their toes together while they looked into each others eyes.

"Nice hat," she said with a cute smile on her face and a wink.

"Yours is magnificent," he replied with stately airs as he winked back. Then they both got up and threw their hats into the branches of Michelle's tree and left them there while they headed down to the docks together.

They seldom disobeyed their parents, and Michelle normally would have worn the hat she threw in her tree, but they both knew that they didn't need to invite any teasing from anyone along the way about Richard's hat. And everything they did, they did together.

There was a small group of boys who had teased Richard about playing the violin since he was a little boy, and now they teased him for only playing with a girl. Nothing too serious, but Michelle and Richard both knew it wouldn't take much to change that, so they did what they could to avoid unwanted attention.

When they approached the lake, Michelle turned and rode her bicycle over to a small group of trees. She leaned her small bicycle against a tree on the opposite side, then she looked at Richard and pointed her finger toward the side nearest to him. Richard obeyed with a curious look on his face. "You have your swimming suit on already, don't you?" Richard asked through the trees.

"Of course," Michelle replied.

Richard looked over to the shore of the lake where dozens of people, old and young, were running around and swimming or laying on the shore in their swimming suits.

"Then why are we standing behind the trees?" he asked.

"It just doesn't seem right to take off 'any' clothes in the open," Michelle said, as she removed everything but her one-piece, old fashioned, dark-blue swimming suit.

Richard didn't quite understand what was wrong since they would be swimming together in a minute, but he respected her feelings and wishes anyway and stripped down to his swimming trunks behind the trees.

They left their clothes sitting on their bicycles out in the open where they could see them and headed over to the docks with their large beach-towels wrapped around them.

The lake was too small for any motorboats but there were a few canoes and inner tubes floating around with children playing in them. There were also people around the edge of the lake picnicking and cooling off in the shade of the trees.

Michelle and Richard walked out to the end of the dock together and they tossed their towels down side by side. Richard looked at Michelle standing there in her long, old fashioned one-piece swimming suit.

Richard thought, "It was probably her mother's or grandmother's, after all they don't have much money."

Michelle immediately noticed the look on Richard's face as he looked at her swimming suit for just that second.

"A proper girl is modest and should not flaunt her body," Michelle said, as though she were reciting something her mother had told her, or something she had read out of an etiquette book.

Richard looked into Michelle's eyes while she spoke. Then he turned and looked at the other girls scattered around the lake and realized that Michelle was a very special girl, as well as his best friend.

Richard smiled, then he stepped up onto one of the large posts at the end of the dock and straightened himself up. He put his feet precisely together, extended his arms, then executed a perfect swan dive into the water without a splash.

Michelle was still watching Richard with admiration as he swam gracefully through the water and climbed up the ladder at the end of the dock. Richard's three years of swimming and diving lessons showed in every move he made.

"Teach me how," Michelle asked with an eager voice when Richard came walking back over to her at the end of the dock.

Without notice, Richard pushed her in. Then he jumped in with her.

As their heads bobbed back up he said, "The first lesson of diving is, 'get in the water'."

Michelle laughed and tried to push his head under but Richard used his swimming skills to avoid her hand and he was over to the ladder and back up on the dock before she could reach him.

When Michelle reached the top of the ladder Richard held out his hand to help her in a gentlemanly way, which she cautiously accepted.

"What's next?" she asked with a smile. Michelle acted totally unaffected by lesson number one and walked back over to the edge of the dock and looked at him.

Richard smiled back as he realized Michelle was a good sport with a great attitude about everything.

Richard taught her each point of diving that he had learned so far, step by step. He explained the proper technique for each one, then he dove in to show her how it was done.

Each time Michelle would dive Richard told her how she did on that particular technique and then he continued on with the next lesson. Within an hour Michelle was beautifully springing through the air and entering the water with beautiful form.

Richard stood and stared while he watched her straight legs and pointed toes glide smoothly into the water and out of sight without a splash. He marvelled how it had taken him almost a year to learn all the little points that go into a perfect dive and Michelle was almost there in one afternoon.

She climbed back up the ladder, walked over to the end of the dock and stood beside Richard, ready for the next critique and lesson.

"Next lesson," she said, while she waited for him to instruct her. She pulled her wet hair back and stood in diving position.

"We're done. That was a perfect swan dive," Richard answered with his mouth still hanging open in disbelief.

Suddenly Michelle's eyes and head turned and she exclaimed, "Look out Richard!" in a frantic voice.

Richard quickly turned around, and as he did, he felt Michelle's hands push him off balance and into the lake. Michelle then jumped in and as both of their heads bobbed above water, Michelle playfully said, "The first lesson of girls is, expect revenge." Then they swam around the lake before climbing up the ladder and drying off.

"I like diving," Michelle said, then she picked up a comb she had brought with her and looked at Richard again. "Thank you for showing me how."

She finished combing her hair out as they walked up the beach. When they reached the group of trees she asked, "Did you have fun?"

Richard replied with a smile and a nod. Michelle really was fun. More fun than anyone he had ever known.

They went back to the dock to dive and swim about twice a week until the summer was over, each diving in turn and judging the other's performance.

Richard taught Michelle every dive he could do off the end of the dock and it didn't take long before each of them received a perfect score of ten on each one.

After the school year started Richard used his allowance to teach Michelle how to play video games on Saturdays at the bowling alley. She started out meek and timid enough, but by Christmas time she was an aggressive competitor and she could hold her own against anyone there.

When the new games started coming to the bowling alley that required that they shoot at each other, Michelle quickly lost interest in video games.

As the quarters ran out one Saturday afternoon she said, "If it's all right with you, I have had fun, but I prefer real things."

Richard completely understood. He knew she felt the same about having to shoot at his guy on the video game, and the electronic games just couldn't compare with all the fun things they experienced together out in the real world anyway. He knew that as long as they were standing in front of a game, he was missing out on some new experience outside with Michelle.

As they walked out of the bowling alley that afternoon Richard sensed that this was the last time they would play video games together.

The next Saturday they both decided that enough time had passed since the drugstore incident and they began visiting the rest of the stores and businesses in town.

It had surprised them how many of the clerks and people in the stores around town had heard about that day in the drugstore, but most of the store owners and clerks were very understanding and they smiled when they saw Michelle and Richard walk in their door together. They had more fun than ever asking their questions now, and they took people's comments in stride while they learned about everything they could in every store.

Though they were a little more careful now about 'how' they asked their questions and 'who' they asked about some of the items. But Michelle still asked about every last one; she just made sure that she was good friends with the clerks before asking about things she didn't know 'anything' about.

When they did find something extra special during the day they would go back and sit between the trees and look into each others eyes, or lie on the grass side by side looking up at the sky, and talk about it.

They talked about everything, there were no limits. They could tell each other anything and they were never embarrassed or worried that the other would make fun of them or embarrass them for any reason.

Sometimes they told each other jokes, but the jokes were never at the other's expense or about each other, even if it was just in fun. There was never an unkind word spoken between the two trees, they were too good of friends to ever let that happen.

The school year passed by and Richard felt like the knowledge he learned while walking through the stores and businesses with Michelle was worth more than the education he received at school. With Michelle everything was real; you could see it, hear it, taste it, touch it, and feel it.

Just a few days after school let out for the next summer Richard realized that they were walking into the very last business in town. It was the radiator repair shop.

"Now where do we go?" asked Richard as he and Michelle walked out of the door and said good-bye to Charlie. He owned the radiator shop where they learned about boiling out radiators and soldering up leaks.

"The rest of the world," answered Michelle as she turned and started walking down the sidewalk toward the city library.

That summer, while all the rest of the children in their neighborhoods were watching television or going to camp, Michelle and Richard spent most of their time reading books together between the two trees. But best of all they lived the books together.

Michelle chose the first book, of course.

It was a book about all the different kinds of dogs and how to train them. After they finished reading it Michelle decided that they should go to a dog show so they could see each of the different breeds for themselves and talk to the trainers who raised them; and they did.

Richard chose the next book, and after they read about trains they talked Richard's mother into taking them to the train station in the next town so they could ride on one together for an afternoon and talk to the conductor and engineer. That's how their summer went, one book after the other, with a fun adventure when they were done with each one.

When Michelle heard that a play would be performed in their town in a couple of weeks she borrowed a script from the drama teacher at the high school and they read it together and acted out the parts. Then they got their parents to take them to the play where they sat side by side watching the actors and they silently mouthed their lines that they had read together.

They read books about how things were done and how everything was made, then they did them or made them whenever it was possible. If they couldn't do something themselves, they found someone who had and they talked to them about it.

Best of all they were friends, and when they were through doing anything, they would always come back and sit between the two trees where Michelle would always ask Richard, "Did you have fun?"

And Richard would always reply by looking into her eyes,

nodding his head and smiling.

Chapter 10: Applause

*M*ichelle noticed that Richard hesitated when it was his turn to select the next book at the library. As his eyes scanned the bookshelves she offered, "Let's do something different."

Richard turned and looked into Michelle's eyes. He knew she already had something in mind by the way she smiled.

"What?" he asked, knowing that a new adventure was about to begin.

"People," was all she said as they walked out of the library and up the sidewalk together. When they started walking toward the east end of town Richard had a funny feeling that he knew where they were headed. There wasn't much out there except for one thing.

"The rest home?" Richard asked as they walked up toward the front door.

"People," was Michelle's only reply as she allowed Richard to open the door for her.

Michelle's eyes glowed while she listened to complete strangers tell her their life story. She would sit down beside them in the entry or walk into an open door and say a few words to get them started talking, then she would sit back and listen with a smile on her face, while Richard sat beside her or stood in amazement.

Richard always thought of old people's conversations as dull and uninteresting but Michelle had a way of asking just the right questions that brought out the exciting or moving events in each of their lives. They would even tell her of their secret loves and desires.

Richard and Michelle visited the rest home every other Saturday during the school year and as the months passed they found themselves the center of attention there. All they had to do each time they went was to say a few words, then sit back and listen to the stories until they became their dearest friends.

Many of the people at the rest home even learned things about one another that brought them closer together and the whole atmosphere seemed to change for the better as time went by.

It amazed Richard over and over how many stories of adventure, wars, loves, music, dancing, hardships, glory, and everything else imaginable were just waiting to be discovered in the rest home.

"And best of all, we can look into their eyes and hear the real stories from the actual people who were there and lived history," Michelle explained to Richard with excitement in her eyes while they sat between the two trees after visiting the rest home one Saturday afternoon.

Richard enjoyed their visits to the rest home but he could tell Michelle was passionate about them.

Even during the next summer when there were so many other places to go and things to do, Michelle and Richard kept going to the rest home every other Saturday. That summer they started making it their habit to pull a few weeds outside and then take in a flower to whoever they talked to that day.

Michelle had an imagination that never quit.

Sometimes, during the summer, when they would return from the lake on lazy afternoons they would walk across the bridge to the other side of the park and lay down on a grassy knoll and look up at the sky and talk. They talked about everything together and nothing was ever too ridiculous or too personal and their imaginations soared.

If there were clouds floating by, Michelle would imagine different animals or people, which always ended up with them laughing together until it hurt. Each time a jet would cross the sky they would talk of traveling the world and going places together.

Sometimes they even talked of love and marriage, though they never talked in first person or about each other specifically. But, on the hot afternoons when they lay on their backs and looked up at the sky and fell asleep, they always dreamed about each other and no one else.

Richard was fifteen-and-a-half and Michelle would turn fourteen in just a couple more months. It was late in the summer but it was still a hot afternoon when Michelle and Richard placed their clothes on their bicycles parked by the small clump of trees.

They walked out to the end of the dock and tossed their towels down side by side like they had a hundred times before. It was then that Richard realized, as he looked at Michelle, that she was still the only teenage girl at the lake with a one piece swimming suit and even though it was her second one since they had met it was still old-fashioned and dark-blue.

Michelle noticed the look on Richard's face as he glanced at her swimming suit the same way he had two years before. She knew that Richard still remembered her words by the look on his face and she smiled as she looked into his eyes.

Richard looked back into Michelle's soft, brown eyes and then he turned and looked at all the other girls scattered around the lake. Now he realized Michelle was a very special young woman, and she was still his best friend.

Michelle climbed up onto the highest post at the end of the dock and executed a perfect one-and-a-half flip with a twist and elegantly entered the water without the slightest splash.

As they put their shoes back on after sitting between the two trees later that afternoon Michelle looked up at Richard and asked, "Will you bring your violin tomorrow?"

Richard knew what Michelle wanted and he was a little reluctant, but by now he felt like he could not refuse her anything that she asked. So he puffed up his chest and lifted his nose just slightly and responded in his most distinguished tone of voice, "Of course, Madame, your wish is my command," as he bowed low with his arm out in front of him.

"Richard wants to take his Bergonzi with him to the rest home tomorrow," Richard's mother told his father while they sat at the dinner table that night.

"What for?" was his father's concerned reply.

"Michelle and Richard have been visiting the rest home on Saturdays and she wants him to play some music for them."

"That sounds like a nice thing to do, but can't you take your spare practice violin, Richard?" his father asked before continuing with his meal.

"It doesn't sound half as good, and Michelle really likes the people there."

"Michelle, Michelle, Michelle. Don't you think you're spending just a little too much time with Michelle?" his father asked, this time with a concerned look on his face.

It wasn't the first time this topic had come up, but this was certainly the most direct assault so far.

"Your mother also tells me your practicing has been slipping a little lately, since you two have been spending so much time together," his father said. Then he gave Richard another look.

Richard knew he had been pushing the limits the last couple of months. He had been spending more and more time with Michelle lately and even though his music studies were still progressing, they had slowed down. He knew he needed to say something to keep his parents happy if he expected them to allow him to keep spending so much time with Michelle.

"If I play at the rest home it will help with my performing skills. My teacher mentioned just last week that I needed to perform more in front of people," Richard pleaded.

"Well, I suppose that's true, but we still need to talk about the amount of time you two spend together," and with that his father went back to eating in silence.

"Don't carry it on your bicycle and don't go anywhere else with it. And bring it straight home," his mother added, with a nod of agreement from his father.

Richard met Michelle the next morning between the two trees carrying his Bergonzi in its black leather case. She walked up carrying a thin paper bag that didn't seem to have anything in it.

After they sat down and put their bare feet together Michelle said, "Thank you," with a twinkle in her eye.

She was referring to his Bergonzi that now sat by his side on the grass.

He smiled back, then asked, "What's in the bag?"

"A surprise," she responded. "For later."

After they wiggled their toes together Richard got a serious look on his face. "Last night my parents commented again about us spending too much time together, and about my practicing."

"I've been thinking about that," Michelle replied.

And without another word they got up and walked to the rest home.

The people in the main entry seemed to light up when Michelle and Richard walked in. They especially noticed the violin case in Richard's hand and started talking excitedly to each other. Michelle had told all of them how wonderfully Richard could play, though he thought she had exaggerated a little.

They formed a ragged circle, with part of them sitting in wheel chairs and the other part in the lounge chairs in the entry.

Richard rosined up his bow, pulled out his violin and started to play. They enjoyed the music and they all listened with smiles on their faces while Richard performed. Most of the pieces of music he played were from his last lesson. Some of the pieces were quite difficult and Richard played them almost flawlessly, one after the other. When he stopped playing they all gave him a warm round of applause. Some of them even cheered and, those that could, gave him a standing ovation.

Richard was about to put his violin away when Michelle stood up and walked over to him and said, "Play this," as she pulled a piece of sheet music out of the thin paper bag she still held in her hand.

She held the music up for him with both of her hands since he hadn't brought a music stand. All of his music was memorized.

Richard looked into Michelle's eyes while she held the sheet music up in front of him, then he glanced down at the music for a minute. He quickly recognized that it was a simple love song.

After only a few bars all of the men and women who were sitting and listening to Richard play began to cry.

Richard noticed as he glanced up from the music that people who never left their rooms started coming out into the entry from down the hallway.

"Again," Michelle requested as Richard came to the end of the piece and the people were still coming out of their rooms.

As he repeated the song he found himself playing each note the very best he could. He found himself playing with more feeling and expression than he ever had before and everyone that sat in front of him or stood in the entry cried with smiles on their faces until his final note died away.

Their silent tears of joy were the loudest applause Richard had ever heard as he loosened his bow and put his violin away.

"Thank you," said Michelle as they left the rest home and walked back up the walkway side by side.

When they reached the sidewalk and turned together Richard looked down and finally noticed that Michelle was holding his hand.

Chapter 11 : Mr. Edwards

The next Monday morning Michelle came over to Richard's house. Mrs. Gaspar answered the door while Richard practiced in the study.

"Good morning, Michelle," Alaine greeter her.

"Good morning, Mrs. Gaspar."

"Would you like me to get Richard?" she asked, and she started to turn.

"No thank you. I came to ask 'you' a question," Michelle announced.

Richard's mother turned back toward Michelle, a little surprised.

"Please come in."

As soon as Michelle was inside and the door was closed behind her, she asked, "If I help you with your housework for a half-an-hour, three times a week, would you teach me the piano for fifteen minutes each day after I finished? I would work very hard, and I do windows."

It took Mrs. Gaspar a minute or so to get over the initial shock, but when she looked into Michelle's earnest eyes, she found herself replying, "I suppose we could work something like that out."

Michelle's piano lessons started the very next day.

During Richard's last half-hour of practicing Michelle and his mother would clean or do housework together. Then they would both come into the study where his mother would teach Michelle how to play the piano.

It was only a few weeks before Michelle could help Richard with the notes and phrases he was learning on his violin by playing them on the piano along with him or by giving him encouragement and advice.

When Richard's playing started improving faster and faster and his mother had more free time than ever, his parents' comments about how much time they spent together stopped.

Richard's parents enrolled him into a private school that fall, and even though they were on a different schedule, by the end of the first week they had settled into a routine.

Michelle's school started later than Richard's, so she would get up early and do her chores before school and Richard would practice his violin right after school so they could meet together between the two trees each day as soon as possible.

The seasons changed and the school year started to pass quickly by. They talked about what happened in school each day and they would share what each of them had learned.

Richard realized that Michelle was a lot more popular than he was and she seemed to learn a lot more from school than he did, even though he was an honor student and got straight A's.

They both had acquaintances at school and were involved in other activities, but nothing really mattered to them except their meetings under the two trees with their bare feet together.

The first cold day of winter that year both Michelle and Richard came walking up to the two trees at the same time. They each carried their homework in one hand and a large pair of thick gloves in the other. They both laughed when they saw what was in each other's hands and they quickly sat down and took off their shoes and socks together so they could try the new gloves out.

They had learned from experience, during their first winter between the two trees, that they needed to bring a pair of gloves to keep their feet warm. Richard also carried two trashbags in his coat pocket to sit on when the first winter storm hit.

The only day they couldn't see each other at all was Thursday. Richard's violin teacher lived in another town and it took all afternoon to drive there, have his lesson, and then drive back. It was on those Thursdays that Michelle started knocking on doors.

Each Friday afternoon when they met between the two trees Michelle would then tell Richard of the people she met and all the things she learned from them while he was at his lesson.

She used the same approach that she had in the stores. She would walk down the sidewalks and look around until she saw something she wanted to ask about, then she would walk up, knock on the door and ask whoever answered the door all about it.

"I wonder how many of them think you are there selling Girl Scout cookies?" asked Richard while they sat between the two trees one Friday afternoon.

"A lot," smiled Michelle, "but I found the most wonderful old man yesterday." Then she straightened up a little, which prompted Richard to do the same. "He only lives a few blocks away from me in the dark-green house with that old black car beside it."

Richard nodded his head. He knew the house. It was probably the smallest, most quaint looking house in town and he had never seen anyone go in or come out of it. It didn't look like anyone lived there except for the garbage can out in front each garbage day as he and Michelle walked by. The old car was an antique but it looked like it hadn't been driven in years with the yard grown over it so much you could barely see it was even there.

"I wanted to know what kind of car it was, so I went up and knocked. It took him the longest time to answer the door, and when he did, it was very slowly."

Richard could tell by the way Michelle talked that this was important to her and he tried to visualize the whole thing while she spoke.

"He is the cutest old man. He looked like a short Saint Nicholas. He wore dark-green, baggy trousers and a red, plaid shirt with suspenders and held a twisty old cane in his left hand that shook slightly as he spoke."

"Yes, can I help you?"

Michelle just stood there for a moment with a silent smile, looking into his sparkling eyes.

"Are you selling Girl Scout cookies?" he asked, noticing her hesitation.

"No, Sir, my name is Michelle Ross and it's a pleasure to meet you," Michelle said as she held out her hand.

With just a little hesitation he replied, "Veryl Edwards, at your service, Ma'am," as he shook her hand in a gentlemanly way. "And what brings you to my doorstep this afternoon?"

"I would like to know more about your car."

Mr. Edwards glanced over at the old car by the side of the house.

"Most people ask me if I want to sell it. You look a little young to be driving, Miss."

"I just want to know about it," was her reply. Then with an innocent, pleading smile she asked, "Will you tell me 'all' about it?"

Mr. Edwards slowly closed the door behind him and walked over to the old 1927 Model T Ford, Tudor sedan with Michelle and explained how he and his wife had driven it on their honeymoon because it was the only car he could afford at the time.

Michelle told Richard how it had cost Mr. Edwards thirty-five dollars, which was almost every cent he had in the world. Then Michelle told Richard how Mr. Edwards and his young bride had travelled all over to see the sights while they sat side by side in that car. Michelle's eyes glistened as she told Richard about Mr. Edwards, the places he had been and all the things he had done.

She also told Richard how Mr. Edwards loved his wife so much, and how she had died a few years ago, leaving him alone.

"He told me that he knows he will see his wife again in heaven and he loves her more than ever now. He's the sweetest old man I've ever met."

Michelle paused for a moment, still looking into Richard's eyes to make sure he understood what she meant when she said, "Mr. Edwards is my friend."

Richard understood, and he was happy Michelle had another friend.

Somehow Richard knew that Michelle having another 'true' friend would never compromise their friendship, and he also knew that somehow, someway it would only help.

School was better this year than any other for Richard. Many of the boys at the private school even had musical interests, so a lot of his troubles seemed to go away.

After school and practicing the violin, Michelle would help Richard figure out problems that he had trouble with while he helped her with the classes he had already been through as they sat between the two trees in the park.

A few days before Christmas Michelle came walking up to Richard in the park carrying a vase. It was about a foot high and six inches in diameter and was made out of strips of copper. Richard could tell it was soldered together like the radiators were at the repair shop they visited but it was painted and glazed over with bright cheery colors and beautifully painted spring flowers.

After she sat down with the vase she said, "This is the special art project I had to complete before Christmas. The one Mr. Edwards helped me with." Then she handed it to Richard for him to see.

Richard knew that Michelle had spent a lot of time working on it with Mr. Edwards while he practiced his violin in the evenings and he could tell that it was very well made.

"It's beautiful," he said as he turned it over in his hands and looked at all the different colors and artwork. "Now what are you going to do with it?"

Richard just knew Michelle had something special in mind by the way she had talked about it over the past few weeks.

"Mr. Edwards and I think that it could cheer up the front counter of the rest home, if they would want it."

"If they would want it?" Richard said sarcastically with

a big grin, knowing very well that they loved everything Michelle took there, and this was the most special thing of all that she had made.

"When Mr. Edwards and I give it to them on Christmas Eve will you bring your violin?"

Richard didn't even answer, he just smiled.

Chapter 12: The Wheel

The first day of summer vacation was clear and sunny with boys and girls running everywhere through the town enjoying their new freedom. Michelle and Richard met early in the morning between the two trees. They had taken off their shoes, sat down with their legs extended, and as they put their feet and toes together, they both seemed to realize at the same time that no matter how tightly they scooted back against the trees their legs were bent now.

Michelle laughed about it, then she pulled out a book with pictures of animals on the cover and large words on the top that said, "Uncle Remus."

"Just because we are growing up doesn't mean we have to stop dreaming," she said as she turned to the first page. And for the next three days they read all about the 'brer' animals and the briar patch in the mornings, then they would swim in the lake in the afternoons.

Richard had decided to split his practicing up this summer. Half in the early morning and the other half at night after dinner.

That Thursday they rode around town on their bicycles in the morning then they parted early so Richard could get ready for his lesson.

Friday morning Michelle came walking up to the trees with a new book in her hand and by the look on her face and how she held it Richard could tell that there was something special about it.

As they sat down and pulled off their shoes, Michelle

told Richard, "Mr. Edwards told me that this was his wife's favorite book. He told me how they would read it to each other over and over and how they couldn't help but cry. It's called "Where the Red Fern Grows.""

Michelle handed the book to Richard and said, "You start," with a big smile. Then they brought their bare feet together and wiggled their toes.

They decided to trade off reading every few pages and they read all morning long, trading the book back and forth between them a dozen times. They only took a short break for lunch and now it was Richard's turn again. As Richard started to read, Michelle began to cry. Richard didn't understand why at first and he just kept reading. Then as he continued he understood and he started to cry along with her.

"Do you want to read now?" he asked, holding back the tears the best he could.

"It's still your turn," she answered, giving him a pathetic look.

"Do you want to stop?" Richard asked hopefully.

Michelle just sat there with tears streaming down her face, shaking her head as she answered, "No".

As Richard continued to read, he started to blubber. His throat choked up and his eyes were swollen by the time he handed the book back to Michelle for her turn.

She almost refused, but she realized it was her duty and she started to read. It wasn't much longer before neither of them cared what they sounded like or looked like as they sat between the two trees bawling their eyes out while they read out loud to each other.

When the book was finished, Michelle closed it and looked into Richard's red, swollen eyes. They looked at each other for a long time, completely exhausted. Without saying a word they slowly closed their eyes and went to sleep.

That summer was spent enjoying life to the fullest. Nothing could keep them apart and everything they did, they did together. As the next school year approached, they found themselves staying out later and later at night, and their largest challenge became trying to keep both of their parents happy with the amount of time they spent together.

Each of their families went on a vacation that summer, but other than that, they were together and the summer was theirs.

It was on a Friday, just a couple weeks after school started. Michelle was almost fifteen now and Richard was sixteen-and-a-half. They went to separate schools, but they still met each afternoon between the two trees. When they had homework they would sit with their feet together wiggling their toes until it was finished.

Their legs were bent even more now than they were at the beginning of the summer. Richard still helped Michelle with the books and classes he had already taken and she still helped him with the problems he could not figure out by himself.

When Richard finished writing in his homework binder he looked up at Michelle. She was sitting against her tree holding up a piece of thread about a foot long with a small piece of raw meat hanging from it.

"What's that for?" he asked.

"Mr. Edwards told me about it," she answered, with an adventurous smile and a twinkle in her eye.

An answer like that meant, "Wait and see. It's a wonderful surprise." Richard found that Mr. Edwards was pretty reliable when it came to special things or things that were just plain fun. Richard tossed his book down and excitedly followed Michelle over to the stream that ran through the park.

She stopped, then looked up and down its banks with a serious look on her face, studying it closely. Her eyes brightened when she saw a small overhang along the bank of the stream and she quickly jumped to the other side and knelt down above it.

"Come here, and keep still," she said with an excited look on her face.

Richard knelt down beside her, peering over the edge

with childlike curiosity, wondering what to expect. He knew it was supposed to be a surprise, but he wasn't quite sure what kind of surprise it would be. He knew she couldn't be trying to catch a fish without a hook.

After about five minutes Richard watched as Michelle slowly tugged back and forth on the thread.

"Got him!" she yelled out with excitement, then she slowly pulled up the line. There was a large crawdad hanging off the end of the string, still holding onto the small piece of meat. Richard drew back at first, then he slowly came closer so he could see better.

"Isn't he beautiful?" she said in the tone of a fisherman who has just landed the big trophy winner.

She admired his claws and tail as she turned it around and around in the air. While the crawdad hung twirling in the air, Richard took a closer look. He never quite knew what to expect from Michelle, so he asked, "You aren't going to cook him and eat him are you?"

"No, of course not, I just wanted to say 'hi'," and with that, they took one last look before Michelle lowered him back down into the water. The crawdad finished the little piece of meat, then he swam backward into the dark recesses under the bank with the tips of his claws still barely showing out from under it.

"Did you have fun?" she asked, looking at Richard after he looked up from the crawdad. Richard looked in her eyes and replied with a big grin. Then she looked back at him with a large smile of her own.

After a minute, her expression changed and she slowly looked around, checking to see if anyone was looking. Then she got up, turned around and started walking over to the far side of the park and into the thick, thorny bushes and trees they called the 'briar patch'. Not long after they met, Richard and Michelle had explored it as much as they could without tearing themselves apart in it. The large, thorny bushes looked every bit as bad as the ones they imagined in the 'Uncle Remus' book they had read together under the two trees.

They only came in here when there was something 'truly

secret' to tell each other.

"What's up?" he whispered as he followed her in. No reply meant it was much too important to talk about at all, until they had reached the center.

Michelle was still smaller and thinner than Richard and he had a hard time keeping up with her through the narrow passage.

"Ow, slow down," Richard called up to her when he got caught on one of the large thorns. It tore a small hole in his shirt that revealed a thin trickle of blood.

Michelle stopped and waited for him to catch up. The brush had grown thicker and harder to get through since the last time they had been here, or maybe it was just because they were bigger now. But they finally made it to the small clearing in the middle of the thorny bushes without too many scratches.

Hardly waiting to catch her breath she said, "Look what I have," as she held out a small, brass key with a mischievous look in her eyes.

"What does it go to?" Richard cautiously asked.

He knew by the look in her eyes that he could expect anything now. Not almost anything; anything. When it came to right and wrong Michelle was normally as good as gold. She would help anyone, give them anything she had to give. She was as innocent and sweet as any girl who ever walked the earth, and yet Richard had learned that she looked at life a little differently than anyone else he ever met and sometimes she did or said things that could shock even him.

"It goes to the gate of Salty Pete's," she replied.

Salty Pete's Family Fun Park was an amusement park that had been shut down and boarded up just before Richard and his family had moved to town.

It had closed down overnight when the owner mysteriously disappeared. A lot of people figured he had been killed or left the country quickly, or something; no one ever knew. So there it sat at the edge of town, still tied up in foreclosures and lawsuits.

Its outer fences and walls were covered with various

signs: 'No Trespassing', 'Danger', 'Violators Will Be Prosecuted', 'Keep Out' and every other kind of 'We Don't Want You' signs they had ever seen. A group of older boys had been caught in there just a few months ago. One of them fell while climbing up the ferris wheel and broke both his legs. They were still fighting it out in court.

"They are tearing it down," Michelle said with a pleading tone in her voice. "My father got the contract yesterday. He left early this morning to find some extra workers because it's such a big job and they will be back early in the morning with bulldozers."

One of Michelle's father's occupations was tearing down buildings. Before he would tear each one down he would normally let Michelle walk through the old buildings so she could remember them. "Because then they would be gone forever," she would say.

"Let's go look at it tonight. Everyone around town has said how wonderful it was and I just want to see it before it's gone forever." She was pleading with Richard, almost begging.

"Does your father know?" suspiciously asked Richard.

She hesitated, then slowly replied, "No," in a meek, but determined, voice.

Richard knew how Michelle felt about things like this. She wanted to see everything. She was normally patient and always waited her turn in line when there was something to see, but if it was something that she could never see again and her chance was slipping, she would do almost anything.

"That's illegal," he replied, trying to get her to think her way out of it.

"We would just look," she said, her eyes pleading.

"What if we got hurt? Like that one boy," he continued to reason.

"We would stay on the ground and just look around. I promise." She grabbed Richard's hand. "Please!"

Richard knew he could not talk her out of it.

This was the first time they had ever snuck out at night. Richard's heart was pounding in his throat as he quietly opened his bedroom door and eased his way out the back with only socks on his feet, tiptoeing the whole way.

They met on the other side of the park, wearing dark clothes just like in the movies. They tried to walk as naturally as possible for the few blocks they had to pass by homes under the street lights. When they finally got past the last house Michelle reached over and gave Richard a big hug. Then she looked him in the eyes and said, "Thank you!"

By the look in her eyes he knew this was really important to her.

When they reached the large gate with the red and yellow signs plastered all over it, Michelle looked around and pulled out the key. There were houses only fifty to a hundred feet away with their lights still on.

"Should we wait?" asked Richard.

"No, just keep a watch out," she responded, just before the lock clicked free. Then she announced, "All clear," as she slowly pulled the chain through the loops.

They swung the large gate open just far enough for them to get in. Its large hinges groaned a little, but Richard thought to himself, "Not bad."

When they were in, with the gate closed behind them, they turned around. It was enormous with over twenty buildings and booths forming a large circle, most of it was overgrown with tall weeds. Both of them looked straight ahead at the huge ferris wheel standing in the middle. "Wow!" said Richard.

Michelle responded, "Isn't it beautiful. It's supposed to be the best part. Let's save it for last."

As they started toward the booths Richard commented, "It looks a lot like the carnivals that come to town each year, but everything here is so much bigger, and look how it's made."

Michelle nodded her head as they walked up to the first booth. The walls were made of thick wood, with carvings and paintings all over them. Richard walked in the back where there were still small metal jugs scattered on the ground and he picked some of them up so he could stack them on one of the pedestals standing there.

"Will the lady test her skill and try her luck for the large stuffed giraffe in the corner by knocking over the jugs?" Richard called out in as theatrical, but still hushed a voice as he could. "Only a quarter. Just a quarter to win the dream of your heart."

He pretended to hold up a large, stuffed animal while he tossed her an old baseball that was laying on the ground against the wall. It was still in one piece but the cover was half torn off and the pieces that remained flapped in the air just before Michelle caught it.

Michelle smiled and pretended to hand Richard a quarter. She took the ball and made some exaggerated pitching movements, then she threw it with all her might.

BAM!

The sound of the ball hitting the jugs and then bouncing against the back wall echoed through the park. They both instinctively crouched down together and looked around.

"Should we leave?" asked Richard, "Someone could have heard that."

"Let's go see," said Michelle, as they walked to the front gate and pushed it open just enough to look out.

All of the houses were still dark and quiet. Even a few more of the lights were out now than before. They waited a few minutes, then Michelle told Richard, "We need to be more careful than that or we won't get to see it all."

"You threw the ball!" he whispered as they headed back through the park.

Richard beat her at darts, though you could barely call them darts anymore since most of the feathers were chewed up or missing, but they tried anyway and she handed him the imaginary prize when they were done.

There was the strong man bell. They both looked at it together, then they looked at each other, shaking their heads, remembering the noise the milk jugs had made.

Next was the funhouse. As Richard peered in he realized

he had not brought a flashlight. "How could I be so stupid," he muttered to himself. He turned around to tell Michelle the bad news and saw her standing there holding up a small flashlight. "I could kiss you!" he said, while he jokingly held out his arms and puckered his lips.

"Not until I'm sixteen," she said, smiling back.

Even though they were just joking back and forth, Richard knew it was true. The day after Michelle had talked to her mother about the drugstore items, she had sat and told Richard everything her mother had said. Her mother had also told Michelle that "No decent girl should kiss a boy until she is sixteen or have sex until she is married," and Michelle had promised her mother that she wouldn't.

Michelle always kept her promises, no matter what. And in a way, knowing this made their friendship that much easier and better, especially this last summer. It was something they didn't have to worry about.

Richard thought it was funny how good Michelle usually was and here she was in the middle of the night breaking and entering, or whatever the police would call this if they got caught.

As they entered the funhouse it gave them an eerie feeling. Richard thought, "It's one thing to go into one of these while a carnival is running, it's another to be here alone at night."

Michelle didn't seem to mind though, so Richard bravely continued on. There were witches and skeletons and everything else he had seen in other funhouses, but it was different with everything quiet and only he and Michelle walking side by side. They walked down the floor that moves back and forth, though it wasn't, of course.

They played and laughed in the mirror room for a long time, each taking their turn holding the flashlight while the other stood there puffing their cheeks and making contortions with their bodies in front of the different mirrors. The one that made them look like snakes with a big head was their favorite and they traded off in front of it a few times until they finally ended up, side by side, laughing at each other.

They exited the funhouse laughing, and they both felt exhilarated as they breathed in the fresh, cool night air. Then they quickly quieted back down when they realized they were outside again. They just looked at each other with a look of 'oops', then they laughed again.

Next came the stage where Richard stepped up and pretended to play a great violin concerto while Michelle threw roses and applauded.

There were big steel cages where large animals used to be put on display. Each took their turn acting out the lions and tigers and their tamers with whips and chairs. Then they climbed up in the monkey tree together and put on a show for the audience. They walked through the rides one by one and talked to each other about many different things.

The fortune telling booth was next and as they walked through the drapes, it reminded Richard of his grandfather's parlor.

Richard had told Michelle about his grandfather while they sat between the two trees and she thought he sounded like the most wonderful grandfather anyone could ever have. "Someday I will go visit him," she said, matter of factly before they pulled their feet away from each other and put their shoes back on.

Richard sat down and placed the flashlight on the table so it pointed up at the ceiling between them. He told Michelle's fortune first.

Richard looked across the table and into Michelle's eyes that were sparkling in the light coming up from the flashlight.

"For me to tell your fortune, Madame, you must put both of your hands on the table."

Michelle placed both of her hands on either side of the flashlight with her palms down. Richard brought both of his hands up and slowly slid his fingers under hers until he held her hands in his.

Michelle smiled and asked, "Is this the way your

grandfather tells women's fortunes?"

"I don't know," replied Richard, "I just made that part up." Then they laughed together for a minute, but they didn't let go of each other's hands.

"I see a beautiful woman," started Richard, in a far away voice, much like his grandfather's. "She is the most beautiful woman in the world."

Michelle could not help but smile back at Richard as he continued, "She is elegant and charming and she is so happy that everywhere she goes, she dances." Richard was repeating the words his six-year-old cousin told him after his grandfather read her fortune in the parlor last year.

"She travels the world and has everything she desires," Richard added. Then he continued in a surprised voice, "And what's this?"

Richard paused, just like his grandfather always did before he would tell someone something very special.

"What?" asked Michelle, playing along.

"She travels with a tall, handsome stranger with short, dark hair, and he is the one who buys her everything and makes it all possible. He succeeds at everything he does and then he gives it all to her." Richard paused again so he could move his eyebrows up and down like his grandfather.

"And who is this stranger?" asked Michelle, pretending to be eagerly eating it all up.

Richard hesitated and then he squinted his eyes and continued in a voice like he was having a hard time seeing the images, "He plays some kind of musical instrument. I can see him standing..."

Then Richard pulled his hands away and said, "That is all the mystical flashlight can tell us this evening, Madame. Fifty cents please." And Richard held out his hand with a smile.

Michelle gave Richard a surprised look like, "That's all?...You coward," but then she smiled and pretended to place the money in the palm of his hand.

Richard pretended to put the money in his pocket and

said, "Thank you, please come again."

Then they stood up and traded places. Michelle placed her hands on the table with her palms up and said, "For me to tell your fortune, Sir, you must place both of your hands in mine."

Richard smiled as he placed both of his hands in Michelle's. She gently wrapped her fingers around his, then slowly closed her eyes.

Her face glowed, and it looked like an angel's to Richard, while he looked across the table at her in the soft light. He had a very funny feeling; the feeling that this 'was' the boy-girl thing now.

Michelle sat silently with her eyes closed and a small smile on her face for about two full minutes. Then she opened her eyes and said, "You will succeed," with a very big smile on her face.

Neither of them had a watch on. Michelle didn't own one and Richard only wore his for formal occasions because it was very expensive. His father had a very successful year financially and he had given it to Richard on his last birthday as a symbol of how very important time was, and not to waste it.

Richard and Michelle never worried about time when they were together anymore, but both of them sensed it was getting time to go.

When they walked out of the fortune telling booth Michelle walked straight over to face the huge ferris wheel and said, "Mr. Edwards told me this ferris wheel was very special."

Richard now realized that Michelle would not have come here just to have fun with some carnival booths and rides, and she probably didn't even know the fortune telling booth was here until they got over to it.

He stood back and watched her stare up at the ferris wheel while she walked all the way around it with an expression of awe. He could tell that she was taking it all in so she could remember it forever. Richard walked over to its large cement foundation so he could look it over as she came around from the other side.

It was gigantic. Richard wondered if there was another larger than it anywhere. The steel columns were anchored to the massive concrete slabs on the ground with bolts as large as his waist, while the seats and open carriages were larger and fancier than anything he had ever seen. They were carved and decorated with everything imaginable, and even though they were very old, they still showed their bright colors and meticulous artwork.

"Whoa," he exclaimed to Michelle as they looked up together.

"Mr. Edwards says this ferris wheel was here long before this was Salty Pete's Park. He met his wife right here when this whole area was grass and trees," Michelle said as she waved her arms in a big circle.

"And they kissed for the very first time way up there at the top." By the expression on her face Richard was almost afraid she would start climbing, but then he remembered her promise that afternoon.

"After they were married Mr. Edwards brought his wife here every week. He would buy an extra ticket and tell the operator to use it to stop the ferris wheel with them at the very top for just a minute." Then she continued, "He said they were here the week before she died."

Now Richard understood. Mr. Edwards was her friend.

They stood there looking at it together, staring up in amazement at its silhouette that covered the whole night sky from where they stood. "I wish we could see it all lit up," Richard found himself saying as he stood and stared up at it.

"I overheard my father say they ran temporary power to it so they could disassemble it tomorrow morning," Michelle answered as she slowly walked away from Richard and toward a green box with a large red handle on it.

"NO! MICHELLE, DON'T!" he yelled, as she reached down and threw the switch.

Chapter 13: The Valley

The police car pulled up to the only store in the town of Leeds. The officer let Richard out of the back seat and they walked in together. The officer turned, took a step to his right and pulled two cans out of the cooler as if it were by instinct and handed one to Richard.

"Two grape sodas on my tab, Mary," he hollered to no one there.

"OK," came a woman's voice from the back of the store.

They sat down together at a small table in the middle of the store where the officer handed Richard one of the straws that he pulled out of a dispenser. Then the officer waited for Richard.

"Thank you," Richard said as he opened his can of pop and put the straw in it so they could take their first drink together.

"You must play pretty well if my mother buys your music," the officer told him.

Richard looked up to see if he was really serious or not. Then they both looked at each other and smiled.

"See you look better already. So you came all the way out here to buy a violin and now he won't sell you one. That is a tough situation, it is."

Richard didn't respond to the officer.

"He is a very different man. He just sits out there carving on those little pieces of wood day and night and doing what he does. He does a lot of strange things too, you know. Come to think of it, I bet he does just about everything out there!"

Then the officer sat back a moment and pondered his own words.

"I know," replied Richard, "He gave me the tour of his shop."

"He gives public tours every once in a while, so my whole family got to see it once," the officer told him before taking another drink. "Pretty impressive, eh? And that valley, whew!"

Richard shook his head with a questioning look on his face.

"If you only saw the shop, Mr. Gaspar, you don't know the half of it," the officer told him.

"What valley?" curiously asked Richard, hardly believing there could be more than he saw at the shop.

"Then you didn't go down the paved road?" asked the officer.

With another shake of Richard's head the officer continued, "Well if you keep on going behind the shop that old dirt road eventually turns into a nice paved one, believe it or not, and it eventually drops down into his valley.

"I don't know why he does that to customers, dirtying up their cars like that," smiled the officer, "maybe to see if people think it's worth driving down it for a violin of his. Maybe he does it for the shock value of his customers seeing fine violins like his in the middle of a dusty desert.

"Well, if you do follow that paved road you will eventually see the tops of large trees. Follow the road further and you will drop down into a sort of 'Garden of Eden', and that's where his house and farm and 'everything else' is."

Richard listened with more interest as the officer continued.

"I remember the first time I saw it. I was called out there while I was on duty. It was late at night quite a few years ago. I heard what sounded like dynamite blasts going on during the evening and figured he had reopened the silver mine again. He has a silver mine for his fittings by the way," the officer said with another smile to get Richard's reaction, which was one of amazement.

"People were calling left and right, but as the law states, 'in the county it's perfectly legal for him until 10 P.M.'. Well 10 P.M. came and just two minutes later, boom!, one more blast went off and that was that. When the next call came in I had to go file a report. It was the last blast, but the law is the law and it was 10:02." He said it with the same tone of voice as when he placed Richard in the back seat of the patrol car.

"I hadn't been down in that valley since I was a boy anyway and I was curious to see what he had done with it over the years. I was amazed. My headlights shone on trees that I had never seen before. Plants that looked like 'dy-nee-saurs' should be eating off them. The closer I got to the house, the more amazed I was. Mind you, it's a desert out there on top.

"Along the road I could see the cotton fields that I heard he uses for his cases and the labels he makes. Good paper is made with cotton, you know," he said as if to show off his knowledge and then he waited for Richard to nod in agreement.

"Why he even makes his shop gloves and aprons out of it! Anyway, to make a long story short, or in my case a little less long," he added with a grin, "everything in this world you didn't see in the shop up above is down there in that valley. There are buildings and areas down there where he refines silver, blows glass and grows everything under the good sun. There's large earth-moving equipment, dump trucks, tractors, machinery, you name it. It's absolutely unbelievable and, one way or another, it's all for his violins.

"I gave him the warning about the noise ordinance, and he politely thanked me and apologized for that one last blast. He said his wife wanted him to finish all the blasting that night, so he placed the last charge even though it was late and he knew it would be close to ten o'clock. I looked up at the silver mine on the side of the mountain and thought that must be quite a show watching the blast and the rocks as they come flying out of the hill.

"Well, we talked a while longer and he showed me around

most of the valley, even though it was night.

"If you only saw the shop, you have no idea," said the officer, with a look of amazement. "When I asked him what it was all for, he answered with the most devoted look you ever saw, kind of like a priest in church saying prayers, "My violins.""

"I don't know, but anyone who would do all that for a pound of wood you hold in your hand and put under your chin must truly love it. I know he doesn't do it for the money."

With that the officer slurped down the last of his soda.

"Were you going to come back when the violin was done, or stick around until he finished it?" asked the officer.

"I was going to stay in St. George for six weeks while I prepare for my next concert and then take it back with me," replied Richard.

"And now?"

"I don't know," answered Richard, shaking his head.

"Well, let's get going while I tell you what 'I' don't know."

Richard followed him back out to the car, wondering what that meant. He actually found himself wanting to hear what the officer had to say next.

"Well I don't know you or your whole situation, Mr. Gaspar," he said as he closed Richard's door and sat himself down in the driver's seat. "But what I told you before about those people driving up and down this road is no hog wash.

"I don't know of anyone, anywhere, who has bought one of his instruments that has not been happy in the long haul.

"I am the law around here, day and night, and I hear everything bad that anyone does, down to pulling puppie's tails, and I know this, I don't know anyone who claims he cheated them."

"Are you telling me that everyone that has bought one of his instruments is totally satisfied and he's never had one brought back or complained about?" asked Richard, not just a little skeptical.

"Oh, there have been a couple bring them back, driving

up the street with their scowling faces, just as I told you. But every time they go out there, no matter who they are or what their complaint, when they come back down the street, they are as happy as kittens with a warm bowl of milk."

Richard thought about the statement for a minute. He knew how people could be. He had been in shops before when people had walked in with instruments that looked like they had been run over by a truck, demanding their money back because the instrument was defective. He had never heard of any maker or dealer who could claim what this officer was saying, 'that everyone was eventually satisfied'.

As the officer let Richard out of the back seat he said, "Here's my advice. If you really can write out a check for a violin of his, do it. Whatever he asks you to do, even if it includes standing on your head and rubbing your belly, 'just do it'. I don't know everything about him, we don't sit down and eat pie together Sunday evenings, but I do know this, 'he loves those instruments he makes'. I've seen it in his eyes. He won't cheat you and you won't be sorry."

The officer stood at the side of the Blazer and smiled as Richard got in, fastened his seat belt and started it up.

"And it will save you a lot of money on speeding tickets," he added with a smile, waving as Richard drove down the road and back onto the freeway.

Somehow Richard felt better, even though the officer had not said anything that should logically change his mind. The Luthier had still burned the check and the Guarneri was still waiting for him in New York, and yet, he thought as he pulled into the hotel, he would sleep on it.

After relaxing in his hotel room Richard pulled out his Bergonzi and started to play. As he ran through his new program he thought about violins and the great performers. He thought about the picture on his grandfather's parlor wall of Nicolo Paganini, the greatest player of all, and his ability to sway a crowd.

There were a few critics who hated Paganini, calling him a 'charlatan' and a 'clown', while there were other critics who listened to him once, then sold all they owned so they could follow him around Europe, living and breathing just to hear one more note from him and his violin.

It was said that Paganini could make his violin mimic an opera singer's voice to perfection, he could make his violin bark like a dog, imitate a flute, cackle like a chicken, and sing a more pure and lovely song than songbirds.

The critics wrote how he would come out on stage and have to wait fifteen minutes for the applause to die down before he could begin playing, then he would play a descending arpeggio that sounded like large, sparkling diamonds being poured out of a silk bag, sending shivers down the spine of everyone there, which sent the crowd into another fifteen minute frenzy of applause; all before he started the program.

Once the program started, he could have them spellbound within a measure, crying after three more bars, then laughing in the aisles and back to spellbound in four more bars, over and over the entire time he played. And when the concerts were over, they would have to carry many of the audience home on stretchers who had passed out from fatigue or ecstasy.

Because there were no recordings made of Paganini, Richard knew that most people today think the reviews were exaggerated and that he wasn't really as good as they said he was.

Violinists today play his violin once a year, when it is taken out of the vault in Genoa, Italy. Though they say it is a great violin, they cannot make it do what the old critics said he could, so they claim his violin was also exaggerated. In fact, some prefer their own instruments more.

Yet he and his grandfather had always believed in Paganini; all the stories and all of the unbelievable claims.

When Richard and Michelle sat between the two trees, and as he told her that he wanted to be the greatest player who ever lived, it was 'that' kind of player, and she had believed in him.

A thought then struck Richard that had never struck him before. "Was it really Paganini's skill or the violin, or was it only possible with them together?"

He put his violin away in the case and got ready for bed as he thought to himself, "She is a good violin; even tone, good volume, a wonderful instrument, but Cercie was right, there is something she lacks that I need. As he drifted off to sleep, he knew the Guarneri was a better instrument than his, with a larger voice and broader range of tone, but it still lacked something. Cercie's words seemed to haunt him and he thought of the teenage Jewish boy with his wife.

"Who are you?" he softly asked, as he turned his head and looked over at his Bergonzi laying by the bed.

Then Richard remembered Samuel's words after the concert, "He will make the instrument you need."

Just before he fell asleep, Richard realized that he was doing something he hadn't done in a long time. He was dreaming.

Chapter 14: The Lady

Richard didn't call the Luthier before he headed back out to Leeds the next morning. He knew he would have to talk to the Luthier face to face and apologize. He hoped he could smooth things out without too big of a scene, but he wondered if the Luthier would even make him a violin now, especially if the money meant nothing to him like the officer had said.

"I will just have to risk it," he said to himself as he drove up the freeway.

When he pulled up to the shop there was a small, white, rental car parked there. "White again," he thought to himself, then looking around at the hot, sunny desert he realized why.

"Another customer. This could be awkward," he told himself.

Richard considered leaving and coming back a little later but curiosity started to creep in as he sat looking at the car and thinking about the boy the day before.

"What kind of people come to buy instruments from this man?"

Richard shuddered as a thought ran through his mind. "What if they are here to order an instrument?"

He looked up on the roof of the shop where the violin still stood in the sun. The Luthier had mentioned that the customer lived in Japan and would make a special trip back when he was called.

A feeling of panic grabbed at Richard as he thought, "If someone else orders an instrument now, it could be three more months! If I'm going to do this, I can't wait that long! And what about the Guarneri? I could never hope to have it held that long without buying it.

But what could he do? What would he say?

"Please, I know I'm the one who swore at you yesterday, but can you have these people wait and make my violin first?'"

He sank back in the seat for a minute, to think. Curiosity started taking over again and he told himself, "Even if they are taking my time slot, I might as well see who it is." Deep down inside, not willing to admit it to himself yet, he was really dying of curiosity.

He couldn't hear anything this time, when he paused for a moment at the door, before very slowly, almost cautiously, opening it.

"Here we go," Richard thought to himself.

The Luthier was handing a large cello to a small, thin, pale-looking woman of probably forty-five or fifty. Her long, black hair was tied in a bun and she was wearing old-fashioned glasses. She reminded Richard of an old school librarian when he was in junior high, except this lady didn't have the scowl.

They both looked over at Richard and the Luthier silently motioned for him to sit on a chair, way over on the other side of the shop. It seemed a little strange to Richard since there were chairs placed all around the entry next to where she would be playing, but since he was here to apologize he didn't hesitate one moment; he placed his case on the table and walked back.

The woman looked at the Luthier with a questioning, almost frightened look on her face as Richard walked past her.

"I believe the adjustments are complete, just as you requested, Miss Gill," said the Luthier. Then he motioned with his hand for her to sit and play the cello.

She just stood there, and she started shaking a little with the same frightened, questioning look on her face.

"It's all right, Janet," the Luthier said, with a warm smile and a small nod, while he motioned to the chair again,

"He plays the violin."

The Luthier said it as if he expected it to calm her and explain everything.

Interestingly enough, it did.

She slowly walked over to the chair, her feeble hands noticeably trembling as she sat down. She placed the cello in a small stand by the chair while she took off her glasses. Her eyes seemed shallow and small, the paleness of her face became even more apparent with her glasses off.

Richard couldn't help himself, and he watched her from between the desks and fixtures that separated him from her. She leaned back, took a slow deep breath and closed her eyes. Next, she slowly reached up with both hands and took the pins out of her hair, letting it flow across her shoulders and fall behind the chair.

Her hands steadied and her face turned to one of resolve as she picked up the bow and vigorously tightened it. The Luthier silently sat down and closed his eyes to listen.

She grasped the cello and held it in front of her, then looked at it with desire. She leaned back slightly and pulled the cello up to her. It was the way she did it that made Richard squirm.

She slid the cello between her knees and laid the scroll by the side of her head as a smooth, warm smile covered her face. She just sat like that for what Richard thought was an eternity.

He couldn't see well from where he was, but he could swear that color was filling her cheeks and all the small wrinkles on her face seemed a little less noticeable as she sat holding the cello. She looked so peaceful to Richard, and for that moment, almost beautiful.

When she lifted the bow in her right hand, her whole body tightened up and she hesitated with the bow hovered over the strings until the waiting almost became unbearable to Richard.

"Boom!" Her body jerked and all her muscles tightened even more as her mouth dropped open and the sound shot through the shop, bouncing off the walls. It reminded

Richard of the dark-brown violin in the concert hall.

After a few measures Richard could tell that she was good, not as good as the young boy yesterday, but still very good.

"She really gets into it though," he thought to himself as he watched her continue playing.

"What an understatement!" he thought, and he rolled his eyes and shook his head.

Her whole countenance changed with each movement and she seemed to be playing for only herself. She bore down on the strings with sweat pouring out of her face and down her thin, white neck, Richard could tell her pulse was racing as she continued.

She swayed with the cello, side to side, flowing with the music. At one point she opened her eyes with a dreamy look, noticeably oblivious to the shop or anyone else in it. She just stared into space.

Then, the cadenza, "Boom, boom, boom," one chord after another, each one sending her into convulsions. Flying spiccato notes rang through the shop as her fingers flew up and down the strings over and over again. She started to let out sharp, short gasps with each set of notes, each time her body shaking. When she was finished she was drenched in sweat.

She relaxed a moment before opening her eyes. Then she looked around.

The Luthier sat motionless with his eyes still closed and Richard didn't even breathe. 'Had he just seen what he thought he saw?' he asked himself, still sitting there motionless.

"Now I understand," he thought to himself. All those old stories of the devil possessing the violin and climbing into the bodies of those who play it. The old religious cries as they burned the violins, violas and cellos in the town squares, yelling, "Tool of the Devil!" The stories of Satan, himself, sitting on Paganini's shoulder as he played, guiding his bow.

Richard thought, "If people played and acted like this back then, I can start to understand."

Miss Gill slowly placed the cello and bow in her large case that stood by the table. Then she rolled her long, black hair back up in a tight bun and placed her glasses back over her eyes that now seemed ten years younger to Richard.

As soon as her cello case closed, the Luthier opened his eyes, stood up and walked over to her. He silently waited for her to comment.

"It will do," she said, in a tone that reminded Richard of the old librarian again. Then she opened the door to walk out, not even giving the Luthier time to open it for her. She turned to the Luthier and in the same tone, but with a little smile, she said, "Thank you," just before she closed the door.

"And now," the Luthier turned to Richard, "how may I be of service to you, Mr. Gaspar?"

It took Richard a moment to collect himself.

"Will I act like that if I buy a violin from you?" he asked with a smile, though there was a hint of fear in his eyes.

"Only if you wish, so choose wisely," the Luthier replied with a serious look, then with a laugh.

"You will know that I have succeeded and that you have *the right instrument for you* when you don't care what you look like when you play upon it.

"So don't worry," the Luthier finished with a mischievous grin on his face.

The words 'right instrument for you' rang in Richard's ears and it gave him hope.

"I'm sorry," Richard said, as he walked up to the Luthier and shook his hand. "My name is Richard Gaspar and I would like to buy a violin."

Chapter 15: The Waitress

"*A*nd I would be honored to make it for you," was the Luthier's reply.

Richard pulled out his checkbook and started to write.

"No, for your instrument, you will pay me when it is finished." The Luthier shook his head and held his hand up.

Richard, even more puzzled than before, put his checkbook away.

"Have you had lunch yet, Mr. Gaspar?"

Richard shook his head.

"Would you like to join me?" asked the Luthier.

"Only if you allow me to buy, and let me apologize for yesterday," returned Richard.

"Very well, then."

Realizing there was no other car than his outside now, Richard quickly offered, "I'll drive."

Leeds only had one place that served lunch, and that was the same small area with the tables in the store that he and the officer had sat at the day before. "Would you like somewhere nicer?" Richard asked, fearing hot dogs and nachos from such a small store.

"This will do. I think the food will impress you, Mr. Gaspar," returned the Luthier.

"That'll be the day," Richard thought to himself as he sat down, just managing to maintain a smile.

It took a little while for the waitress to finally come. As they waited Richard said, "You can call me Richard if you like, and what shall I call you?"

"Until I start your violin please call me Jonathan, but once I begin, please call me Luthier."

"Jonathan," Richard said in a solemn voice, "I am truly sorry for my outburst yesterday, and I do apologize."

"Done," was all the Luthier said in reply with a smile on his face.

They sat and waited quietly for at least ten minutes before the waitress finally came from the back of the store with the menus. Richard was starting to show signs of impatience by the time she arrived at their table.

She looked a little tired as she approached and wore a forced smile on her face. She took their order, and when she started back, a couple of other people came in and sat down. She stopped and took the other people's order before delivering Richard's and the Luthier's to the cook.

"Does it normally take this long?" Richard asked as he thought of the service he received in his favorite coffee shop in New York.

"We have time today," the Luthier replied with a smile.

"Where do we go from here?" asked Richard, referring to the violin.

"The violin on the roof will be finished in a few days and I have already called Mr. Haito. After he leaves, I will select the wood for your violin and begin carving."

"I have heard of people selecting the wood for their own violins, do you allow that?" Richard asked.

"I do upon occasion, but for your violin, 'I' must select it," replied the Luthier, as he tilted his head back and looked up, as though he were looking up at the wood hanging from the ceiling of his shop.

Richard thought of Michelle as the Luthier looked up.

Michelle was looking up the stairs at the brightly lit glass doors that led into the police station. She looked like it was judgment day itself as she stood with a meek, solemn look on her face.

Richard thought to himself, "She must have just realized what she has gotten us into."

She looked over into Richard's eyes and said, "This is

going to change things."

And as always, she was right.

They had known each other for over three years now and they had spent almost every free minute they had together. At first Richard's mother was just happy that he had apologized and had a friend, any friend. But as time went by, both Richard's and Michelle's parents became puzzled and then concerned at the inordinate amount of time they spent together, especially this last summer now that they were older.

"A boy and girl spending that much time together can only lead to trouble," Richard had heard his mother tell his father one afternoon.

"We've never done anything bad!" Richard thought to himself while he listened to them talk. "Why won't everyone leave us alone!"

'Everyone' included some of the boys that had started teasing him the very first week of school this year. They must have talked to the boys at Richard's previous school and learned his old nickname, "Girlie boy," from them. They had given it to him when he first met Michelle, when he was thirteen and she was eleven. Even though he was now sixteen and the other boys were looking at girls differently, they still teased him with the nickname now and again, and he hated it.

The trouble was, Richard's parents only seemed to hear about the negative things that people had to say. The complaint was usually about Richard and Michelle being out too late together. No one seemed to comment about the good things they did.

They would help people find things and carry their groceries out to their cars when they went to the stores. They pulled weeds at the library and out of the flowerbed at the rest home, then they would pick a single flower and place it in the vase Michelle had made when they were done. Richard knew that many people around town just enjoyed seeing them walk by each day with smiles on their faces.

"But, I guess those people don't talk to my parents," he thought to himself, "only people like Mrs. Becker."

Some of the things that got back to their parents were considered a little questionable by those who told them. And maybe they did some things that weren't quite appropriate, but most of it boiled down to them just 'simply spending too much time together'.

"After all, they are old enough," he could clearly hear Mrs. Becker's voice, while his mother talked on the phone at the breakfast table. That was the morning after they had been at the lake late the night before.

"Where did you go last night, Richard?" his mother asked, after she hung up the phone. His father was out of town on a business trip as usual.

Richard thought how it must have looked walking home last night and replied, "We went swimming at the lake."

"At eleven forty-five at night?" she asked.

Thinking ahead Richard responded nonchalantly, "It was still hot, and we hadn't been swimming in so long we decided to wear our swimming suits under our clothes and walk down to the lake."

"Mrs. Becker says Michelle was all over you and had her arm around you as you walked by."

Richard, looking truly innocent replied, "Michelle hurt her foot on a broken bottle at the lake and I had to help her home."

A cut foot was a pretty easy thing to verify with Mrs. Ross, so his mother stopped the questions there.

While shaking her head, his mother repeated the same line she had said a dozen times over the past two months, "It just isn't right, Richard." Then she continued, "It's one thing to go out swimming on the docks at night with the boys, and it's another with a girl, alone at night."

"How?" asked Richard innocently, trying to close the conversation before it went on too long.

His mother looked a little frustrated, and not wanting to pursue the particulars of boys and girls at that moment she said, "It just is, and you know it."

Richard knew it. As Michelle and Richard stood on the moonlit shore of the lake the night before separated by the small group of trees, he knew it.

As they each removed all of their clothes while facing opposite directions, he knew it.

Michelle told him that skinny dipping together would be 'OK' if he promised to look the other way until they were in the water.

"A promise between friends is a promise, no matter what," she had told him a long time ago while they sat between the two trees. So there was nothing in this world that could make Richard break a promise to Michelle.

Richard hesitated before he started undoing the first button on his shirt. "What if someone sees us?"

"No one is going to see us. I've been out here a dozen times and the only time someone came out here I could see their headlights from a mile away."

Richard could tell she was already facing the other direction and pulling off her clothes by the sound of her voice.

"You've done it 'here' before?" he asked, surprised.

"Are you ready?" she asked.

Richard could tell she was ready and waiting.

"I guess so," he sheepishly replied as he removed his clothes.

"Are you ready?" she asked again, never willing to accept any halfhearted answer from Richard.

"Yes," he almost squeaked out.

"Then let's go."

Down they went, into the water with their backs to each other, walking just a few feet apart. Richard's heart was thumping. He didn't know if it was because he was afraid of getting caught, or because there was a fifteen-year-old girl standing behind him like this, even though she was his best friend.

They slowly walked into the warm water.

"This is a lot warmer than I thought," said Richard in surprise.

"Isn't it wonderful?" she replied, as she pushed off

backward into the water.

Richard followed her example and pushed himself back into the warm water. Then they floated out into the middle of the small lake together, side by side.

"What if someone sees us now?" asked Richard.

"Then we'll swim to the other side and run for it!" Michelle answered, with a little excitement in her voice.

Richard thought of his wallet in his pants on the shore.

"Oh great," he said, "then they would know who we were, and we'd have no clothes either."

After a moment he heard her simple, soft words float over to him, "Trust me." She almost never said those words, and he knew this was very special to her.

He was ashamed of himself; he knew they were best friends, no matter what. So he tried to relax and forget about everything.

"It is beautiful," Richard said as he looked up at the stars in the night sky.

He kicked his feet just enough to keep moving beside her while they floated together in the middle of the lake.

"I love the feeling of floating effortlessly and seeing forever," she told him in a soft, dreamy voice.

Richard looked at the stars and thought about Michelle's words. It was a nice feeling, but mostly because she was there.

After a while they started to slowly circle the lake. They tried to stay a few feet apart, but as they turned, their hands touched together. Richard started to draw his hand back, but Michelle gently held on.

They circled the lake four times, holding hands and looking up at the stars and the moon together. They talked about life and many of the things they had done, then they floated again in silence.

Richard was glad he came; he was also glad Michelle was his friend.

"We better get back," Michelle said as they came around to the grove of trees again.

So they slowly separated and paddled back to the shore, both looking at the stars once more while they swam. It was a warm summer night and they didn't feel any chill at all when they rose out of the water.

Richard thought this would sure look funny to anyone who could see them there, walking up to the trees, back to back.

Michelle screamed in pain. Richard had never heard her scream before and turned by reflex, before he could even think. There she stood. In the full moonlight standing on the shore, about ten feet away from him. She was turned sideways and he could see something large and dark on the left side of her stomach as she turned and bent over in pain.

It took Richard a moment to realize that he was looking at a birthmark on her stomach. He had never seen it before because of her modest swimming suit that she always wore. His eyes then looked down as she picked up her injured foot. A large piece of a broken bottle fell to the ground. She stood on her right foot while she pulled the remaining glass out of her left foot with her trembling fingers.

Blood dripped onto the broken pieces of the bottle still imbedded in the dirt and sand below, as she let out a soft whimper. They then looked into each other's eyes as she slowly dropped her foot to the ground and stood up. It seemed an eternity to Richard as tears welled up in her eyes and flowed down her cheeks.

Michelle slowly turned back around, and without hesitating, she painfully started walking back up to the trees. Richard turned around and was soon behind the trees drying off and getting dressed. He didn't know what to do and he worried about her the whole time.

"Are you OK?" he pleaded for an answer.

"I don't know," came her tearful reply. "I'm so sorry I made us break our promise."

Richard could hear Michelle quietly sobbing on the other side of the trees.

Richard thought back to the look in her eyes with the tears welling up in them while they stood looking at each other and he knew it was not her injured foot that had made her cry. It hurt him so bad to even think of what she must be going through and it seemed like forever before he heard her voice again.

"OK," a hurt, soft voice came from the other side of the trees.

Michelle was sitting down, trying to clean off the dirt and sand from her foot, as she looked up at Richard. He looked down at her with tears in his eyes and he picked her up. Without a word he carried her back down to the lake and lowered her enough to wash her foot off in the water and he held her until she was through.

The wound was deep but they both knew it would heal with time.

"Here it is," the Luthier said with a smile as the waitress walked up to their table.

As she approached, she tripped, just catching herself in time. Richard jerked back with a disgusted look on his face that remained there while she slowly put the plates down on the table in front of them.

"Thank you," pleasantly said the Luthier, giving her a smile as she walked away.

Richard settled back down when he smelled the steaming hot food in front of him. He took a bite and realized the Luthier was right, he was impressed with the food anyway.

While they ate, Richard talked about violins, what he liked in particular instruments and what he didn't like. He named off many of the finest instruments in the world and told the Luthier what he thought of each one.

After they finished their meals Richard cautiously asked, "Do you mind if I come out and watch you work, or if I visit while the violin is being made?"

"You are welcome to come out as often as you like," the Luthier responded, surprising Richard with his answer.

Richard had heard that all the old masters were very secretive and that's why their recipes and processes had been lost. Besides that, all the other makers Richard had ever met acted as though they each had their own secrets and this Luthier seemed to be the most eccentric of them all.

After they had finished their meals, the waitress placed the bill on the table. It was a little crumpled, some of the words were misspelled and the total came to eighteen dollars and twenty-three cents. Richard placed a twenty-dollar-bill on the table and asked the Luthier, "Are you ready?"

The Luthier glanced down at the bill and the twenty dollars sitting there together. He slowly pulled out a twenty-dollar-bill of his own and placed it on top of Richard's.

"I said I was buying," said Richard with a questioning look on his face.

"Tip," was the Luthier's reply.

"Are you kidding?!" Richard replied, thinking of the waitress' less than spectacular performance.

"It is impossible to understand what those that serve us go through," replied the Luthier, then he turned around and walked out to the Blazer.

Richard stood there a minute, first looking at the Luthier, then back down at the forty dollars sitting on the table. He shook his head and reluctantly left them both behind and followed the Luthier out.

Richard got in and started the engine while the Luthier continued, "When I was young I started working in a restaurant, cleaning tables and washing dishes. I noticed this one young woman who would walk to work each day. It didn't matter the weather or what shift she worked, she walked. If she worked an early morning shift I would see her kiss her three small children, dressed in ragged clothes, good-bye as they continued on to school from the restaurant. Sometimes the uniform she wore looked acceptable, sometimes it looked weathered. She wasn't beautiful and never flirted with the customers like the other waitresses, but she was always pleasant and always worked hard, though I could tell she was usually too tired to do her work well.

"I watched night after night as customers would complain that she was too slow, or how they ordered her around and talked bad about her. Some even seemed to get pleasure out of making her jump to their every demand, only to leave no tip at all.

"But," I thought, "if you average it all out she really didn't deserve much more than she got because of how slow she was and the mistakes she made."

"One night I walked back to the employees' table and watched her count her meager tips for the evening. She then laid her head down on the small pile of coins and started crying. I was a young, hard worker and a blind stupid fool."

Tears were welling up in the Luthier's eyes now as he spoke. "I asked her, 'What's wrong? I work twice as hard as you do, and I don't get any tips.'" As I stood there, she looked up at me with eyes that were red and swollen.

"Don't you know?!" she cried with disbelief at my comment.

"What?" I replied.

"She unbelievingly shook her head, bursting out in tears again, and pointed up to a small sign taped on the wall which I had never noticed before. It looked like it had been there forever and seemed to blend into the wall. It was the minimum wage for employees, and the minimum wage for waitresses. Her wage as a waitress was about half of mine and not enough to support anyone.

"I took every dollar I owned out of my wallet and emptied my pockets. I placed it all on the table in front of her and walked out. I didn't even wait for my last paycheck. I left, knowing that I could never work there, or in any restaurant, again. And to this day I ask God to forgive my soul for being so heartless and for hurting her like that."

Richard and the Luthier drove silently back to the violin shop. When they arrived, Richard handed the Luthier a piece of the hotel stationery with his room number written on it. Then he drove away, back down the old dirt road.

Chapter 16: The Samurai

A few days later Richard received the call. The other violin was finished and would be picked up before noon. The Luthier said that if Richard was available and would like to come out that afternoon, he could get started on his violin tonight.

Richard had been constantly grinding away at his music since his last visit to the shop and had only left his hotel room a couple of times.

He worked on each note individually, then he methodically put the notes together bar by bar. When that was done he would work on it movement by movement, forward and backward, before he would play the entire composition. He would then memorize everything, and finally, make it music.

He knew his system wasn't everyone's favorite, but that was how he worked, and it seemed to work for him.

"I'm right on schedule," he thought to himself, as he closed his violin case.

Richard thought about all he had accomplished so far and figured he could use a short break. So he bought a few maps of the area that morning and decided he would take the long way, or the "scenic tour," as the literature called it on his way to the violinshop,

He drove up the freeway and looked around. Everything looked just a little different this morning and had a peaceful glow about it. The morning air was still cool so he opened the windows and let the fresh, clean air circle around him.

He hadn't realized just how nice Southern Utah was, compared to the large cities he was used to, until now. Though he also knew that in a couple of hours the desert would be almost suffocating with heat.

He took another deep breath of the cool morning air and looked around as he took the exit off the freeway that would bring him around to the violin shop from the other direction.

He couldn't believe all the colors that he had missed before on his way to the shop. There were huge, red mountains surrounding the desert floor and valleys on one side of the road while mountains layered in colors as though an artist had taken one brush at a time and swiped them across the canvas were on the other. The sun rose higher in the sky as he drove on and the shadows and blazing colors changed; it was truly spectacular.

Richard could clearly see into what was called Zion Canyon, well over twenty-five miles away. "Those sheer cliffs and mountains must look amazing when you stand there and look up at them," he thought to himself. And since he was planning on being here for more than five weeks he thought he just might.

The Blazer wove its way up around the hills and the bends in the road while the scenery changed constantly. After a few minutes a reservoir appeared on his left where swimmers and boaters were enjoying the cool water. On his right was a large fairground, complete with a racetrack and horses running on it.

He continued driving and passed over the Virgin River on a bridge. Richard thought it looked more like a muddy stream than a river and the water carried thick, brown-red silt that swirled in it as it churned its way through the sand and rocks.

"If that water is their idea of what a virgin looks like, someone should have a talk with them," he thought to himself with a chuckle.

He smiled as he drove on and looked at each of the small towns and retirement communities along the way. He understood why this was fast becoming one of the most desirable places to retire today, especially in the winter months.

Soon, he found himself thinking like a tour guide, "...and on your right are the peach orchards originally planted by the pioneers. While, on your left are the old cotton fields and grape vineyards. Originally this area was settled as the 'Dixie Wine and Cotton Mission' by early Mormon pioneers." He laughed when he found himself quoting the visitors' guide word for word.

Small towns were nestled between the mountains and the houses seemed to follow the winding path of any precious water. He looked up at huge plateaus that looked like they were pushed straight up millions of years ago and marvelled at them.

He drove through the towns and noticed that there were large, modern homes built next to small adobe and rock ones, with people living in both, and their children playing together in the yards. It made him feel good.

There was a sign for a hotsprings 'complete with massage,' that caught his attention next.

"That couldn't hurt any," he thought, as he rubbed his neck.

Southern Utah may be an area to relax, but Richard was still practicing over twelve hours a day, so he mentally put it on his schedule. Almost before he realized it, he was looking through the railings of a bridge which suspended him hundreds of feet over the same Virgin River again.

"And if it was before it isn't now," he snickered.

He just couldn't help himself, and he imagined he wasn't the first one who thought it. "Who would call this the Virgin River anyway?"

He took some side streets and wandered around the next small town a little. He was just getting the feel of the town when he stopped for lunch. It was a small, ordinary fast-food restaurant but as he walked out he smiled to himself when he thought of the larger-than-normal tip that lay back there on the table.

"He must be getting to me," Richard thought to himself

as he climbed back into the Blazer, but he didn't seem to mind this time. Richard pulled up to the violin shop just as his watch beeped two.

"Perfect," he thought, and he grabbed his violin.

As he walked in, there was music playing.

This time the music came from a record player in an elegantly carved, old wooden cabinet that stood against the wall in the entry.

Neil Diamond was singing, "...some people never see the light until the day they die."

Richard noticed there was an extra long violin case sitting in the middle of the table where he had set his violin before and he looked over to the Luthier who pointed to another bench closer to the workshop area. Richard assumed the case contained the violin that had been on the roof the last time he was here as he placed his own violin on the other bench.

"Good afternoon, Richard," the Luthier greeted him with a smile as soon as the music faded away.

"Good afternoon, Jonathan. Or is it time, Luthier?" Richard asked with a smile, questioning whether the Luthier had officially begun.

"It is time," replied the Luthier. "Though I must ask if you will excuse me when Mr. Haito arrives. His jet was delayed and he was not sure what time he would pick up the violin."

"Of course," replied Richard, just a little curious to see yet another customer, possibly the last before his own violin was finished.

"You have told me what you 'want' in a violin," spoke the Luthier. "It is now time to decide what you 'need'."

The Luthier looked at Richard with a piercing gaze, squinting his eyes as though he were examining him.

"I keep hearing those words lately, first from my old sponsor, Samuel Jackson, then from my best friend, Cercie Copala, and now you. Are you all in this together? Do you all know something I don't?" Richard questioned the Luthier.

"Every player must find what they 'need' before they

can become a virtuoso. They must be able to thoroughly enjoy, and be moved by the music, with no compromises or reservations. Whether it is joy or sorrow, pleasure or pain, ecstasy or melancholy, the music must fulfill them one way or another. Otherwise, it is just notes. One can play at any level and be a virtuoso."

Richard thought of the lady playing the cello during his last visit. "She must be a master virtuoso according to this definition," Richard thought to himself with a smile.

The Luthier continued, "A 'True Master Virtuoso' is one that can then share those feelings with others."

"The lady on the cello?" Richard questioned.

"Miss Gill plays only for herself, and that is what separates you from her. You must find what you need, then share it with the audience."

Richard realized that what the Luthier was saying was true, but he couldn't think of anything more than what he had told him back at the store. "What do I need?"

"For most musicians it is a certain tone in the instrument that makes them feel the way they need to. It inspires them, you might say.

"Some require a mellow tone that gently pushes away the cares of the world and caresses and soothes their soul.

"Some require a hard, authoritative voice, like a strict schoolteacher. It keeps them in line, it drives them and makes them practice, achieving their satisfaction only when the piece is strictly perfected.

"Some want only the loudest, booming voice with no soul at all, their instrument becoming a slave to their ambitions, so they may take all the credit for themselves and satisfy their ego."

Richard could not help but think of the dark-brown violin at the concert hall as it was put away into the dark leather case.

"There are some who require something else, something more. Sometimes it has nothing to do with the instrument at all, something that simply fulfills them and allows them to fully enjoy the music, something that..."

The door of the shop suddenly flew open and there stood a stocky, Japanese man with a stern look on his face, followed by his wife and daughter.

"Haito san, Mrs. Haito, Sara, welcome!" The Luthier greeted them with a bow, then shook each hand as they entered. To Richard it seemed a strange mixture of Japanese and American greetings.

"Let me introduce Richard Gaspar," the Luthier said while motioning toward Richard.

"Of course, we enjoy your work," Mr. Haito replied, a little too matter-of-factly for Richard's taste. "And this is my wife and my daughter." Then each of them bowed slightly in turn toward Richard.

"Don't they have names?" Richard found himself wondering while he greeted them.

"Is it finished?" Mr. Haito asked in a stern, but anxious tone directed at the Luthier.

The Luthier motioned toward the case sitting on the bench.

Mr. Haito instantly turned and walked over to it. He opened the case and looked down at a blood-red violin. "It is beautiful, of course," he said as he lifted it out.

He pulled out a jet-black bow with Japanese characters engraved on the frog and tightened it up.

He then stood back with a stance of 'ready, aim, fire,' and started to play. He warmed it up with some of Paganini's most difficult caprices, then took it through a series of songs from mellow to aggressive when he suddenly stopped. He then looked at the Luthier with a stern look in his eye.

"It is a wonderful instrument, but you cheat me!" Richard almost jumped back as Mr. Haito flared at the Luthier, holding the violin and bow out toward him.

"Isn't this instrument as good or better than the example you played upon when you ordered?" the Luthier calmly answered, looking Mr. Haito in the eyes.

"It is just slightly better! You charged me more than double the price! Seventy-five thousand dollars!" His voice was getting louder with each word.

"Impossible! No one has ever paid that much for a new violin," Richard thought to himself and he backed away a little, just in case Mr. Haito blew.

Richard thought about the police officer's words a few days ago and now wondered if they were really true, or if this would be the first time someone drove back down the street with a scowl on their face and maybe even a little blood on his knuckles.

The tension in the room seemed like it was about to snap.

"Look at the case," the Luthier calmly suggested.

Mr. Haito glanced back over at the case, his eyes tight and his jaw set firm. Then he looked back at the Luthier. Richard thought the case was beautiful. It was extra long and covered with black and gold silk with small, highly colored silk ribbons that were tied in a curious manner around it. On the top were Japanese characters running vertically, embroidered in gold. They overlaid a beautifully colored Japanese-style scene with mountains and gardens. It was nice, and fitting, thought Richard, but certainly not worth an extra thirty-five thousand dollars.

Mr. Haito stood there seeming to challenge the Luthier where he stood. Just when Richard thought Mr. Haito was going to lunge for his throat the Luthier said, "Play it with the top open," pointing back over to the case.

Mr. Haito almost snapped back, but instead he stopped and turned his head toward the case again.

Richard then noticed two square bars running along the lid of the case hidden by the colored ribbons. They had tapered pins running through the center of each of them. Mr. Haito set the blood-red violin down beside the case and looked at the bars and pins.

"I believe you know how to do it," the Luthier said as Mr. Haito stood there looking at it with a strange expression on his face.

Mr. Haito closed the main lid of the violin case and quickly removed the tapered pins out of their holes and lifted a smaller, upper lid.

In the top of the violin case, in what looked like an elaborate shrine, hung two Samurai swords, one above the other, with a small dagger beneath them. They were beautifully inlaid and adorned with gold and jewels, with writings and engravings covering everything in the most exquisite fashion.

"My father's swords!" cried Mr. Haito as he dropped to his knees with his head bowed. He stayed there for a moment, then raised back up, looking at them closely as though he could not believe it. "But how? They were destroyed when the bomb was dropped and my father was killed! Are they real?"

He looked at them like they were ghosts and he seemed afraid to even touch them. Mr. Haito turned back toward the Luthier, still waiting for an answer.

"You tell me, you are the expert," the Luthier replied.

Mr. Haito then carefully picked up the long sword with reverence. He was considered by most sword dealers and collectors to be one of the world's top authorities on Samurai swords. He held the scabbard with his left hand and slowly slid the blade out on its back, not allowing the fine edge of the blade to touch the scabbard as it exited.

"It is still perfect," he said as he looked down its length and width with pride.

Upon examining the pattern between the hard and soft steel called the hammond, he declared, "I remember it well, this cannot be copied or imitated. This sword was made by my ancestor, the greatest swordmaker who ever lived!" His eyes glistened as he turned it over and over in his hands, only touching the handle while he carefully examined everything about it.

Then he told his wife without even looking up, "Get my briefcase!" as he continued to admire and inspect everything about the sword.

When she returned carrying his briefcase he told her, "Open it and hand me the white silk cloth. Hurry! Hurry!"

While holding the blade with the silk cloth, he pulled out the small pin hidden in the handle and pulled the handle off of the sword, revealing its roughly forged tang.

"Just as it looked the day he forged it seven hundred years ago!" Mr. Haito declared, as he inspected his ancestor's signature there. He then replaced the handle and its pin, turned the sword over and dropped the silken cloth onto the blade. There was no hesitation as the cloth dropped into two pieces as it fell upon the blade. He started crying, then looked up into the Luthier's face. "It is not possible, they were destroyed."

After a pause of silence, Mr. Haito continued, "How? They could not have been stolen, I spoke with him only two days before the bomb, and there was nothing left after. Did anyone survive? Did my father know something might happen and entrust them to someone? Who? How did you get them? How much did you pay? They are worth millions of dollars! Somehow I will get the money. Somehow I will pay you!"

After a long pause the Luthier smiled and said, "They are yours."

After another silent pause, the Luthier continued, "Now try the violin."

Mr. Haito just stood there struck dumb with a grateful, but still questioning, look on his face. Realizing no answers would come from the Luthier, he picked up the violin.

This time the music was totally different. It was sweet and peaceful, and as he played, tears of joy ran down his cheeks and across the belly of his violin.

After replacing the swords in the top lid and pushing the long, tapered pins back in their holes, Mr. Haito lovingly wiped off the violin and its bow and carefully placed them back into the lower compartment.

"These swords and this violin can now be handed down to my daughter Sara and then to her children," he said as he smiled at his daughter who still stood silently by her mother.

"I beg your forgiveness, Luthier, I am ashamed," he said, bowing his head. "I must pay you more, or now I will cheat you," he said as he stood looking at the Luthier.

"I have nothing to forgive you for. I am your servant, and

always will be."

"Thank you," said Mr. Haito with the deepest gratitude. Then he bowed low and walked out carrying the long violin case.

Richard was sure that those were the two swords he had seen in the back of the shop. "He had just given this man two fake swords! Or was he just reworking or remaking the scabbards?" he then wondered, "Or was the Luthier making copies for himself?"

Richard couldn't decide.

Richard turned to the Luthier after Mr. Haito drove away and asked, "What will he find when he chemically analyses them and carbon dates them?"

"Exactly what he expects to find," smiled the Luthier, with a content look on his face.

"Why didn't you just show him the swords at first?" asked Richard.

"I do things the way I feel will make my customers appreciate my instruments the most after they leave my shop. I'm willing to take a few risks in order to accomplish that."

Richard thought about the check the Luthier had burned just a few days before, then the look on Mr. Haito's face just a little while ago.

Richard then turned to the Luthier again and said, "I see."

Then he asked, "Will I look like that when I leave this shop?"

Chapter 17: Exiled

"*W*here were we?" the Luthier asked Richard.

"...allows them to fully enjoy the music. Something that..." replied Richard with a big smile, mimicking the Luthier's last words before Mr. Haito arrived.

The Luthier smiled back at Richard, "Very good. Something that...makes their world right."

"I think I see what you mean," Richard commented. He was referring to Mr. Haito.

Then they both laughed together.

"It does feel good to give people what they truly need. It makes the world just a little more right," said the Luthier with a gleam in his eyes.

Then continuing again, the Luthier added, "Some believe you cannot play a truly romantic song until you have loved. Those same people believe your music cannot make people cry until you have truly suffered."

These words of the Luthier struck a powerful chord inside Richard.

Salty Pete's Park was a flat open field with only a few trees still standing by the time Michelle's and Richard's verdicts were read to them at the courthouse.

The huge ferris wheel had lit up the entire night sky with the bright colors of its carriages and the other lights shining down on the neighborhood around the park. Richard and Michelle had just stood paralysed in awe as they looked up at its beauty and grandeur against the night sky. They couldn't believe that it was going to be torn down the next day and they both secretly wished that they could sit up at the very top and kiss for the very first time.

Even though they hadn't done any damage or tried to run when the police came, Judge Becker wanted to make an example of them.

When they found out that the town gossip, Mrs. Becker, was also the judge's wife, they realized it was going to be much worse than they thought.

"After all", the judge said, "it just isn't right for a boy and girl to be out alone together at that time of night. We also have to set an example, to keep this kind of blatant disrespect of the law from ever happening again. That park was clearly marked, and they knew there were still lawsuits pending from the last group that went in there."

Mrs. Becker sat in the courtroom with smug glee written all over her face as the judge handed down their verdicts and punishments. Richard and Michelle could even see her lips move in sequence with the judge's statements when he read the verdict.

In the end, their punishment all boiled down to this: there was a restraining order placed upon both of them so they could not see each other unsupervised for a period of six months. During which time, they each had to perform 200 hours of community service.

"Six months?!" Richard had actually stood up in the courtroom and screamed with tears flowing down his cheeks, pleading and shaking his head. "Please, Sir. No! Can I pay a fine instead? I will pay anything!" Richard was thinking of his buffalo nickel set.

"One year! And we will not have any more outbreaks in this courtroom or I'll have you locked up!"

Michelle and Richard looked at each other and cried in horror.

When the paperwork was finished at the courthouse they looked at each other one last time. They were not even allowed to say good-bye to each other as they stood at opposite ends of the counter. They just looked into each other's eyes.

After each of their parents had signed the papers and picked up their copies, they both left and went to their separate homes.

This didn't just change things, it destroyed things.

Both of their parents acted as though this verdict was a relief to them. There were no fines to speak of and they had both worried that neither Michelle or Richard would ever have any other friends of their own age or gender.

Neither of them did.

The community service didn't seem so bad of a punishment at the time the judge delivered it to them. After all, they had done those chores together just to see the happy looks on people's faces.

But, now that they had to do it separately, it became miserable, painful drudgery. Every time Richard bent over to pick weeds or help someone, it seemed to remind him that Michelle was not there.

After he put his last handful of weeds into the wheelbarrow at the end of the first week, he thought, "To be separated for a year, never to be able to have a private conversation with Michelle is bad enough, but two whole months without seeing her at all!"

He was thinking about how both of their parents had agreed it would be better if they were not allowed to see each other at all for two months to try and break them of this obsession with each other.

They were not even allowed to write letters or notes to each other.

Each weed that Michelle pulled became a physical struggle. She had no strength. She could barely eat anything anymore without choking on it. And when she finally got something down, more often than not, it came back up and she would almost pass out for lack of air in the process, which happened once.

Her mother had heard some noises coming from the bathroom and then there was a silence that struck fear into her. She jumped up and ran as fast as she could, finding Michelle on the floor unconscious, just in time to clear her throat and give her mouth-to-mouth. After that it was as though someone had taken a large syringe and simply sucked the life out of Michelle.

The moment the judge said, "One year," Richard's life and dreams just fell apart like the small toys you push the button in on the bottom and the stick figure on top collapses.

Nothing mattered. Nothing tasted good. Nothing looked good. It may have been daytime outside to everyone else, but to Richard the sun was not shining, and even if it were, it could not get through. Then when night came it only darkened his mood.

Richard had managed to eavesdrop on a phone call between Michelle's mother and his after a month had gone by. Michelle's mother spoke of how Michelle would come home from doing her service hours and sit on her bed for hours, silently holding her little dog. Then she would cry into his fur and wipe her eyes with him until he was wet as a mop. Dehydrated and exhausted, she would then roll over on her side and whimper and shake until she fell asleep.

Sometimes, in the middle of the night, after she finally got to sleep, she would scream out, "Richard!" then she would not be able to get back to sleep again.

Her mother told how Michelle would never answer their questions about what happened in her dreams and she would just lie there and shake for the rest of the night.

"Her teachers send home notes all the time about how she just won't do the work and how she sleeps in class all the time. She's flunking school!" Michelle's mother added as she cried into the phone.

"So is Richard," Mrs. Gaspar replied.

Then his mother told how George and her couldn't even force Richard to play his violin any more.

"In fact, he can't now," his mother said while she burst out crying.

She was referring to the cast on Richard's right arm. She told how they had gone for a walk together as a family, to try to cheer him up a little and get some fresh air, and then how he tripped off the sidewalk. "He just simply fell off the side. You know, where it raises up along Elm Street?"

"Yes," was the reply. "Where it's about four feet high by the ditch?"

"Right there," replied his mother. "He fell down onto the street and into the gutter. It's lucky there weren't any cars driving by just then.

"The strangest thing was, that he didn't even try to stop the fall. He just fell off, limp as a rag, on his arm and hit his head. Now he has a concussion and a broken arm on top of everything else. He just laid there as though he didn't feel a thing, like it didn't matter at all with a glazed look in his eyes.

"At the hospital, the doctor told us Richard was suffering from low blood pressure and that he had lost twenty pounds," she said with a scared sound in her voice.

She choked up and it took her a minute to continue, "I think we should take him to a psychiatrist but, so far, George won't allow it. He says Richard will get over it. But I don't know, Margie, I'm scared."

"Do you think we should let them see each other?" Margie asked.

Richard's heart almost flew out of his chest and he could feel the blood pumping in his ear as he held the phone against it. He waited for the reply and began softly pleading, "Please, God."

"George says not for another month. Maybe just before Christmas," was his mother's reply. "He thinks by then they'll get over it."

"Or be dead," was Margie's reply. "Oh, my gosh. I'm sorry, Alaine. I didn't mean that," and she hung up.

Richard quietly set the phone receiver back down. He had thought about it. He almost wasn't sure sometimes why he hadn't died.

But then he would think to himself, "This will end. It's only another month and I will be able to see her again."

He hadn't even seen Michelle's face since that day in the courtroom.

He would try to gather hope and start counting down the days until the two months would be up. But each day by itself seemed so long and dreary, and everything around him seemed so worthless and meaningless.

He thought of the book "Where the Red Fern Grows," how Michelle and he had cried together as they read of Big Dan and Little Anne. Now he thought of them, how she was smarter but he would protect her if anything went wrong.

Richard cried again as he thought of Little Anne crawling up and lying down on Big Dan's grave and dying of a broken heart.

Richard sank to the floor in a heap as he closed the door to his room, after listening to the phone conversation. He started to go into deep depression and rolled on the floor in pain.

Then he sat up. He looked over at the two pictures hanging side by side on the wall above his desk and screamed, "No! I will not give up!"

He looked at the pictures and said to himself, "It is only one more month, and I 'will' see her again!" as he pounded his fist on the floor and burst into tears of resolve.

He did see her again.

It was two days before Christmas. Each of their parents had told them two weeks before exactly when and where they would meet in the hopes of cheering them up. And of course it did.

Michelle and Richard were told that they would each receive ten dollars to buy each other a Christmas present since neither of them had any money of their own. They would be allowed to shop separately and when they were done they would be allowed to exchange their gifts and open them by the fountain in the center of the mall because Michelle's parents were leaving town for the holidays the next morning.

"Try to think of something that she likes, and have a few alternate choices because many of the stores sell out right before Christmas," his mother and father had advised him.

"OK," was Richard's reply.

The next morning Richard asked his mother if he could make Michelle a special present he had been thinking about, as well as the one he would buy her. She answered, "Yes, of course."

Then Richard added, "I will just need some string, cardboard, tape and glue, other than the pens and paints and things I have in my room."

He kept his bedroom door closed with his desk pushed up against it the whole time. He worked on the present day and night and he finished it the morning before they were supposed to meet.

"Just in time," he thought, as he made the last finishing touches on it right before lunch, then he ate his first full meal in over two months.

Richard was excited and anxious while they drove to the mall that evening. He knew exactly what he was going to buy her and held the ten dollar bill tightly in his right hand with the large cardboard box in his left.

Once they got to the mall he headed straight to the music store. He walked down to the sheet music aisle and picked out her most favorite songs. Even though some of them were old, the store had the ones he wanted.

"Maybe that's why they still have them," he thought to himself, as he looked at all the other empty shelves in the store.

His mother and father stood watching him and they seemed to be happy with his choice of presents.

"You will let her come over and play our piano again, won't you?" Richard asked.

"Yes, of course. As long as one of us is home and has time to watch you," replied his father, nodding his head, "until the rest of the year is over."

"Thank you," was Richard's sincere reply.

He was the happiest he had been since that night at the ferris wheel over two months before.

His parents turned and smiled at each other when they saw his face light up. It had been a terrible drain on them, and they hoped the worst of it was over.

"You are going to act reasonably from now on, aren't you?"

His father's question reminded him of all their discussions about tonight.

"Yes, Sir," Richard responded. "I wouldn't do anything in the world to spoil tonight."

"Good, Son. It's about time," his father said with a smile.

When the sales tax was added onto the price of the music, Richard was about twenty cents short and he started to take one of the songs back to the rack.

"That's all right," his father said as he handed the cashier another dollar bill and took the change and receipt, since Richard's hands were taken up with his sheet music and cardboard present.

Richard headed straight for the fountain in the center of the mall with his parents trailing behind. They noticed a small, jingling sound coming from the box as he hurried, and they wondered what it could be.

It was almost Christmas and there were hundreds of people wandering the mall, hurrying to buy their last minute presents. Richard looked at every face, trying to see Michelle at the first possible moment.

They waited for over an hour until some of the shops started to turn off their lights and close their doors.

Richard hung his head down and started to sob as the lights flickered off around him.

"I wonder what happened?" Richard's mother asked his father.

"I don't know," was George's reply.

"I hope they didn't get in an accident or... Oh my Gosh!" his mother let out a gasp.

The sound of his mother's voice startled Richard and he lifted his head, just as Michelle and her parents walked up and stood in front of them.

There she stood. It was Michelle, but Richard barely recognized her. Her face was pale and her cheeks were sunken in. Her glazed, malnourished eyes also looked sunken in and they had dark rings around them. She had always been thin, but she looked as though she had lost one-third of her weight, and her elbows were now larger than her arms. And she had no hair!

There were only some small, ragged wisps of her light-brown hair left. Less than a half-inch long at the most.

Richard flinched as he thought of the pictures of starving African children. They looked good compared to her.

He had lost almost as much weight as she had, but she was so much smaller to begin with. When he looked down from the tufts of hair on the top of her head and into her eyes, he realized Michelle was still there, inside.

They both started crying as Richard stood up and they looked at each other.

Trying to act as though nothing was wrong, Michelle's father spoke. "We are sorry we're late. Even though we had an appointment with the jeweler, he was so backed up, we had to wait for over an hour and Michelle wouldn't leave until it was finished."

Michelle smiled and held up a small package in front of her with both hands, close to Richard, and smiled.

Richard took the small present from her and their fingers touched for the first time in over two months. That small touch felt more wonderful than he ever imagined it would, even more wonderful than he had built up in his mind as he sat in his room alone, waiting.

"I feel I have to explain," started Michelle's mother as Richard stood there silently with the small present in his hands.

"The night after we told Michelle about this meeting at the fountain, I went to her room to call her to dinner. When I walked in she was sitting on her bed with her dog. She was sitting there looking like 'this'," as she lightly placed her fingers on top of Michelle's head, "and she had all of her hair in her hands, holding it out for me to see, and she asked me, 'Please sell my hair.'

"I don't know if she read it in a book or heard stories somewhere or what, but there she sat, holding it out for me to take it from her. She told me that ten dollars was not enough for the present she wanted to buy Richard and she just knew that this would make up the difference.

"It had to, she said." Michelle's mother was crying now.

"I tried to scold her and punish her for it, but I didn't have the heart. Then I tried to find someone to sell her hair to. I tried to find the people who make wigs, but our town is small enough that I couldn't find anyone. I asked everyone we knew, but I couldn't find any place that bought hair.

"Finally I went to her yesterday and I told her I was truly sorry, but I couldn't sell it anywhere. She cried in my arms and I didn't know what to do. Joe and I couldn't scrape together more than a few dollars to save our life. Then Michelle said to me, 'Ask Mr. Edwards, he'll know someone'.

"So with nothing else to do, I took it down to him. When he saw the box of hair he immediately asked me whose it was. When I told him it was Michelle's he gave me an understanding smile and took her hair that I had put in a shoe box and he said he would take care of it. He said he knew some people.

"I went back home and told Michelle what Mr. Edwards had said and she cried with joy, 'I knew he would know where to sell it. I knew he would. He's my friend!'

"Later that evening he came walking up to our house. Michelle had been sitting on the couch all afternoon waiting for him and for the first time in two months she fell asleep with a smile on her face.

"I heard his cane on the sidewalk before he knocked and I answered the door as quietly as I could. He stood on the porch with the copper vase Michelle had made for the receptionist's desk at the rest home filled with over a hundred dollars in one dollar bills and loose change. 'The people I sold the hair to didn't have any larger bills,' he said, as he handed it to me. He walked over and gave Michelle a gentle kiss without waking her up, and then slowly turned and walked away."

After a long pause Michelle's mother finished, while crying and trying to smile, "And so, here we are."

Richard, without his eyes ever leaving Michelle's, said, "Thank you."

He looked down at the present in his hands and said, "But you first." Then he gave her that special smile she had given him so long ago.

"Together," she said in her simple way, smiling back.

Richard put his present in his shirt pocket and picked up the large cardboard present he had made and held it out for her to take. She reached for it, and when she started to take it from Richard, he noticed her arms shaking and that a worried look came over her face.

He knew that even though it wasn't very heavy, she wouldn't be able to hold it. With Michelle still holding onto the present, Richard slowly placed it on the flat shelf behind the seat that circled the fountain. It was just below eye level for both of them.

She stood motionless, waiting for Richard to pull his present out of his pocket and begin.

"OK, now," he said.

He carefully opened the wrapping paper that surrounded the fancy, sterling-silver rosin holder he had seen in the violin shop on the other side of town. It had little branches and leaves circling the top and an engraving of Paganini on each side. On one side was his portrait and on the other, a finely engraved picture of him playing for a crowd. On the lid was engraved the words, "Maestro Richard," in large fancy letters. On the bottom was engraved in smaller letters, "My friend."

When Richard opened it up, sitting on top of the rosin was a buffalo nickel.

Michelle could hardly pull the tape off that held her present closed. The box Richard had made opened from the front like a small cabinet. Her mother bent down to help her, but Michelle seemed determined to do this herself, so they all stood back and waited and watched as she finally peeled the tape off that held it shut. As she swung the two halves open, both sets of parents let out their own exclamations and gasps at the same time.

There sat the Bergonzi violin with its bow sitting on a special stand meticulously made out of cardboard and painted with flowers and birds. The box was painted dark-blue inside with two trees that stood out from the doors, one on each side. In the top of the box hung his entire buffalo nickel collection from thin dark-blue threads.

They looked like stars hanging in the night sky, with the words written above them, "Everything I am or ever will be, I give to my friend," and at the end of the words was the watch his father had given him, with the word "Forever" painted under it in gold. Then Richard handed Michelle the sheet music he had bought for her and smiled.

Michelle looked up from the box and smiled back at Richard with the same smile that made him feel like a million dollars when they sat between the two trees.

Just then, the rest of the lights went out in the mall.

Richard's father was the first to speak. Looking at Michelle's parents, he said, "We'll talk about this," and he closed the doors on the box and picked it up.

Michelle's parents, somewhat in a daze, nodded back in agreement. Then each set of parents took their own child in their arms and headed out of the mall. Richard, with his silver rosin holder and Michelle, with her music.

Chapter 18: Tommy

"*I* don't need any more love, and I certainly don't need any more suffering," Richard told the Luthier.

"So, what do 'you' think I need?" he asked the Luthier, unable to come up with anything that could inspire him now.

The Luthier just stood silently waiting for Richard to continue. After thinking for a few more minutes, Richard said, "Other than a great violin, I just can't think of anything you could find in this world, or anything you could make in your shop, or in your valley I have heard so much about, that I need."

"Then it will be my job to find out," said the Luthier.

After a moment of silence the Luthier's face changed expression and he slowly turned around.

"Almost as though he had heard something," Richard thought, as he watched the Luthier look up at the wood hanging from the ceiling with a far away look in his eye.

Richard looked up at the wood also. He heard some of the pieces of wood click together now and then, as they swung back and forth in a small, gentle breeze created by a large fan that was always running.

Richard hadn't heard anything out of the ordinary.

Richard noticed the Luthier was looking toward one particular set of wood as it hung there in the back. Thinking of the stories he had heard about the old violin makers, he asked, "I have heard that Jacob Stainer, one of the earliest Master Luthiers, would tap the trees in the forest with his walking cane to see how the tree sounded, or some say, to see if it had a soul." Then Richard paused waiting for an answer from the Luthier.

"It is true, he did," was the Luthier's reply in a matter-of-fact tone.

"What do you hear?" asked Richard.

"When it's ready," was his reply. Then as if to change the subject, the Luthier pulled down two pieces of wood that hung directly above him. He held one in his left hand between his thumb and middle finger about one-third of the way from the top. Then he tapped it with the other piece of wood about one-third the distance from the bottom, sending a beautiful ringing sound throughout the violin shop.

"Wood is a wonderful thing," the Luthier continued. "It is amazing what it can tell us if we listen and it is amazing what it can do if handled properly."

The Luthier and Richard then sat down at a workbench so they could talk more comfortably.

Richard looked at the large rack of small metal scrapers that were neatly sitting on the bench. He knew that they were used to smooth the shapes and curves of the violins, instead of sandpaper. Richard admired the many different interesting shapes and sizes as he sat listening to the Luthier talk.

"Trees are marvelous, once you get to know them.

"There are so many things in life to experience if we will but close our eyes to the world in front of us and listen.

"Close your eyes and listen, Richard," asked the Luthier. "What do you hear?"

"Come on, Ricky. Close your eyes," pleaded Tommy, as he and Richard walked down the middle of the school hallway together. Richard stopped in front of the vice principal's office and turned back toward Tommy, "That's an old joke. I'm not falling for that one."

Tommy and Richard were sharing a locker until the maintenance department at the school could finish fixing and painting the one he was assigned to.

It was over a month after the start of the next school

year, and the twelve months of supervised visitation were over. The trouble was, Richard had not seen Michelle since the first week of summer vacation and so much had happened since they had exchanged their Christmas presents by the fountain...

"It is his to give," said Richard's mother as they drove home from the mall. "We gave the violin and bow to him when we bought it."

"So he could play it! Not give it away! We haven't even finished paying for it yet!"

"That is true," replied his mother.

"Do you know how much that set of nickels is worth?" his father asked both Richard and his mother at the same time. They didn't answer, none of them really knew and his father had never added it up.

The first three that his grandfather had given him were the most valuable and George had bought most of the others, one at a time, on his business trips. If he could find one they didn't have he would present it to Richard each time he came home. He almost never told Richard how much they cost, but Richard remembered one of them costing five hundred dollars. He remembered it well because his father and mother had argued over it for a week.

"Five hundred dollars for a nickel?" she said, coming as close to yelling as she ever did.

"He needed it to complete the set!" his father had replied.

Then his father continued, "That set is at least worth three thousand dollars! Not including the ones my father gave him!"

After a long silence it surprised Richard when his mother said, "It shouldn't matter the cost, it is the thought that counts."

His father just stared back at her in disbelief.

When the arguing was done and Michelle had returned with her parents from visiting her grandparents, the decision was made. Michelle could keep everything but the Bergonzi and its bow.

It really was OK, because between Michelle and Richard, it really was the thought that counted.

It was remarkable how quickly they both started putting back on the weight they had lost and looking like their old teenage selves again. Richard's mother even bought Michelle a couple of hats to wear while her hair grew back.

"They are actually rather stylish," his mother had commented. Richard looked at Michelle while she picked them out and looked at herself in the mirror and he agreed.

They were allowed to see each other twice a week for two hours as long as one of their parents was always in the room or accompanying them wherever they went.

It wasn't quite as bad as they thought it would be. Usually within fifteen or twenty minutes Richard's mother would sit down at the other end of the parlor and read while they quietly talked together.

Michelle also learned each of the songs Richard had bought her for Christmas on the piano in the parlor, then Richard played the songs with her on his violin.

When Richard went over to Michelle's house they would play with her dog and read books together while her mother did her housework and the paperwork for Joe's business.

They also realized that they could do their community service hours together if one of their parents was there. It didn't take very long for Richard and Michelle to talk both of their mothers into donating time at the rest home and the library.

They were even allowed to spend some of their supervised time working in Mr. Edward's yard where he and Michelle's mother got to be good friends.

Michelle's and Richard's lives finally seemed to settle into a routine again and both of their parents were happy with how it was going.

Richard's service hours were completed before Michelle's, but he continued to work with her until her hours were completed. After that, they kept doing the service they enjoyed, since it gave them more time together, though it got harder and harder to talk their mothers into donating their time. But, all in all, they were happy again.

They were never left alone together, and over time it did change things. They could only talk about sitting under the two trees and diving off the docks. They had no private place to go and tell each other their most secret thoughts and they could only talk of riding their bikes through town, asking questions from the clerks about new things. As the next few months passed by, a mellow, numb feeling seemed to take over.

When the bad news came, it didn't hurt nearly as much this time. In fact, they seemed to take it as just another addition to their melancholy.

Michelle's father received a very large contract in another city one week before school let out. The job was scheduled to last all summer, maybe even a little longer. Since it was temporary, and he needed Michelle's mother to take care of the books, they planned on leaving their house vacant and living with Michelle's aunt and uncle for the summer.

"Besides, they have a daughter named Crystal. She is only a year older than you, and you could get to know each other and be friends," Michelle's mother had told her just before they left.

They were allowed to hug each other good-bye and as they parted, Michelle whispered into Richard's ear, "When I return, we will be free!"

Richard wrote his first letter to Michelle that very afternoon. He had never written anyone a letter before other than thank-you cards and notes to his relatives. He read it over and over and it seemed strange to him. He couldn't figure out what he wanted to say, so he just said the same things over again that he had told her a hundred times. He signed it at the bottom, "Yours truly, Richard."

He received her first letter less than a week later. She wrote him about driving for hours with all of their things piled on top of them because it wouldn't all fit in the trailer. The city was much larger than theirs and there were many big, wonderful stores and places to go. Then she wrote of Crystal, her cousin, who looked a lot like her, only older, and how Crystal liked boys. And she signed it, "Your friend always, Michelle."

Richard felt bad when he read "Your friend always," realizing that was the way he should have signed his letter. He wrote her back again, and so it went throughout the summer.

Michelle gradually wrote Richard about more and more exciting things that Crystal would introduce her to, and eventually of their adventures together.

Richard's letters gradually got shorter and shorter because everything he wrote was just the same thing over and over again. He just didn't do anything new without her there.

His father was out of the country almost the whole summer on business trips and his mother never seemed to do anything without him while he was gone so he never got to go anywhere all summer long.

Richard had even walked down to the docks to see if there was anyone he could swim with, but no one was there that day and he never tried again.

The last letter he wrote to Michelle was just before the end of summer and it read, "Everything is OK. Your friend always, Richard."

Michelle kept writing him, though her letters seemed more reserved and they were a little shorter than before. She never asked questions or said anything about him not writing back to her anymore.

School started and Richard had an even harder time fitting in this year. There had been quite a bit of teasing after that night at Salty Pete's Park, but he was too numb to even feel it or care at the time.

Now, as the new school year started, Richard felt it and it was enough to keep him totally ostracized.

"Come on Ricky, close your eyes!" Tommy repeated again, as they stood in the middle of the hall. Tommy had seemed OK while they shared their locker together, but Richard just didn't know him that well.

"Of course, I don't know anyone at this school very well," he thought to himself, as he stood there. "We're right in front of the office so it couldn't be that bad, and maybe I'll get a laugh out of it too."

So Richard stood still and closed his eyes.

"Keep them closed, no peeking," cheerfully said Tommy. "And put your hands behind your back."

So Richard, with a halfhearted smile, put his hands behind his back. It had been a dull afternoon anyway.

The instant his hands were behind his back, two boys grabbed them and wrapped duct tape tightly around his wrists over and over again, while someone else brought a woman's bra down over his head and around his chest.

While the three other boys held him, Tommy took out some bright red lipstick and smeared it all over Richard's mouth. Then the four boys drew back together and cried, "Girlie boy!" while they pointed and laughed. Then they pushed him down onto the floor and ran.

Richard started crying immediately while he lay squirming around, trying to get up without the use of his hands. There were quite a few boys and girls gathered around him now, but no one helped him up.

After finally getting to his feet he looked around at all the faces looking at him. Most of them were laughing. Some tried not to, but they couldn't seem to help it when they looked at him.

Richard headed down the hall as fast as he could. He turned around to push the large swinging doors open with his hands, then he ran out. He lost his footing as he turned around and started down the stairs. Just before his body rolled up and hit the ground he looked up and saw Michelle looking down at him.

"No, God, please not today," he said in his mind as he rolled over on the ground and came to a stop right beside her. "Why today? Why not any other day?" Richard just lay there, curled up in a ball with his eyes closed, wishing this would all go away.

Michelle could hear voices coming from inside the school and said, "Get up Richard. Let's go."

Then she helped Richard to his feet and brushed him off as they walked away.

Chapter 19: The Kiss

Richard closed his eyes and listened as the Luthier sat watching him. "I hear the fan blowing air through the wood hanging from the ceiling. I hear the pieces of wood tapping against each other as they swing. I can hear a truck out on the freeway. I just heard a bird chirp out in the orchard." Then Richard hesitated.

"What else?" softly asked the Luthier.

"I can hear a creak or moan coming from the shop walls."

Just then, the sides of a can buckled loudly from the back of the shop.

"Probably from the temperature changing," thought Richard.

"And I just heard the sides of that tin can in the back pop as the air expanded inside it," Richard said with a smile, since it was pretty loud compared to the other things he could hear.

After another long pause, the Luthier asked, "And do you hear the spider wrapping up a small bug in the corner behind us?"

At first Richard was going to say, "Of course not," but then he thought better of it and he tried to listen more carefully. He cleared his mind and sat there listening for a while, trying to concentrate on any sound behind him. He knew this Luthier was getting at something and Richard found himself doing whatever he asked.

So Richard listened more carefully and after a minute he did hear a little sound, almost like a small chewing and wrapping sound coming from the corner of the wall and floor behind him.

"Yes, I do!" he exclaimed, "Just off to my right!"

"Very good," said the Luthier.

In a somber tone the Luthier continued, "It is said that a Shaolin Priest could tell you whether that spider was missing a leg as he wraps his web."

"That's impossible," said Richard as he opened his eyes and looked at the Luthier in disbelief.

The Luthier remained sitting in his chair with his eyes closed. He then stopped his slow breathing for a moment and a small, mellow smile slowly spread across his face.

"His third leg back on his right," said the Luthier with a calm assurance in his voice. Then he opened his eyes and looked at Richard.

Richard got up and hurriedly went over to where the spider was. It was dark in the corner and Richard pulled out the small flashlight that hung on the end of the rental-car key chain. He knelt down and looked very closely at a small house spider, hanging in its web, holding a small bug that it was busily winding up to save for a snack later on. Richard looked around it and noticed that it was missing its third leg back on its right.

Richard knelt there in disbelief. "It's impossible." Then he thought about the Samurai swords and wondered if the Luthier had really made them after all.

"Who are you?" Richard turned and asked in a fearful voice. "What are you?"

"I am a 'Master Luthier,'" he calmly replied.

"That means you can forge and fake seven-hundred-year-old Samurai swords that fool the best authorities in the world, along with their chemical tests and carbon dating? That you can hear better than the famed Shaolin Priests? That you can make instruments that can take over people's souls?"

Richard thought, "This can't be happening. This can not be real."

He just could not believe what he had been seeing and hearing the past few days, and now as he looked at the Luthier, the Luthier seemed to have an evil smile on his face in response to Richard's declarations and accusations.

"And are you now going to pull my heart out of my chest with your bare hands, and like the ancient Aztec priest, hold it out in front of my face still pumping, so I can see it before I die?" asked Richard, as he stepped back from the Luthier, now shaking in fear.

"That is next," replied the Luthier.

Michelle pulled the bra off of Richard and threw it into the next trash can sitting along the curb as they walked by. Then she unwrapped the duct tape from around his wrists and threw it away.

His wrists were already red and swollen from the boys wrapping the tape so tight and his arms ached from falling down the stairs. They continued to walk in silence as Richard hung his head down. He didn't dare look at Michelle and he couldn't figure out anything to say to her.

When they came to the road leading to Richard's house Michelle turned the other way, leaving Richard walking up the sidewalk alone for a moment. Just as he realized she wasn't beside him anymore she tugged at his arm and gently pulled him toward the park.

He still hung his head, but now because he was ashamed. It had been so long and so much had happened that he had all but forgotten about the two trees. He couldn't believe he had forgotten, as she beckoned him to follow her into the park and over to them.

Everything over the past year just seemed to overwhelm Richard and pull him down further than he had ever been before. He realized he had let her down. He thought of how he had stopped writing to her. He thought of her letters, how she was doing things and meeting people and having fun while he sat in his room and stared out into the yard, alone.

He thought of how he must have looked as he stumbled down at her feet in front of the school. It could have only been worse if she had seen him on the floor as everyone laughed at him with his hands behind his back, a bra over his chest and lipstick smeared on his face.

What would she think when she found out just how much of an outcast he really was? Then he remembered the lipstick still on his face.

"How I must look to her!" he thought to himself, and he hung his head a little lower as he stood between the two trees praying that this could all go away.

Michelle reached down and opened her purse, took out a handkerchief and started wiping the lipstick off of Richard's face.

Then she lifted up his chin until Richard looked her in the eyes.

"You look awful," she said, slightly shaking her head.

"And she always means more than she says," he thought to himself.

Michelle then gave him a little smile and said, "Close your eyes and promise you won't open them until I am completely finished and I tell you to open them."

Richard hesitated. Words just like that had changed his life forever, only minutes ago.

"But, this is Michelle," he thought, and he hoped 'she' was still his friend.

"I promise," he barely choked out.

As if his reply were her cue, Michelle went to work. She pulled out a cotton cloth from the purse that hung by her side along with a small bottle of makeup remover and started removing the lipstick from Richard's face.

While Richard stood there and as she wiped his face off, he realized that she had a purse. He also realized that her hair had grown almost all the way back in, and it now hung to her shoulders and had the small curls around the bottom again. He almost broke his promise, he was so anxious to see how she really looked.

Michelle finished by blowing the remaining fumes away from Richard's face. His face felt cool as the cleaner finished evaporating. The smell gradually went away and Richard waited for her words so he could open his eyes and see her again.

Then something warm and soft touched his mouth. He

wondered what it could be when it remained there for a moment. Then he could feel her soft, warm breath against his cheek as he felt his lips starting to twist slightly and move back and forth. Richard almost burst out loud as he realized, "Michelle is sixteen and she is kissing me!"

Michelle did not stop. She rotated her head the other direction, without her lips ever losing contact with his, and she continued moving them slowly and softly.

There they kissed, standing in the shade between the two trees for five full minutes with nothing touching but their lips.

Then, with a soft, little smack, Michelle stepped away.

"OK, you can open your eyes now," she said as she stood back with a smile on her face.

She then put her thumb and forefinger up to her chin, seeming to scrutinize him, and said, "You look much better now."

And he was.

Chapter 20: The Ceiling

Richard still stood there staring at the Luthier. Feelings he had kept down inside of him all of these years suddenly emerged and exploded, making his whole body shake.

He thought of the ancient Aztec priest again with his sharp, obsidian knife, "And that is something even 'you' cannot do, Master Luthier!" he yelled at the top of his voice while shaking his head defiantly.

"Is that so?" replied the Luthier curiously, as he looked deep into Richard's angry, scared face. "And why is that?"

"Because there is not one there!" Richard yelled back at him with tears streaming down his face in torrents.

Then Richard dropped to the floor as though every bone had been pulled from his body and he repeated the words, "Because there is not one there!"

When Michelle and Richard stood back, he opened his eyes and realized that she looked different now. There she stood, straight and tall, with her beautiful, light-brown hair flowing down, with the small curls just touching her shoulders. She was wearing a bright, pastel summer dress with flowers on it that fit the smooth, flowing form of her thin, womanly-shaped body perfectly. She had a white, stylish purse hanging from a very thin strap on her right shoulder in a way that seemed to give her a sophisticated air.

As they looked into each other's eyes, Richard knew that they were still friends and big smiles spread across their faces at the same time.

His heart was still beating fast from her kiss and he could feel his whole body tingling. She smiled and looked at him with tender eyes that said, "Welcome back."

Richard knew by the look in her eyes that he didn't have to apologize for anything. He looked at her and realized that he had truly underestimated her friendship. There were questions he was going to ask her and things he was going to tell her that he had saved up ever since that day at the amusement park, but right now none of them needed to be said.

"You look taller now," Michelle said with a smile.

Richard thought that it was only the feeling he had while he stood looking at her. Then he realized that it had been four months since they had seen each other and he was sure that he was standing taller now than he had ever stood in his life.

"I am," replied Richard with a firm voice neither of them had ever heard before, and he straightened himself up and stood even taller while he smiled back at her.

Michelle took a small step toward Richard, and he took a large step toward her. Just as Richard slowly started to rotate his head and moved a little closer, she smiled and stepped back.

"Do you remember the day after we were tossed out of the drugstore?" Michelle asked.

"Yes," he replied, almost laughing as he thought of the look on the clerk's face while Michelle had innocently asked her questions.

"I told you how I promised my mother that evening that I would not kiss a boy until I was sixteen."

Richard nodded his head. He remembered.

"What I didn't tell you was," she hesitated a moment to give Richard that sweet, playful smile of hers as she looked into his eyes, "I promised myself that 'you' would be the first boy I kissed."

Then the expression on Michelle's face changed as Richard stood there with his face only inches away from hers. She hesitated just one more time before she added,

"I also promised myself that you would be the 'only man'."
   This time Richard kissed her.

   They walked away from beneath the shade of the two trees holding hands, asking and telling each other all the things they couldn't with their eyes. They wandered through the park until they stopped by the stream where Michelle had pulled out the crawdad.
   Richard noticed Michelle was bubbling over and seemed to glow more with each step she took away from the stream.
   "She is the best thing in this world," he thought to himself. Then, as he turned and looked at her again, he realized, "She is the only thing!"
   He looked at her with these thoughts running through his mind and she looked back at him with longing in her eyes. She seemed to know what he was thinking and she felt the same way.
   A big smile spread across her face and large tears welled up in her soft, brown eyes.
   "Be my love," was all that she said.
   They quietly stood on the path, looking into each other's eyes, smiling and remembering that very first day they met.

   After the tears dried on their cheeks and each of them took a long deep breath, Richard asked, "What do we do now?"
   Michelle gave him an almost mischievous smile.
   "What?" asked Richard
   "We 'always' keep our promises," she said, looking for his response.
   He slowly nodded yes.
   "And we are still too young to get married."
   He nodded again, this time with a serious look on his face, holding back a smile.
   "So, what do we do?" he asked, not quite sure what she was leading up to.
   Michelle didn't even hesitate. She grabbed Richard by

the shoulders and pushed them back and forth a little as if
to loosen them up, then she patted both of his arms at the
same time with her hands to straighten him up again.

Michelle stepped back, stood like a little tin soldier, and
said:

"I, Michelle Ross, truly love you, Richard Gaspar, and I
always will. I will live my life to make you happy and will
love no other." After a slight pause she quickly added,
"And I promise to be good until we're married," ending
the phrase with a smile.

Richard stood just a little straighter and taller and
replied in a slow, serious tone, "I, Richard Gaspar, truly
love you, Michelle Ross, and I always will. I will live my
life to make 'you' happy and will love no other." Then
with the same little pause that she had used, he continued
while bobbing his head back and forth and side to side,
"And I promise to be good until we're married."

They both laughed together, and when they were done,
they sealed it with a kiss.

They walked through the park holding hands and they
talked about life, love, and about the future. But instead
of talking generically like they had while laying on the
grassy knoll over the years, everything they said now was
first person, 'you' and 'I'.

They walked over by the 'briar patch' and Richard peered
into the dark, gnarly bushes. The path had grown over
and it was now totally blocked with large, sharp thorns.

"I guess I'll have to tell you my secrets somewhere else,"
Richard said with a disappointed look. "Or if you like, I
will come back and cut these away. Kind of like a
community service project," he smiled as he pointed to
the large, thorny branches that blocked the path.

"We don't need secrets anymore. And you can talk to
me anytime, anywhere!" replied Michelle. "We are free!"

Michelle tilted her head back, opened both of her arms
and ran up the path and across the small bridge. She
ran across the grass and directly into the sprinklers that
were spraying the grass in the middle of the park.

Richard followed her example, running and repeating

the word 'free'.

They stopped right in the middle of the sprinklers and gave each other a big hug and then a kiss. After they separated they joined hands and twirled around and around while the sprinklers continued to drench them with cool water.

Their hands eventually slipped and they both laughed and smiled at each other while they fell backward onto the wet grass. Richard lay on the grass for a moment, a little dizzy from twirling around and he smiled again as he watched Michelle get back up and circle him around and around in the sprinkler.

Even though Michelle was growing into a mature woman, Richard knew that she would always be his friend. He thought how good it felt to finally be with Michelle again. He also marveled how she could take the worst day of his life and turn it into the very best.

Michelle came running toward Richard breathing hard and full of life, her feet sloshing through the wet grass. She splashed the water in his face as she jumped right over Richard and then ran over to a park bench which sat along the sidewalk. She jumped up on it with her arms stretched out and energetically cried out, "Free!"

Richard smiled, rolled over and turned around just in time to see her wet feet slip out from under her on the slick, flat slats of the metal bench. It threw her helplessly backward, through the air, and then down onto the concrete.

He watched in horror as her wet hair slapped the ground and her head hit the sidewalk with a sickening thud.

He closed his eyes as her head twisted to the side and the rest of her body came falling randomly down on top of it.

The whole world seemed to go quiet as Richard got up and ran toward her.

It seemed like an unbelievably morbid dream as he frantically screamed out, "Michelle!"

Michelle didn't move when Richard ran to her side and stood there dripping on the sidewalk.

He knelt down beside her crumpled form and watched as her whole body relaxed. His eyes went wide and he stopped breathing. Then he shook his head back and forth in disbelief as he looked at her lying on the concrete in a lifeless heap.

Richard carefully rolled her thin, motionless body over and then he froze and stared in shock. He could tell by looking at Michelle's face that she was dead.

There was no chance for words, no last look in her eyes, no parting kisses or hugs, just death.

He thought of their dreams and all their future plans they had just made together as he gently untwisted her body, one limb at a time, and rotated her head back around how it should be.

His shaking hand held her head while he unwound the wet, light-brown hair from around it. He slowly pulled each strand of hair off until her clean, white, expressionless face lay there below his.

"God!" he pleaded, as he picked up her right hand in his, "Please, don't take her! Don't keep her from me again! I can't live without her!" was his desperate prayer as Richard knelt on the sidewalk holding Michelle in his arms.

After a moment he closed his eyes and shook his head.

When nothing happened he opened his eyes and looked down at her again.

She lay silent and peaceful.

His whole face took on the sorrow and loss that he felt as he leaned down and slowly kissed her soft, placid lips. He knew in his heart and deep within his soul that she was all he lived for and as he looked down into her face he vowed to her over and over again, "...and I will love no other, and I will love no other..." until he noticed her fingers getting cooler in his hand.

Richard turned when he heard the door of a house slam shut across the street. Mrs. Becker was standing on her porch looking at them. Richard knew she had probably watched the whole thing through her front window.

"Stay away from us," he screamed as Mrs. Becker started

toward the park. "Stay away from us!" he repeated even louder and more frantic, as she continued to scurry across her yard.

Mrs. Becker quickly crossed the street and kept on coming toward Richard while he held Michelle's lifeless body.

"Go away!" screamed Richard.

"LEAVE US ALONE!" he cried out, as he picked Michelle up in his arms. Mrs. Becker just kept bearing down on them.

Richard stood up and turned. Still holding Michelle in his arms, he started to run. He looked back and saw Mrs. Becker hurriedly pursuing them across the grass yelling, "Stop!"

Richard ran across the bridge and over the grassy knoll until he reached the far end of the park. Then, in a blind rage, he held Michelle's body tightly against his chest while he screamed in torment and ran as fast as he could, straight into the briar patch.

He ignored the large thorns and sharp branches as they tore away at his shirt and pants and dug into his arms and face.

The ground was soft and his feet dug in while his legs trudged forward beneath the branches that held up the large, razor-sharp thorns. They entered deep into his flesh and they tore away at him, piece by piece, while he continued toward the heart of the briar patch.

The thorns got larger and tore even deeper as he advanced, but he ignored the pain and held Michelle tighter and tighter against him and would not give in.

"We're almost there," he choked out to her lifeless body as he pushed on with all his might.

He felt nothing as his blood drained from the wounds that covered every inch of his body now. The branches and thorns tore at his face as he looked down at her lifeless body clutched in his arms. It was only then, when a large ragged branch hit the side of his head, knocking him unconscious and leaving two large long holes in his left cheek, that he stopped running.

It was only then that his and Michelle's bodies tumbled down together at the edge of the small clearing in the center of the briar patch with his arms still around her.

Richard sat on the floor of the violin shop, sobbing and repeating the words, "Because there is not one there!"

The Luthier slowly walked over to Richard and put a gentle, sympathetic hand on his shoulder and told him, "I will find what you need."

Richard drove back to the hotel very slowly, almost reluctantly, that afternoon. He had cried like a baby on the floor of the violin shop, and he didn't know what he was going to do now. This had 'all been taken care of' years ago when his psychiatrist looked him in the eye and said, "You are ready," meaning, Richard could now accept all the tragedy of his childhood and get on with his life.

Richard had repeated the words, "I am ready," as he walked out that door so many years ago, and he 'had' walked away with the ability to remember Michelle without bursting into tears or going into a rage. And he had never looked back.

Until now.

"If Mrs. Becker hadn't run back to her house and called the police and ambulance immediately, Richard would not have lived," Dr. Staheli told George and Alaine Gaspar as they stood outside the emergency room waiting to see if their son would live or die. "By the time he arrived at the hospital Richard had lost most of his blood and his heart stopped beating for a few seconds until we could start it again."

George Gaspar had never heard a doctor talk so bluntly before, but later, when he saw Richard lying on the bed after all the operations were over, he understood why.

Richard had not even regained consciousness when Michelle's coffin was lowered into the ground while both Michelle's and Richard's parents watched together in disbelief. That was the only time both his parents left his bedside before he finally opened his eyes in the hospital and realized what had really happened.

His badly torn body slowly recovered as he lay in the hospital bed week after week, but his life did not. When he learned that his heart had stopped on the operating table, he said to himself, "It never started beating again."

The days went by and Richard stared up at the ceiling, while he became more and more miserable with each passing moment.

He had very few visitors other than his parents. His mother eventually told him that Michelle's parents were moving to another town where Joe had gotten a permanent job offer. "They seem so miserable and down lately," she said, shaking her head.

"It's probably the best thing for them right now, to change their surroundings, and do something different," his mother told him while he lay in bed, still unable to move more than a few inches.

"You need something different, too," his mother said with a cautious smile. "Don't get upset, Richard, but I've tried everything else. After all, if it wasn't for her, you wouldn't be alive."

"No! No way!" Richard tried to scream, but he only mumbled through the bandages and braces that still held the left side of his face together. His mother ignored his protests and gave a small wave toward the door, as if to encourage someone in.

"Come in, Mrs. Becker."

If Richard were able to, he would have either run back into the briar patch again or strangled Mrs. Becker right then and there. But all he could do was lay in his hospital bed, helpless.

"Hello, Richard," Mrs. Becker said with a small smile. "I know how you must feel about me."

"You have no idea!" Richard screamed at her while he struggled to move his arms that were bandaged and braced together to the point he couldn't move them. Then he tried to kick his right leg because that was the only thing he could move a little.

"I'm sorry!" she blurted out with tears in her eyes. "I knew the only way I could ever tell you that was if I did it while you couldn't run away."

These words were different than Richard had expected, but he still struggled on.

"When you two were together at first, I saw things that bothered me. It reminded me of my husband and myself. We did get in trouble, big trouble, and it destroyed our lives for years."

"So you destroyed ours!" Richard tried to scream, but doubted she understood the words.

Reacting to his outbreak, she continued, "After hearing your questions at the drugstore, I thought you two would wind up in the same kind of trouble someday, and I thought if I could just slow you down a little, I would be helping you out. So I made it my goal to get you both separated, for your own good."

Then she burst into tears. "I really only wanted to help! Please forgive me! Once I saw how miserable you two became when you were separated, I knew you had something special, more than we had, but I didn't know what to do or how to say it. I also figured you hated me so much that you wouldn't listen.

"I cried when I saw how she helped you that afternoon as you two walked by. Most people can only dream of that kind of relationship. I am truly sorry I watched you; you looked so happy together.

"When I came out, believe me, it was only to help Michelle. I wouldn't have hurt her for anything in this world."

After apologizing, Mrs. Becker turned and walked away.

That was the last time Richard ever saw Mrs. Becker. Later in his career he had found out from Samuel that it was Mrs. Becker who had called and told him that he must come listen to a young man named Richard Gaspar play the violin.

All these things, and more, started running through Richard's head as he drove back to St. George; back to his hotel room.

Richard's eyes were red and swollen when opened the door and set his violin down. He now began to wonder again, after all these years, if it would have been better if Mrs. Becker hadn't seen them and had left him in the briar patch to die.

While he lay on the bed, he became more and more confused, and his mind began spinning around and around. He finally fell asleep out of pure exhaustion, wondering if the dream would start again.

When he opened his eyes he looked up at the ceiling. It was still dark but he knew what was up there by the dead, calm feeling that hung thick in the air. He cowered back in fright, feeling like a little boy as he pulled the covers up over his head.

Then the moaning started.

Softly at first, then louder and louder. Next Richard could hear their individual voices screaming, "Help me! Do something!" Then, each of the voices would fade away into a pitiful cry for "Help!"

Richard knew what he would see when he removed the covers. But the voices just kept calling him over and over. A woman's voice, a man's voice, a small child's voice, one after the other, over and over again.

"Go away!" he yelled out, but his voice only seemed to encourage them on in their pleadings.

"Help us!" some would chant together, sometimes with all the others joining in.

"Go away!" he screamed again, knowing that they wouldn't, or couldn't, until he lowered the covers and looked at them.

Above Richard's head in the hotel room, hung rows and rows of people, each hanging from the ceiling by ropes tied in nooses around their necks. Each one fighting and struggling with their hands tied behind their backs, trying to get free. They were kicking their feet and swinging around.

A large man right in front of Richard gurgled out, "Cut me

down, boy." Gasping for air, he continued, "I can't wait any longer. For God's sake boy, cut me down!" He was fighting and kicking the whole time, with his eyes bulging out and blood running from the corner of his mouth.

Next to him was a beautiful woman with long black hair and blood dripping down from behind her ear. She couldn't speak because the noose was too tight around her neck. Her feet were loosely tied together though she wasn't kicking. She just hung there with a pitiful look on her face, staring at Richard.

Richard stood up and walked through the screaming and moaning people, one after the other, until he approached the other side of the room.

His mind eventually blocked the sound of all of the yelling and screaming voices out until he distinctly heard a very soft and gentle, "Please," come from one of the rows of people. He couldn't believe he could hear it with all the other people's loud voices, but he did. Then he heard it again, "Please," and he ran to where the voice came from. Somehow this voice was different. It seemed to call to 'him'.

In the middle of the kicking and screaming people, hung a young woman. She was dead and lifeless, hanging perfectly still and silent from the rope that was tied around her white, elegant neck. Richard got the impression that hers was the voice and that she had just died. She had light-brown hair that hung around her shoulders and a flowery summer dress on with a white purse hanging from her right shoulder by a very thin strap.

And as always, Richard then woke up.

Chapter 21: Wood

Richard considered calling the Luthier to cancel his appointment at the violin shop today because of his dream. He considered cancelling everything.

Richard had not thought of suicide since he was in the asylum and nothing they could say there had convinced him to want to live.

It was only when he remembered the words of their vow that he had decided not to kill himself. That was the only thing that kept him alive while he was there and the only reason he had to live: because he had promised her, "I will live my life to make you happy."

His word to Michelle was more important to him than life 'or death'. He also knew, as he contemplated his future while in the asylum, that Michelle believed in him. He also thought of the words that she had spoken to him under the two trees the day after they met, "I believe you will become that greatest player in the world."

Even though he thought Michelle was talking about their future together, she had still used the words, "You will succeed," as they sat across from each other in the fortune teller's booth in Salty Pete's Park.

"She believed in me, and she was never wrong!" he said to himself in the asylum, more resolved to do his part than ever before. He may have failed her in other ways but he would not fail her now! And so he had practiced and lived and breathed violins night and day 'for her'.

"And now I am almost there!" Richard said to himself as he stood up in his hotel room and shook his fist at the ceiling.

Richard felt resolve like he hadn't felt in years. Dreams or no dreams, he would live his life and he would succeed! For her!

He opened his case, pulled out the small, silver rosin holder and while looking at the inscriptions and pictures of Paganini, he said, "We will show the world!" He then picked up his Bergonzi and played Paganini's twenty-four Caprices flawlessly before heading out to the violin shop.

Richard had a hard time not speeding as he drove through the town of Leeds. He had to fight the desire to put his foot to the floor on the Blazer's gas peddle over and over as he headed up the road. He had put the Blazer on cruise control while coming up the freeway, when he looked down at the speedometer.

He fought the desire to go faster and faster all the way through the small town and he was glad he did when he passed the police car that was hiding behind the old mechanic's shop. Richard was going seven miles an hour over the speed limit, but the officer probably let him go because Richard was wearing a big smile on his face as he passed by.

Richard's tires skidded as he came to a stop almost in front of the door of the violin shop. He hurriedly grabbed his Bergonzi and then burst through the front door and headed across the entry.

Richard almost threw his violin onto the entry table and ran over to where the Luthier sat and asked, trying to keep as calm as he could, "Master Luthier, if the fan is turned off, will the wood still swing?"

The Luthier smiled.

"I see you have been dreaming, Richard," replied the Luthier.

Richard felt an overwhelming satisfaction flow through his entire body. He sat down beside the Luthier and let out a big sigh.

"So you see it too?" asked Richard, looking up at the wood hanging from the ceiling.

"I see a lot of things," answered the Luthier.

Richard looked into the Luthier's eyes and continued, "I know you see it. What does it mean?"

"It means you and your wood are ready for me to start your violin."

The Luthier stood up and very solemnly walked over to the switch that controlled the large fan that slowly blew air between the pieces of wood that hung from the ceiling.

Richard looked up at the wood and watched it gently sway back and forth in the breeze. Some of the pieces gently touched against each other as they moved, making a gentle clicking sound in the breeze.

The Luthier turned off the switch and the breeze slowly died down until the shop was completely calm. The air around him seemed to take on the atmosphere of a tomb or catacomb, and a chill ran up Richard's spine as he tried to shake off the feeling of his dream.

Richard watched as the swinging pieces of wood settled down a little. But some of them continued to swing the same even without the breeze blowing through them.

The Luthier stood by the switch and watched Richard the whole time after he turned the fan off.

After a few minutes, Richard noticed that some of the pieces of wood completely stopped swinging, while others right next to them swung freely, back and forth in the motionless air.

Richard looked to the Luthier for an answer, but the Luthier just closed his eyes and slowly walked under the wood with the same look on his face that he had the day before when he listened to the spider.

The Luthier stopped walking, then he opened his eyes and looked up at the ceiling for a moment. He turned and picked up a stepladder that was leaning against the wall and set it under the pieces of wood that were hanging perfectly still and climbed up the ladder so he could pull them down.

It was the same wood that Richard had noticed the Luthier look at after Mr. Haito had left.

The Luthier examined the wood he held in his hands

and with a large smile he said, "It is ready."

The Luthier walked back over to the switch on the wall and turned the fan back on, and immediately the feeling of death and stillness faded away.

Richard stood spellbound. After all these years; after the torment of his dreams, the drugs and therapy, everything he had questioned about his sanity was really happening and he had seen it with his own eyes!

Richard was willing to believe anything now and he looked at the Luthier with expressions of relief and gratefulness.

Then, he thought of the many different pieces of wood that had stopped swinging when the fan was turned off, and he asked, "How do you know which pieces of wood to pull down, out of the ones that don't move?"

The Luthier lovingly picked back up the pieces of wood that he had pulled down from the ceiling and he looked at them with a tender smile.

In a very soft and gentle voice he answered, "Please."

Chapter 22: The Lesson

Richard laid on the bed in his hotel room that night, and he looked up at the ceiling with a calm, peaceful feeling. Somehow he knew he would never have the dream again.

When he did fall asleep, images of Michelle and the lake started floating into his mind and he realized he was free to dream of Michelle again after all these years.

The Luthier invited Richard to visit the violin shop anytime he wished and he told Richard that he was free to ask any questions, "...though there are some I cannot answer," the Luthier told him.

At this point Richard doubted that was possible.

"You seem to know everything," stated Richard the next morning as he watched the Luthier sort out the violin wood that lay before him. The Luthier picked up one of the pieces and tapped it so the sound would ring through the shop.

"Beautiful," he said. He smiled and did the same with each piece of wood until they all lay before him on the bench in the order that he would carve them.

"Did you dream well last night?" asked the Luthier.

Richard thought it was a strange question at first, but he was getting used to these kinds of things by now and answered, "Yes, yes I did," as he remembered his dreams of Michelle.

"Very well then," said the Luthier.

Just an instant later, with his index finger and thumb,

the Luthier snatched a small gnat out of the air that was flying around his light and held it up by the wings for Richard to see. Richard was not surprised at all this time at the Luthier's demonstration of skill or speed.

"I can believe anything now," he thought to himself, as he looked at the small bug kicking his legs between the Luthier's fingers.

"Then it is time you knew the truth, Richard. I do what is necessary to make my violins the best they can be, whatever it takes. I will go to the ends of the earth, sparing no expense, to make one small improvement in their materials or quality. I will also do whatever is necessary to make my customers appreciate them to their fullest."

"What I am about to tell you may or may not change your mind about me or your violin, but I must do it for Truth's sake."

The Luthier then carried the small bug, with his tiny little legs still kicking out from between his fingers, over to the small spider's web in the corner. The Luthier stooped down and said, "Here is a treat for you, Ben."

With that, he tossed the little insect into the web, right next to the spider.

The spider, with its seven legs, quickly walked over and started winding it up.

"He is my friend," said the Luthier. "I knew he was missing that leg long before you entered my shop the first time.

Richard looked puzzled. "But you could hear him rolling up that bug yesterday."

"And with a little practice so could you," reminded the Luthier.

"But you just pulled that bug out of the air. I just watched you."

"And so could you, with practice," replied the Luthier. "But the greatest Shaolin Priest and I together cannot tell you which leg is missing, only by listening. I need you to believe so I can make your violin the one you need."

Richard now stood dumbstruck. Was everything he had seen a trick? Was the Japanese man a setup? Could the

Luthier have even pulled Mark and Cercie in on it?

And yet the sound and the volume of the two violins. How about Sam? How about Richard's dream? No, it wasn't possible, and yet here the Luthier stood telling Mark he had lied, or at least exaggerated. Was the Luthier a fake or not?

"Before you accuse me of being a charlatan, as some do Paganini, let me continue," the Luthier said as he walked back over to his bench and sat down.

"How great do you believe Paganini could play?" asked the Luthier.

"He was the greatest player who ever lived," replied Richard.

"Do you believe he could play faster and technically better than anyone else?"

"Yes, I believe that," answered Richard, "and so did my grandfather."

"Could he make his violin sing like an opera singer?"

"Yes."

"Bark like a dog?"

"Yes."

"Cackle like a chicken, sing like a bird, or cry like a child?"

"Yes, yes, yes," Richard replied, remembering and still believing all the stories he had heard as a child.

"Could he make the audience laugh?"

"Yes."

"Could he make grown men cry?"

"Yes."

"Could he lift the spirits of the depressed?"

"Yes," answered Richard, nodding his head.

"Roll on the floor with agony and despair?"

"Yes," whispered Richard.

"Could he give them what they needed?"

"Yes."

"And so will I, to you, if you will but believe."

Richard sat there a long time pondering what was being said.

"Believe what?" asked Richard. "And since you just told

me you lied about the spider, how will I know that what you tell me is the truth."

"I did not say I lied about the spider, I just said he was my friend and that I knew him before you came."

"You said not even the greatest Shaolin Priest and you together could tell me only by listening," said Richard.

The Luthier smiled as he heard Richard repeat the words correctly.

"A great Shaolin Priest uses more than his ears," replied the Luthier.

Richard was getting confused and angry now, feeling the Luthier was teasing him.

"Well, can you or can't you hear if that spider's leg is missing?" demanded Richard.

"I can never tell you. You must decide for yourself," replied the Luthier.

Richard still wasn't sure, but one word still kept whispering in his ears while he sat at the bench looking into the Luthier's eyes, "Please..."

"The reason I have put you through this and seem to taunt you now is because of what I am going to do next," said the Luthier.

"What next?" Richard wondered.

"He has already insulted me, humiliated me, shocked me, tormented me and now let me down. Or maybe he's let me down and picked me back up? What could possibly be next?"

"I am going to teach you how to play the violin," said the Luthier with a smile.

"You're what?!" hollered Richard, who considered himself one of the three greatest players in the world.

"It's time you learned how to play the violin," smiled the Luthier again.

Richard was appalled, but before he blurted out his reflex answer, he stopped and thought it over.

"Can this Luthier actually be better than me? I can play faster and more accurately than anyone recorded in history, but could I pull that gnat out of the air by its wings? I have perfect pitch. Can he really hear the leg missing? Or, is everything just a charade, or a bag of tricks?" Then he thought, "What about my dream?" Richard believed 'that' was real.

Richard slowly relaxed and looked into the Luthier's eyes. It started to feel a lot like the first time he and Michelle had put their feet together between the two trees. He took a deep breath, sensing that this was for keeps.

"What shall I call you? Teacher? Master?" asked Richard humbly.

"Luthier will still do," he replied with a large smile. "Let's begin our lesson."

Richard instinctively started to get up and walk toward his violin.

"You won't need that," quickly commented the Luthier.

"Do you have a better one, here?" asked Richard with a smile, wondering what the Luthier would pull out for him to play.

"You will not need a violin," replied the Luthier.

With a puzzled look, Richard sat back down.

"You can already play the violin as well as Nicolo Paganini," the Luthier said.

Richard looked back at him, waiting for a laugh or some other indication that he was joking.

After a long pause Richard realized that the Luthier was not joking.

"You seem to be knowledgeable about Paganini's life and the stories that surround him. Do you recall how it is claimed he never practiced after he was eighteen years old? That his performances were practice enough?"

"Yes," replied Richard. Richard knew the stories well.

"He spread those stories, as he did all the stories good and bad about him. They were all true, in a way. But the real truth was not that his performances were enough, but that practicing was too much."

Richard almost thought he understood the words of the Luthier, but then he realized he didn't.

"Just ponder that as we go on," continued the Luthier.

"Have you heard it said that when he was a young boy he spent two years with only his bow in his right hand and he didn't pick his violin back up until he had mastered the bow?"

"Yes I have, and I have always admired that kind of dedication and the ability to isolate one thing and perfect it," said Richard, thinking of how his own way of practicing followed this philosophy.

"Paganini carefully spread that rumor so that other players wouldn't feel bad at their lack of skill. Since no one else was willing to hold a bow in their right hand for two years, it gave them an excuse for why he was so much better than they were. While they sat in the audience, they could still say to themselves, 'If I did nothing but hold a bow in my hand for two years, I could bow as well as he does.' Without that rumor they would have said, 'I can never play like that. I hate him.'

"It is part of the reason why he would dress and talk the way he did. He wanted to leave the impression that he was possessed of an evil spirit or that he was the devil himself standing on stage. The audience would then believe he was more than a mere mortal standing before them and they were willing to believe he could do anything. Back then, it was easy to convince someone you were possessed." The Luthier then added with a smile, "It is very difficult for me today."

Richard started to understand and let out a little laugh.

"The belief that he or his violin, or both, were more than mere mortals also did something much more important.

The Luthier paused and his face became very solemn, "And what I am about to do is 'very' important."

"Are you a man of your word?" asked the Luthier.

"Yes, I am," firmly replied Richard.

"Then, close your eyes and promise you won't open them until I am completely finished and I tell you to open them."

Richard's eyes opened wide.

"Those were Michelle's exact words. How..." Richard started to blurt out, but the Luthier put his index finger over his lips.

"I promise," Richard replied.

"Good. Now close your eyes and take a deep breath."

Richard did as he was asked. He closed his eyes and took a deep, relaxing breath.

The Luthier continued with a slow voice, almost like a hypnotist, but different. Richard had been hypnotised before and he was certain that he was not hypnotised now, and yet a strange feeling came over him.

"Imagine yourself over a hundred and fifty years ago when Nicolo Paganini, the greatest player in the world, is still alive and in his prime.

"You have never heard 'HIM' play before and you have travelled far to be here tonight.

"You have dreamed of this day your whole life. You have heard all the stories and rumors and now you sit in the audience waiting for 'him' to perform so you can confirm all of your beliefs you have held since you were a little child.

"You sit in your seat and realize that you and everyone around you paid three times the usual amount for your tickets tonight and still the hall is packed to capacity with the crowd of noisy people inside and throngs outside pushing up against the doors, waiting for just a note or two to float out." Richard listened and could hear the wood clicking together above his head, then the breeze going through it seemed to grow stronger and stronger and the clicking louder and louder as the Luthier spoke. The temperature in the room seemed to get warmer as Richard imagined the crowd around him, sitting in the old concert hall with no air conditioning in it.

"You are now sitting in your seat, in the audience, anxiously waiting for 'him' to walk out on stage.

"'How deformed is he?' you ask yourself. 'Will he walk with a limp? How twisted is his spine? Does he hunch over? Will it show at all? Did his parents really lock him in his room night and day with only his violin to play upon and then starve him until he performed flawlessly for them? Did it, after all those years, permanently deform his body as he grew and is his twisted body what allows him to play relaxed where others have to stretch?

"'Did he use his possessed violin to lure a beautiful dancer through the streets of the city and into his lair where he strangled her with her own G string so he could put it on his violin to play those evil songs with?' Or, you wonder, 'was it how others say, that as he sat in prison after killing her, each of the strings on his violin broke until none were left? Then did he pull her G string out of his pocket, place it upon his violin and play upon it until he bewitched the jailers and escaped? Does he now wander the streets at night looking for another victim?

"'Does the devil stand beside him as he plays, guiding his bow? Will I see his shadow? Will I cry as he plays his love songs? Will I laugh? Will I lose control?'

"Then, the lights go dim."

Was it Richard's imagination or did the violin shop just get darker? Yet the Luthier remained right in front of Richard the whole time, so close at times that Richard thought he could feel his breath.

"After a long wait you hear a little commotion and the crowd hushes instantly in anticipation."

Suddenly Richard could no longer hear the fan blowing or the wood clicking together in the violin shop and the atmosphere gradually changed until he felt like he was deep within a silent crypt. Richard listened, but he could no longer hear anything as he sat there, not even the walls creaking or the trucks on the freeway.

Then he felt a strange presence enter the room, and he was tempted to open his eyes, but he had promised.

"Now this is weird," he thought to himself, but he was also enjoying it.

"The concert hall goes pitch black," the Luthier announced, and so did the violin shop, sending a cold chill and tingle up Richard's spine.

"Then the lights come back on, dim, and they finally settle in to a low glow, setting the mood for something 'evil'. No one in the audience knows why, but they all feel it together. It is as though something is all around them, surrounding them and closing in."

Richard found the hairs on the back of his neck raising and somehow knew the feeling the audience felt. Then Richard thought he heard the muffled scream of a cat from the back of the shop. It was so soft he wasn't sure. Then again louder. The feeling of something all around him, coming toward him and closing in was even stronger now.

"A figure from the shadows on stage starts to move. You almost think you remember seeing it before the lights went down, but you are not sure if it has been there the whole time or not. As you wonder, the figure moves forward and there is a commotion in the crowd."

Richard then heard the Luthier move back slightly and stand up. Then he heard other footsteps! They were slowly moving toward him from the back of the violin shop!

"He is tall and lanky, almost gangly. His face is thin and white and looks like a skull cradled deep in his long, ratty, jet-black hair as he turns his head toward the crowd with an evil smile."

Richard listened carefully and thought he could hear the sound of long hair rustling against material as the Luthier spoke. "He wears an old-fashioned black set of tails. His white hands are so large and also accentuated by the four inches of his wrists sticking out from the sleeves of his tuxedo.

"His hands are 'enormous', you realize, when he waves his fingers one at a time and brings them down against the strings of his violin."

There was no doubting it, Richard could hear fingers touch across all four strings of a violin while the Luthier spoke.

"The light is just bright enough for you to make out the large silver ring with the deep-red, oval-shaped ruby set in it. It is the ring that he only wears when he seduces women or when he wants to possess the souls of those that listen to him play."

Richard immediately thought of the box sitting on the shelf below Paganini's picture in his grandfather's parlor.

His grandfather was the only one Richard had ever heard the stories from about the ring. When his grandfather died and left the ring and painting to Richard he had taken them both to many dealers to have them authenticated and appraised, but no one had ever heard of the ring or of the painter before, and they could not authenticate them.

Even though the ring and painting were the correct age Richard wondered if his grandfather had made up the stories because of all the dealer's reactions to his grandfather's stories about them. And yet the Luthier was describing the ring perfectly and he also knew the stories!

"He walks to center stage, and he moves slowly with a strange limp." Again Richard could hear the footsteps, as they came toward him even closer. "He walks slightly hunched, with his left shoulder lower than his right, and he looks your way with an eerie look on his face and an evil smile.

"'It is true, you say to yourself! It really is him!'"

The violin shop then exploded with the crying voice of a violin, far beyond Richard's wildest dreams. It was like no violin Richard had ever heard before in his life. As the double stop notes wound their way up past the end of the fingerboard, it made him burst out crying with joy.

Paganini stood before him, he knew it!

Then, as the notes staccatoed back down, Richard could not help but laugh; they sounded like sparkling diamonds being poured out of a silk bag.

"Laughing and tears together, it was true!" Richard told himself. He knew Paganini was as great as they had said!

Richard knew this Luthier was supernatural but to bring Paganini back to life? Yet, there was no mistaking it: the phrases, the flying spiccato, the lightning speed, a barking dog, a songbird, and a chicken.

Richard laughed out loud as all the sounds came from the strings of a violin only a few feet away, then he laughed again when they were all done because they sounded so real to him.

Without a pause, almost on top of the other sounds, he heard a beautiful woman's voice float out from the violin. "The opera singer!" Richard told himself. And it was true. The most beautiful, pure soprano voice he had ever heard, lingered and floated through the violin shop. Then an alto voice joined in. This one was just as beautiful, but it sang Italian words, pure and true.

Richard almost opened his eyes out of pure shock. He didn't understand. He could imagine Paganini playing double stops and imitating two voices, but he had never heard of a violin that could sing words! The tears flowed down Richard's cheeks as he sat back and listened in ecstacy.

Everything was true! Everything his grandfather and all the critics had ever said about Paganini's playing. He was hearing it for himself! Would the Luthier let him open his eyes? Was it worth breaking his promise to see the great Nicolo Paganini brought back to life?

Suddenly the music stopped and there was silence.

"Richard, there is someone here I would like you to meet. Please open your eyes."

Richard's eyes flew open in an instant.

"Richard, this is my wife, Sheryl. Sheryl, meet Richard Gaspar."

When Richard's eyes focused, he saw a woman with flaming-red hair in a black dress, holding a large white and black house cat.

"It's a pleasure to meet you Richard," she said with a smile and a nod.

Next to her stood the Luthier holding a violin with bright, red varnish that matched his wife's hair in one hand and a bow in his other.

Richard sat staring with his mouth wide open, then he stammered, "You?...You?" He shook his head and stammered over again, "You can play like 'that'?"

"Yes, and you are much better than I am," was the Luthier's reply with a mischievous grin.

Chapter 23: The Secrets

Sheryl walked over to the switch with her fiery-red hair swishing as she turned the fan back on.

"You're not going to tell me that your playing was a trick?" asked Richard.

"No, it was no trick," answered the Luthier.

"Very few people in the history of the world know the 'Three Master Secrets' of playing the violin, viola, or cello. They go far beyond desire, skill and technique. These three secrets separate the 'Master Virtuoso' from all the other performers in the world."

The Luthier paused, and Richard found himself feeling the same way he imagined Mr. Haito felt just a few days ago as he stood staring at the two swords hanging in the lid of the black violin case. Mr. Haito's words ran through Richard's mind, "They are worth millions of dollars! Somehow I will get the money. Somehow I will pay you!"

The Luthier looked at Richard and continued, "These three secrets are priceless. They have value beyond your wildest dreams."

"How much?" asked Richard, knowing that if he could play like the Luthier he could take on the world.

"I will give them to you, as you become ready," answered the Luthier. As if that were her cue, Sheryl kissed the cat and lowered him to the ground, then she walked through a door that led to the center of the violin shop. After the door closed behind her, the Luthier said in a dreamy voice, "She is the most wonderful wife in the world."

The Luthier then stood there with a happy, far away look in his eyes and seemed to ignore Richard.

When the Luthier finally snapped out of his daze he asked, "Will you join us for lunch when Sheryl comes back out and I will tell you the first two secrets?"

Richard answered, "Yes, please."

Sheryl came back out wearing a soft cotton blouse with light-yellow stripes, Levi overalls with flowers embroidered on the pockets and tennis shoes with white socks coming up just shy of her ankles. To Richard she seemed to transform from an elegant, sophisticated enchantress, slightly older than the Luthier, to a bubbly, young country girl many years his younger, just by walking through that door.

"It's not the room, it's the clothes," the Luthier told Richard when he noticed his reaction. "But we will get to that in its turn," he said, as he took Sheryl's hand in his and walked toward the front door of the shop. The Luthier opened it for her and said, "After you, my dear."

Sheryl and Richard both walked out, with the Luthier following. Just before he closed the door, the cat Sheryl had been holding came running out with his long tail barely making it in time. The cat ran past them, then it circled around and stopped in their path.

"Oh, I'm sorry," said the Luthier, while looking at the cat. "Richard, this is Mooch, the cat."

Richard swung his arm down and bowed to the cat and said, "Good afternoon, it's a pleasure to meet you, Mooch."

With that, the cat walked over to him, and as cats do, 'allowed' Richard the privilege of petting him for a moment.

It was hot outside and Richard was a bit surprised they were going to walk anywhere.

They walked down the dirt road behind the violin shop until it turned to pavement, which was the opposite from anything Richard had seen before.

"Usually the pavement ends and the dirt road starts as you head away from civilization," Richard thought to himself. "But, there is nothing usual about this Luthier," he realized as his foot stepped off of the rough dirt road and onto the smooth, black asphalt.

The pavement made the temperature outside seem even hotter. Richard started to perspire and wondered how far it was to the Luthier's house.

Just as Richard was becoming uncomfortable and considered commenting about the heat, the road twisted and started heading down. He saw the tops of beautiful green trees as he turned the corner and he was hit with a cool breeze coming out from them. The temperature cooled even more as they headed down the road, with Richard looking everywhere around him in wonder.

The vegetation changed from the harsh desert cactus and sagebrush to the soft, green plants of the forest, complete with a small stream running through the middle of them.

When they reached the valley floor it continued to keep him spellbound. There were honeybees flying in and out of a hole in a rock cliff to their left and a small pond of water on the right surrounded by sunflowers. The Luthier left the road and walked over to the sunflowers so he could pick one and hand it to Sheryl with a kiss.

Mooch the cat took the opportunity to run over and chase a bee as it flew through the flowers, then he laid down and rolled over on the soft grass. When he looked over and saw them start to leave him behind, Mooch ran up next to them, but followed truantly, wandering and chasing everything he could find.

When Richard first saw Sheryl and the Luthier standing together they gave him the impression that they had been married for many years. Now, as they walked together beside him, they seemed like young lovers who had just met. The thought brought back good and bad memories so Richard pushed them from his mind.

The Luthier turned to Richard while they walked and said, "My shop must be in the desert to cure the wood and dry the varnish so I can make the best possible instruments and so they will last for hundreds of years. At the same time, some of the plants I must have will only grow down here.

"My family and I love the cool water and the lush trees, and this is one of the few places on earth that can supply us with all that we need."

As the Luthier spoke those words the valley opened up into a paradise and Richard looked all around him in amazement.

He was standing in front of gardens that lined the road and grew every kind of vegetable he knew of. Further beyond the gardens he could see lush, green lawns and trees surrounding a beautiful house. It looked like a mixture of a Victorian and country farmhouse; colonial-blue with white trim, complete with a large, white porch that wrapped around it.

Beyond the house were small, individual vineyards dotting the hillsides, giving an unbelievably picturesque setting. The two large mountains on either side totally blocked the view to the rest of the world and high on the one to his right, Richard could see what must be the silver mine the officer spoke of.

Richard found it was very easy to forget that there was any other world out there beyond the mountain tops he could see from where he stood on the valley floor. As they walked toward the house, Richard could see beautiful horses off in the distance, prancing though a pasture.

There were also small shops by the house that seemed to each serve a different purpose, just as the officer had mentioned. He looked around one last time before stepping up on the porch with the Luthier and his wife. Richard was about to ask about the winepress in the corner of the porch when he realized he had not said a word since they were at the shop. He had been so engrossed in thought, then too amazed with the valley as they walked along.

Finally Richard spoke, "Do you make your own wine?"

"Yes, though only for my instruments. The rest of us drink our own blend of grape juice."

Sheryl asked, "Would you like to try some, Mr. Gaspar?" as they entered the house together through a massive, but elegant, round-top door, filled with small panes of glass.

"I would be delighted. You may call me Richard if you like."

"And you may call me Sheryl. Please have a seat while I pull some grape juice out, and finish preparing lunch."

Richard looked around the large, spacious home with high ceilings and a copious amount of windows and he noticed the signs of children. Then he remembered that the Luthier had a son, named Skyler, in the National Guard. He was still amazed that the Luthier had a family. He knew most Master Luthiers had in the past, but he still envisioned an old, grey-haired man, alone at his bench carving away when he thought of master instruments, and he still had a hard time imagining anything else.

"How many children do you have?" Richard asked.

"Skyler, eighteen, Tessa, sixteen, and Colter, eleven," replied the Luthier.

"Skyler is at boot camp, while Tessa and Colter are swimming down at the lake with friends, otherwise we would introduce them to you," Sheryl added, as she brought out three glasses on a platter with a large bottle sitting in the center. She carefully lowered them to the table sitting between Richard and the Luthier.

"Allow me," said the Luthier as he picked up the bottle and pulled a large cork from its mouth. The bottle was large and thick, with fiery curls of brownish-red transparent color swirling throughout it. It gave Richard the impression of the ancient Egyptian glass he had seen at the museum in Cairo.

The three glasses appeared to be made from the same kind of glass, only they had a mixture of blues and greens with other wisps of colors mixed in. Richard wondered if this wasn't indeed some ancient wine being poured before him. His glass was poured first, but he waited so they could all pick up their glasses together.

"To your success," said the Luthier with a smile.

"And to yours," was Richard's reply.

Then the Luthier turned to Sheryl and said, "She's already

succeeded."

They all smiled and after a moment they all drank together.

The drink had a unique blend of sophisticated flavors but it was cool and refreshing at the same time. Richard was pleased; it was very good even though he could tell it contained no alcohol.

"It is wonderful," Richard remarked. "Thank you."

Richard noticed the flavor in his mouth develop and change as the time passed between sips. It was as though a rainbow of flavors filled his mouth. It reminded him of the fragrances that surrounded Cercie as she hugged him.

Richard listening to the Luthier and admired the glass he held in his hand as the flavors changed in his mouth.

The Luthier told him, "I love to blow glass; those were some of my first pieces."

"You blew this?" Richard didn't even know why he questioned by now; it had come out by habit.

"Right over there, next to the garage," the Luthier replied as he pointed to a large glass blowing oven made out of hundreds and hundreds of strange bricks assembled in a way Richard had never seen before.

"It's much more fun than it is work," the Luthier said as his fingers played with the colors and texture of the glass he held in his hand.

"And I love to stomp grapes," Sheryl said with a smile, moving her legs in winepress fashion.

"And both are wonderful," Richard replied, referring to the glass and the wine, or juice, or whatever it could be called. Richard knew a lot about wine but he still couldn't decide what the wonderful drink was that he held in his hand.

"Please excuse me, gentlemen," Sheryl said as she started to rise from her chair to go back to the kitchen. The Luthier instinctively rose first and helped Sheryl up with his hand. Richard was a little embarrassed, as he had let his manners slip a little over the years. He was used to performing for the press, but he socialized as little as possible because he was always alone.

Richard couldn't help but notice the look in the Luthier's eyes again while he watched her leave. "This guy is in serious puppy love," he thought to himself. "I wonder if they are like this all the time?"

Richard had a hard time shaking the thoughts off as the Luthier began to speak seriously.

"You already possess half of the first secret; you only require the second half."

The mention of 'the secrets' perked up Richard's attention and he was on the edge of his seat instantly.

"The first half of this secret is simply believing that you can. There are many people in this world who 'want' to be the greatest, some may even believe they can be and they work very hard and get very far, but deep down inside they fall short. Something inside keeps them from truly believing they can, especially when they compare themselves to one as great as Paganini. Something tells me that you have acquired the belief that you can succeed. You only lack the second half."

The Luthier purposely paused there for a painful length of time, waiting before he went on.

"Yes?" prodded Richard, anxious to hear the rest.

The Luthier acted as if that was what he was waiting for, and he replied, "The second half is 'knowing that you can'".

Richard thought about the words. They were simple and yet they had a ring of truth to them. He believed he could. Michelle had believed he could, and he was willing to do all he could to succeed for the rest of his life. And yet, as long and hard as he practiced, when he looked at the final goal he still wondered if he would succeed.

"How can I 'know' that I can?" asked Richard.

"You can only 'know that you can succeed' by knowing the other two secrets," the Luthier replied with a smile, "Sheryl and I will give you the second secret, while we eat lunch."

Then the Luthier led the way to the dining room.

Richard turned the corner, where he was greeted by Sheryl, who offered with a smile, "Please, have a seat."

Richard could not help but burst out loud with a laugh, then a shock of horror tore through him while Sheryl and the Luthier stood there with an offended look on both of their faces. They stared at him in disbelief.

He wondered, "They can't be serious, can they?" And yet they were so different from anyone he had ever met in his life.

Trying to compose himself the best he could, Richard tried to straighten his face and solemn his expression. He burst out laughing again as Sheryl smiled and he realized they weren't serious.

In the fine dining room, where Richard would normally expect to see an elegantly carved table and chairs, sat an old park bench complete with peeled paint and weather-beaten wood full of slivers. Sitting on the table at each of three places were cans of dog food and cat food with plastic forks stuck in each one. There were large specimen cups full of yellow liquid set at each place with two small bags of more dog food and cat food sitting in the center of the table.

Sheryl and the Luthier sat down at two of the places on one side of the table and motioned for Richard to join them on the other. He reluctantly sat down, but assumed there was a purpose for all this.

"I assure you all the food here is not animal food and that you will not be poisoned," Sheryl said with a smile, and with that they offered a short prayer.

"It'll need more than that before I'll eat it," Richard thought, as he opened his eyes and looked at it again.

"You may want to start with some salad," offered Sheryl as she pulled some lettuce out of the cat food bag and placed it in a cat dish set in front of her, then she passed the bag to the Luthier. Next she picked up a can of motor oil and poured it on the lettuce.

Richard still hesitated when the Luthier offered him the cat food bag.

"This is a joke, right?" he asked as Sheryl was about to put the fork of lettuce with the motor oil dripping off of it in her mouth.

"It is nice, clean salad dressing, I assure you," answered the Luthier. "We went to great pains to carefully prepare each container so it would be totally cleaned and disinfected, without disturbing its appearance." With that said, he and Sheryl both put a large fork full of salad into their mouths, then looked at each other and smiled.

"Mmm, it is good," Sheryl commented after she finished swallowing, with the Luthier nodding in agreement.

Richard still hesitated while they both continued eating.

"If you will care to join us, we will tell you the second secret," the Luthier said between mouthfuls.

Richard had a hard time giving in, but he finally did, and he grabbed the cat food bag and poured out some lettuce into his dish.

After Richard had taken his first bite, the Luthier continued with a look of satisfaction on his face, "Superb, isn't it?"

Richard only gave him a puzzled look.

"Please, try an appetizer," Sheryl offered, as she held up a can of dog food with toothpicks sticking out of it.

When he saw the sincere look on Sheryl's face, he couldn't refuse, though he almost did when he looked at the can again. But finally, he pulled out a toothpick with a square piece of something stuck on the end and he stared at it.

It was only after Sheryl and the Luthier had both taken a bite of their own appetizers that Richard decided he was really going to take a bite of his. He stared at the little dog pictured on the side of the can while he lifted it to his mouth.

The Luthier declared, "Fantastic!" just as Richard closed his eyes and pulled his appetizer off the toothpick between his teeth.

"It is quite good!" he thought to himself, when he finally chewed it up and swallowed.

"Let's have a drink," offered the Luthier as he picked up his large specimen container.

The cup had a hospital sticker on the side and a patient number written on it in ball point pen. The Luthier's was a little darker than Richard's with a different number and name written on it. The Luthier grabbed his cup and waited for Richard and Sheryl to join him.

"To your health!" he said, as Sheryl and he raised their containers up in front of them.

Upon seeing Richard's hesitation, the Luthier prodded him on, "As soon as you drink, I will tell you the second secret. It is worth it."

Richard thought it over for a moment before he raised his container and they all drank together.

The liquid was warm! He involuntarily spewed it out of his mouth and all over the table in front of him.

While Richard was wiping off his mouth the Luthier looked at Sheryl and said, "Wonderful and inspiring," holding up the glass for all to see.

"Though, possibly, a little too warm," he added as he looked at Sheryl with a shake of his head and a smile.

"Enough is enough!" Richard exclaimed, even though he realized it was just apple juice. "What are you getting at? What else are you going to make me eat?" asked Richard as he stood up from the table.

"Superb! Fantastic! Wonderful! Inspiring! I weep with joy at the very thought of it!" The Luthier stood and was almost yelling as his fiery eyes glared at Richard. "And yet that is what you want the critics to say?!"

Richard stood there trying to grasp what the Luthier was getting at. "I don't play my violin standing on a toilet!" declared Richard. "I don't make a clown of myself! And I don't..."

"Set the stage," interrupted Sheryl.

"The second secret is 'Set the Stage'," clarified the Luthier.

"Did you notice how quickly your opinion of us went from that of admiration and awe, to that of disgust and loathing? Stop and think before you say anything more. How long has it been since you sat in the chair in the dark and listened to me play the violin? Who did you think I was? What would you give for people to think of you that way and more?"

Then there was silence. The Luthier sat down again as he and Sheryl watched to see what he would do. Slowly Richard sat back down and the Luthier continued, "The drink in the parlor. Was it good?"

Richard slowly nodded as Sheryl reached under the table and lifted up a bottle of store-brand grape juice.

"It cannot be!" declared Richard.

"It is," replied the Luthier. "No virtuoso can take the leap and join Paganini as a Master Virtuoso without setting the stage."

Chapter 24: Setting The Stage

*I*t took Richard a long time to finish his dinner, but the Luthier insisted that it was necessary, "For the 'Master Virtuoso' must learn to judge a performance, regardless of the stage it is performed on."

The only change to the menu was a cool drink of their own grape juice in a blue, hand-blown glass, which Richard enjoyed even more than the first juice.

He also found it much easier to eat when he ignored the table or just closed his eyes as he chewed and swallowed.

After dinner, Richard and the Luthier sat across from each other at the picnic table and talked.

The Luthier began, "Some criticize Paganini for how he set the stage. Some say he started the rumors about himself to make him seem supernatural for his ego. Some say he powdered his face and darkened his eyes to make people feel possessed so they would 'have' to buy the expensive tickets. Some say he had assistants play notes on an organ slightly lower than the ear could detect to give the audience that eerie feeling that something was all around them for sensationalism. Some will say he had assistants open the heater vents or open windows at just the right time to imitate depression and tingling feelings so he could capitalize on them and exaggerate the mood."

"Are you suggesting I do these things?" asked Richard, remembering his feelings he had while he sat in the violin shop with his eyes closed.

"No. You cannot reinvent the wheel, you cannot

rediscover America, you cannot be the first man to step on the moon. You cannot be Paganini.

"You must use who you are, deep down inside, to succeed. Find out who you are, Richard Gaspar, and then use that to set the stage, and never perform until the stage is set."

Richard knew, deep down inside, that the words the Luthier was telling him were true. He remembered the day he played in the rest home, before Michelle held up the music in front of him. He knew he played his music well that day, but until she looked in his eyes he was nothing.

He knew he was the great violin player, 'Richard Gaspar', on the outside, but deep down inside he still knew he was 'nothing'.

Richard exited the hospital four weeks after Mrs. Becker had visited him. The nurses pushed him in a wheelchair even though he could manage by himself now. It was a cool and cloudy day with a small breeze that sent a chill through Richard as he was pushed out the doors and up to his parents' car which was parked by the curb.

"I think we should just go home," Richard's mother pleaded as he carefully climbed into the back seat.

"I never got to say good bye," Richard answered after the door was closed, and he leaned his forehead against the window and looked out.

No one said another word while they drove back to their small town.

As the car slowed down and entered the city limits, Richard's father tried reasoning with Richard again, "It's clear across town, Richard. We can take you there some other time, maybe even later this afternoon, after you get settled back in."

Richard answered his father with silence and his parents looked at each other in despair, knowing it was hopeless to try and talk him out of it. His father shook his head as he turned onto the street that led to the cemetery on the hill.

Richard pressed his forehead against the cool window and watched the familiar streets and houses pass by.

He looked at each and every sidewalk that they had walked down while they searched for new adventures. He looked down the streets as far as he could, knowing what was at the end of every one and he remembered what they had done there together. He looked up at the sky and the clouds from the car window and he thought of all the things Michelle had seen and said about clouds while they lay side by side on the grassy knoll in the park.

His thoughts darkened and started back into depression when he thought of the two months he spent entirely alone after the ferris wheel, and how his life became so empty that it was worthless to him.

Richard had managed to survive in the hospital. The new surroundings had not reminded him of Michelle and he had gotten by. At least it was somewhere they had not been together, so the hospital didn't have memories attached to it, good or bad. Now everything he saw was theirs, somewhere they had been or something they had shared together and it tormented him.

The car pulled up and stopped at the curb. Richard slowly opened the door of the car by himself and looked out across the tombstones. He had gone through some physical therapy already but he also had a long way to go. He was still very stiff every time he started to move and everything he did hurt.

Richard eased his stiff, sore limbs out of the back seat and slowly stood up. His whole body ached when he started to walk, but he soon limbered up a little while he followed his parents to the recently covered grave where Michelle was buried.

"Your father helped Mr. and Mrs. Ross sell the buffalo nickels so they could pay for the funeral and buy the headstone. It's the very nicest you could imagine and it should be placed in another week or two," his mother told him, as Richard walked up to the mound where a small brass plaque simply said, "Ross, Michelle," above some numbers and letters that represented the plot location.

Richard knelt beside the mound and put his hands on its side. He looked down at his badly scarred and misshapen arms and hands from the briar patch and closed his eyes as he remembered that day.

When he thought about the briar patch and the thorns tearing at his arms and legs he thought to himself, "I would do it again if I could only see Michelle one more time!"

Richard opened his eyes and looked up to the cloudy sky above him. "Why did this have to happen?" he asked God, if He were really there.

"Is there a God?" Richard questioned. "If there is, why would he take Michelle? Why take her from me just as we were free?"

Richard started sobbing and his parents both came up to him and softly put their hands on his shoulders.

"I am nothing without you, Michelle," he cried out loud. "Nothing," he said again, as he remembered the two months he had spent alone, without her.

Richard remembered how he was before he met Michelle. He remembered how he thought of no one but himself before that day, and now he thought of no one else but her, "And now she's gone!"

"There is no God!" Richard looked up and screamed, while shaking his fist. Then he looked back down at the mound and started digging into it with his bare hands.

His parents had to physically pull Richard off the mound and restrain him as he fought and screamed out of control. They had to drag him to the car by force and put him in the back seat. His father tightly held him while his mother drove the car back to the hospital and asked for a psychiatrist or any other kind of help they could give him.

That evening was Richard's first in the asylum and it took him almost two years before he said the words, "I am ready," and walked out the door.

Richard dropped his head into his hands while he sat at the picnic bench in the Luthier's dining room. Nothing had changed since the day he had fallen apart and broken down sobbing on the floor of the violin shop.

He knew his dream of the people hanging from the ceiling was gone, but now his heart was back, and it was broken and torn to shreds. Richard's body began to shake and his head started swimming while he sat in front of the Luthier.

He knew this was what the Luthier meant when he spoke of pulling his heart out of his chest and showing it to him before he died.

"Why must you torment me?" Richard sobbed, as he lifted his head and looked the Luthier in the eyes.

"I am only here to help," he replied.

"You keep tearing me apart inside. You give me hope, then you dash it to pieces. Over and over again."

Richard couldn't control himself. "I see you and your wife so happy together, then you remind me I am alone and that I am nothing. You give me hope only to tell me the solution is hopeless. No matter what you know or who you are, I just can't take it any more," and Richard put his head down on the table and cried.

The sun was behind the west mountain, but the sky was still light when Richard raised his head from off his arms and looked around. The large house was silent.

When he slowly stood and looked down at the picnic bench with the cat food cans still sitting there, he realized Sheryl and the Luthier were right. Everything surrounding the performance was as important as the performance itself, for the performer as well as the audience.

Every time he had stood on stage to perform it was for Michelle and to make her happy. And every time he looked out into the audience, Michelle was not there.

He used to dream of finishing his finest performance, and at the end of the fifth and final encore bow she would suddenly appear in front of him and give him a kiss. But now he realized that without her to inspire him before he went on stage, his music would always be hollow and devoid of feeling.

He may be the great Richard Gaspar, violin player, on the outside, but he was nothing inside. Nothing. Just like the thirteen-year-old boy playing the violin in his study before his music stand fell over.

He walked over to where they had sat and drunk the grape juice out of the hand-blown glasses earlier and silence hung in the air, thick as fog. He felt so alone.

He closed his eyes and listened more carefully. He listened, just as the Luthier had told him to in the violin shop; he closed his eyes and listened and waited.

Nothing was there.

He had never experienced this feeling of loneliness accompanied with total and absolute silence before. There were no cars driving by, no banging of doors, no people talking, no fans running, nothing.

Richard realized he 'was' alone.

He looked over to some pictures on the wall and saw Sheryl and the Luthier together. Then Richard looked toward the large front door and knew that if Michelle would walk through that door right now, his life would never have a moment without music and laughter again. He started to dream that it could happen; after all, this was the Luthier's house.

But after a few minutes had passed by, Richard realized that nothing was going to happen and he decided to walk outside. He swung the massive front door open and he thought he heard music, very faint and sweet.

"Come sit down, Richard," said the soft, sweet voice of Sheryl. She was sitting on a porch-swing looking up at him.

He slowly walked over and gently sat down beside her.

"Who was she?" Sheryl asked with a kind, understanding voice.

"Michelle Ross," was his reply. "The most perfect, wonderful girl in the world." When he looked at Sheryl's face, he added, "For me."

With a sweet, pleasant smile, Sheryl asked, "What happened?"

She asked in such a way that Richard could not refuse to tell her everything.

When Richard finished talking, Sheryl smiled with a look of understanding and comfort that soothed his fears and gave him more hope than all the years he had spent with psychiatrists.

"I am truly sorry you have had to go through what you have," she said. "If Jonathan died I know that I could never remarry. I know the feeling of true love. Legends talk of it. Novels write of it. Everyone hopes for it, but it is truly a rare gift and once you have it, nothing else will do."

"When I married Jonathan, I knew it was for keeps. There was no 'till death do us part' in our ceremony. As we knelt across the altar and took our vows, it was forever. We live and we will die, happily ever after. No matter what.

"I don't know what you think about life or God, but this I know. Life is not always fair. God allows some terrible things to happen in 'this' life. But there is more to you than just this physical body."

Then Sheryl placed her hand gently on top of Richard's. "And somehow, God will make it up to you, if you never give up."

Chapter 25: Dancing

*T*he violin started to take shape day by day. The blocks were glued to the mold and then they were shaped. The ribs were cut and scraped, then bent on a hot piece of metal called a bending iron until they fit the mold perfectly. Then the ribs were allowed to relax and they were bent again, until they would match the shape of the mold and blocks forever.

Everything the Luthier did seemed to be in expectation of forever. Richard had been giving a lot of thought to the words Sheryl had said while they sat on the porch together.

Richard asked the Luthier during one of his many visits to the shop, "How long should a master violin last?"

"If loved and cared for properly, at least five hundred years, if not forever."

After a minute the Luthier added, "I have also seen instruments destroyed in a single moment."

"What do you mean? Destroyed in a fire or wreck?" asked Richard.

Richard sat on a padded chair watching the Luthier carve the small channel around the edge of the violin's back where the three small strips of wood, called purfling, would be inlaid.

"That and other ways," replied the Luthier. "I have seen great instruments that touched me deeply and made the most beautiful music in the world go into the hands of people for only a moment and never be the same again. No matter how they are adjusted, no matter what strings are put on them, they never sing with their true voice again. Usually instruments can be brought back simply by being played on by someone who loves them, but I have also seen where they can not."

Richard could see the sadness in the Luthier's eyes; it was as though he were talking of a friend who had died. "Do you believe violins have souls?"

The Luthier looked back at Richard with a solemn look. "You have been dreaming again, haven't you?"

"Yes I have," was Richard's reply. Then he smiled at the Luthier and waited for his answer.

"I believe 'true master instruments' have something special. Call it a soul or whatever you like. Unless made as a copy or an inferior instrument made without love, each instrument has its own personality. It goes far beyond what I can do with chisels and gouges, scrapers and varnish brushes.

"I love making violins and I believe that what I do is a gift from God. I believe that every talent we possess is a gift from God, but I do not put the soul in the instrument. After all I can do to make an instrument the best I can, the most important part comes from God and the player.

"I *can* 'set the stage' if you will, but what truly matters comes after I lay down my tools. I take full responsibility for the quality of the instruments I make, but if there is something truly special there when it is played, it comes from the player."

Over the next week Richard settled into a routine of practicing in the morning, visiting the violin shop after lunch and then practicing in the evening until he retired. Each day he visited with the Luthier he saw the progress of the violin. It was his desire to see every step of the process.

The Luthier was the only one who worked on the instrument, just as Richard had imagined. Each day Richard would find him carving away the surface of the wood, revealing the shape that was taking form beneath.

One afternoon, as Richard walked in the door, he was

surprised to see Sheryl standing at a large workbench, ready to assist the Luthier. Richard walked over and they seemed to ignore him so they could concentrate on the task at hand.

The overhead fan was off and the shop was very warm. Suddenly, they both pulled two glue brushes out of a glue-pot and started around the violin; the Luthier working around the edge of the back and Sheryl on the ribs. The brushes raced with incredible speed and fluidity and they finished the task in only seconds.

The Luthier then flipped over the ribs and had them accurately placed and aligned on the back with the help of small, wood, locating pins. The assembled pieces sat in a fixture like Richard had never seen before and the Luthier had the top of the fixture securely fastened in another instant, finishing the job.

Before Richard realized what was going on, his violin sat with the back completely glued to the ribs. It amazed him how they worked together and completed a task in seconds that he had seen take as much as an hour in other shops.

"There are only two operations that require another person's assistance in making my violins and I always use my most trusted assistant," the Luthier told Richard as he looked at Sheryl with a thankful smile. "I trust her with my life as well as my instruments."

Over the next few days, when Richard took his afternoon break from practicing and drove out to the violin shop, he started having strange feelings that he couldn't explain.

The Luthier noticed the change in Richard and he stopped working one afternoon so he could turn to him and say, "To watch one's companion for life being operated on is difficult, if you will allow me the analogy.

"Many physicians will not operate on their own wife. When they are finished operating it becomes very difficult for them to look at their beautiful wife and not see her as veins, muscles and tissues."

Richard nodded his head and he started to understand.

The Luthier continued, "It is also difficult for some men

to watch a doctor give their wife a physical."

"I suppose you are right," agreed Richard.

He had always looked at the great 'master violins' as a complete work of art. This was the first time he had ever seen the pieces of one lying separately on a table. And knowing that the pieces of wood sitting on the bench in front of him would become his instrument, and that he must look at it as a work of art when it was completed, he agreed with the Luthier's analogies.

"If you feel you need to ask anything or would just like to visit, you are always welcome. But you may find it more comfortable for you if you only come and watch when it feels right to you."

"I believe you are right," replied Richard. "Besides I have wanted to do some sight-seeing and maybe even shoot a round of golf."

Then Richard left the Luthier to the task at hand and headed back to St. George.

Richard enjoyed travelling around Southern Utah each day when he took his breaks from practicing during the next two weeks. It seemed to breathe new life into him as he looked out across what they called 'Color Country'.

There were a few people who recognized him as he drove and hiked around, but for the most part, he blended in and could go about anywhere and be treated just like everyone else.

"It feels good for a change," he thought to himself as he looked out over a colorful, rocky valley from the top of a small mesa he had climbed. Then, as he thought of the concert stage with its excitement, along with the attention and applause, he thought, "But I wouldn't want to get used to it. At least not just yet."

Almost every night, as Richard laid his head down on his pillow, he dreamed. Most of his dreams were about Michelle and the good times they had together, while other dreams he had made no sense at all, but they still left him with a pleasant feeling when he awoke.

At the end of his third week in Southern Utah, he had a

very special dream. It was even more vivid and real than the dream about the people who hung from the ceiling. Only this dream was different. Much different.

In his dream, he awoke from a long sleep in the middle of the desert. The sun came up and soon the sand was scorching hot. He became almost mad with thirst while he still lay on the parched ground, looking around at the cactus and sagebrush. He got up, wondering what he was doing here, and started walking across the endless expanse of sand until his legs gave out.

He fell on his knees and started to crawl, while the hot sand burned his hands and knees. Just when he felt like he could go no further, he looked out across the desert and saw a woman. He could barely see her at first because she was so far away and the heat waves rising from the sand blurred his vision.

Richard squinted his eyes and finally noticed that the woman was spinning around, far off in the distance, and slowly moving his way. After a minute or two he could tell that the woman didn't have any clothes on, not even shoes to protect her feet, but it didn't seem to matter to her as she danced across the sand. She held both arms outstretched and her head was tilted back with her eyes closed. She smiled while she spun around and around, wandering across the sand.

Richard felt ashamed as he watched her, but he couldn't look away. He was so miserable and she looked so happy, dancing across the sand with her eyes closed and a smile on her face.

The sand was still scorching hot and it blistered Richard's hands and knees. The sun grew even hotter as she approached him and it beat down on Richard until he was ready to completely give out. His arms were ready to buckle, but he kept watching her come closer and closer, still spinning and smiling with her arms stretched out and her eyes closed. Her soft, swirling hair would have reached her waist if she were to stop spinning.

He recognized the pure, golden-brown color. It was longer now, but it still had the small curls on the end.

Then, when she turned around, Richard could see she had a birthmark on the left side of her stomach.

She twirled around for the very last time and she softly whispered the word, "Free."

Richard woke up late that morning and he immediately jumped in the Blazer and headed up the freeway toward Leeds. He had the windows open and he noticed that the desert air was already getting hot when he pulled onto the dirt and gravel road that lead toward the violin shop.

Richard pulled the Blazer to a stop and looked up.

He couldn't see anything on the roof from where he was, so he threw open the door of his Blazer and ran over to the Luthier's ladder.

"It must be here, I just know it," he told himself as he worked his way up each rung.

He worried about what the Luthier might think when he heard him climbing up the ladder, but he didn't care and he didn't let it stop him.

Richard's eyes peered over the edge of the roof and he could see the beautiful silhouette of his white violin against the azure sky. It was soaking in the rays of the hot, desert sun.

The violin was a beautiful, creamy-white color, waiting for its first coat of varnish. It had a flowing shape and a beautiful form without a blemish or stain on it, except on the left side of the belly, where the wood was a little darker and had a distinct discoloration or 'birthmark'.

Chapter 26: The White Violin

The white violin was more elegant and beautiful than Richard could have imagined.

Its form was perfect, with sweeping curves and style. Richard realized that, just like in his dream about Michelle, he could not stop looking at the violin while it stood in front of him on its stand. It seemed so beautiful and happy soaking in the rays of the sun. He seemed drawn to it and found he could not resist.

He finished climbing the ladder and slowly walked over to the violin. He knelt down beside it, then reached out his hand to rotate it on the stand. The white violin slowly turned and to Richard it seemed so happy and free basking in the sun. He knelt down, mesmerized, just staring at the violin while he turned it slowly around and around.

After a while, when he finally realized that the hot sun was beating down on him, Richard reluctantly stood up and walked back over to the ladder.

There had been music coming from inside the violin shop while he was on the roof looking at his violin and now, as a new song started to play, it caught his attention. He stopped partway down the ladder and listened. Its melody floated through the walls of the shop and into Richard's soul.

He recognized the song before the words even began. It was one of Michelle's songs that he had given her for Christmas. He could still remember the cover of the sheet music. It was a picture of the three 'Lettermen' sitting against a boat washed up on shore with the blue sky behind them...

    Young and foolish,
    Why is it wrong to be
    young and foolish...

Richard knew every word by memory and found himself softly repeating each one while he thought about Michelle.

    ...smiling in the sunlight,
    laughing in the rain,
    I wish that we were young and foolish again.

As the words drifted away, Richard stared back up at the violin and its birthmark and a thought crossed his mind. He started to wonder what was really going on. He wondered if he was still lying in the hotel room back in St. George, dreaming all of this.

Or, he thought, as his mind wandered still farther back, was he still lying on the bed in the hotel room the night of his last concert after talking with Janice and Julia from the Herald. Had Sam's words about 'needing' something triggered his mind and started him dreaming again?

Or, was this some kind of joke or conspiracy among his parents and friends? They all knew what songs he had given to Michelle. They all knew his feelings about her. Could they even have talked to Joe and Margie Ross and found out about Michelle's birthmark?

Then as he thought about Mark and Cercie, his mother and father, Michelle's parents and Sam, he realized they would never even consider being involved with anything like this after the torment he went through in the asylum. He felt ashamed for even thinking it as he climbed back down the ladder.

"So what is going on?" he asked himself, as he slowly walked back to the Blazer and sat down. "Is this Luthier more than just a man? Is this all some kind of miracle?"

Richard thought it over and figured it was probably best

if he just drove back to the hotel so he could think about everything before talking to the Luthier again. He put the keys in the ignition and started the Blazer.

He started to back out as he looked from the small flashlight hanging from the key chain to the white violin on the roof, and he realized he had to know! He had to know 'now', and he knew that there was a man on the other side of that door who had all the answers!

Richard didn't know what he felt as he turned the knob on the door that would lead him to the Luthier. He felt he had to know; he also felt an uncontrollable curiosity that had to be satisfied. He felt raging anger and frustration, determination, love and hate. He felt every emotion possible as he walked in the door, except...sympathy.

Richard opened the door to the shop and started walking toward the Luthier, sitting at his varnish bench surrounded by all kinds of varnish making materials. He was bent over with his head lying on his arms like he was asleep.

The Luthier hadn't even responded to Richard, or looked up when he opened the door and walked in. Richard walked closer and looked down at the Luthier as the next song on the record player started to play.

The Luthier remained at his workbench with his head lying in his arms, but now Richard could tell that he was crying, shaking his head in torment and writhing in pain.

After only a few notes, Richard understood. He remembered the last time he had heard the song and he started to shake, though he maintained control. He remembered his own torment and despair while he listened to the song coming from the janitor's portable radio in the asylum...

Richard was lying on his bed, shivering in the middle of the night. He was all alone and he couldn't think about anything but Michelle, but when he thought of her now, all he could see was her still, lifeless face in his arms.

When he finally became exhausted enough to fall asleep, nightmares tormented him.

He was halfway between consciousness and sleep that night when the music started floating down the hall...

> Once upon a time,
> A girl with moonlight in her eyes
> put her hand in mine
> and said she loved me so,
> but that was once upon a time
> very long ago...

Most of the time Richard spent in the asylum was a hazy blur in the back of his mind now, but he still remembered 'that' night as he laid on the cold, hard bed listening to the words of the song.

> ...how the breeze
> rustled through her hair,
> how we always met
> as though tomorrow wasn't there...

"Stop it!" Richard screamed, as he put his hands over his ears and got out of bed.

> ...we were young and didn't have a care,
> where did it go?...

"Stop it! I can't take any more!" he yelled at the janitor, whose radio was playing the song while it sat on his cleaning cart. The janitor just continued mopping the hall floor, not seeming to understand or care what Richard was screaming about.

> Once upon a time...

"Stop it!" Richard cried, as he burst into tears and started banging his head against the bars in the door trying to get the memory of Michelle's death out.

The janitor even turned the volume up and the song kept on playing, in spite of Richard's screams and protests. The words seemed to go on forever and the janitor ignored him even more while Richard sobbed and continued to beat his head against the bars until his face started to bleed.

> ...everything was ours,
> how happy we were then,
> but somehow once upon a time
> never comes again.

Even when the music stopped playing on the radio, it kept running through Richard's mind. It tormented him over and over again as he dropped to the floor and beat himself unconscious against the door in a pool of blood and tears.

"Richard is an extreme risk patient here at the asylum. He has tried to hurt himself again and again ever since he came here, and last night we believe he tried to kill himself," the doctor told George and Alaine Gaspar when they questioned the straightjacket and restraining bands the hospital had put on Richard.

The doctor continued, "He was making progress until last night, but his reasoning capabilities have now become disrupted to the point of requiring constant sedation."

Richard's parents looked at each other in disbelief and Alaine broke down in George's arms and cried.

"This latest outbreak seems to stem from a certain song that was played on the radio by a janitor here last night. The song was, "Once Upon a Time.""

Richard thought of the pain and misery he suffered while spending the next two years in the asylum. Memories, nightmares and hopelessness.

"Somehow," Richard thought, "the Luthier knows."

All of his doubts and questions turned to sympathy for the Luthier, as he remembered the two years of torment he spent in the asylum. Richard thought of his nightmare again and the word 'please' ran through his mind. He looked up at the wood hanging from the ceiling of the shop and realized what the Luthier saw every time he looked at it.

Even though Richard had said the words, "I am ready," the day he left the asylum, he had gone back to the park so he could stand between the two trees and remember Michelle before he got on with his life.

Before he even entered the gate, he could see a large playground right where the two trees had once stood. There were children playing in it and somehow that seemed to soften his grief, but it still left him with a hollow feeling that he had never been able to completely get over.

Richard thought of how much the Luthier loved the trees themselves and he wondered what the Luthier felt when he had to chop them down and split them up in order for him to make his violins many years later.

"Somehow the Luthier knows and feels what I went through and felt during those two years in the asylum and all the years since," Richard thought, as he slowly backed away.

The Luthier still sat at his bench with his head down, weeping, while he listened to the song.

It reminded Richard of the waitress the Luthier had talked about in the restaurant. Richard remembered the picture of her in his mind as she lay sobbing on the table after the Luthier had hurt her, and now Richard felt he understood the words that the Luthier had said, "It is impossible to understand what those that serve us go through."

Before the last words of the song had died away, Richard was in the Blazer driving back to St. George and his hotel room. He knew he would not be back until the violin was finished.

Chapter 27: The Violin

"Your violin is ready for you, Mr. Gaspar," came the Luthier's voice over the telephone.

"It seems strange to hear the Luthier talk so formally again," thought Richard, and he simply replied, "Thank you," and hung up the phone.

He packed all of his belongings and checked every square inch of the hotel room to make sure he was not leaving anything behind. He folded up his music stand and put all of the sheet music together for the concert and he thought, "I'm ready."

Over the past few weeks, since he had talked with Sheryl, he had done a lot of thinking. "There is more to life than just what we see around us and somehow God will make it right in the end."

He also thought about the art of violin making over the last couple of weeks while he waited for the white violin to be varnished and strung up. The Luthier's ability to take trees that had been dead for ages and seemingly bring them back to life as great musical instruments that could touch people's lives and thrill audiences gave him hope.

He then thought of himself, and the good that he could do using 'his' talents to make the world a little better place with his music; just like Michelle had done for him with her life.

He felt like he had slowly regained his heart as he dedicated each song to Michelle. He also found, as the days went by, that he only thought and dreamed of the good things now, the fun times they had when she was alive, and especially, their first kiss.

Without the nightmare to haunt him anymore and with finally finding someone who could sympathize with his pain and loss, it was as though Richard's mind had finally been cleared of all his bad memories and regrets and he could finally get on with his life, emotionally as well as professionally.

Richard grabbed the door handle and turned it while he said to himself, "I know who I am. I am Richard Gaspar, and I can live with that now."

He held up his hands in front of his face and looked at them and said, "There is more to us than just this physical body, and someday I will see Michelle smiling and running and we will be together again. Until that day, I will live my life to make her happy and I will make her proud of me!"

Richard drove up the freeway with a smile of contentment. He wasn't worried at all about the violin.

"Maybe," he thought, "the instrument really doesn't matter."

He had noticed that his Bergonzi had started sounding better and better as his outlook on life did and he was now playing better than he had ever played in his life. He had even given a lot of thought to how he could 'set the stage' in a way that could be acceptable to the critics, while thrilling the audience.

As he pulled off the freeway and onto the Main Street of Leeds, he felt like he was ready to take on the world.

"Even if the violin isn't as good as the Guarneri, it has all been worth it. Two years in the asylum and possibly a hundred-thousand dollars over the years for therapy never made me feel like this."

Suddenly it struck him. "The Luthier never told me the third secret!"

It was only then, that Richard realized he still 'needed' something. He thought of the Luthier playing in the violinshop, and now he remembered how each note had sounded to him. Even with the stage set, the notes themselves were different, and he knew it.

Terror seized Richard, and he thought, "No, I still don't play like the Luthier, let alone Paganini."

He knew he was good, but when he stopped and compared himself to Paganini, or even the Luthier again, he knew he still fell short.

"And yet the Luthier said I was better than him! What is the last secret? Will he tell it to me now?"

Richard settled back down a little as he pulled onto the old dirt and gravel road and looked over to his case that contained his Bergonzi and he spoke out loud, "What is the last secret? What do we lack, old girl?" He smiled at the case and he wondered what the answer was, as he pulled up to the violin shop.

"He must tell me! I have to know!" he thought as he picked up his Bergonzi and walked to the door for perhaps the last time.

"I wonder what he will be like today?" Richard thought, as he remembered the angry face of Mr. Haito before he saw the swords. "Whatever he does, I'm going to remain calm and smile. I want that last secret!" Richard said to himself as he opened the door and walked in.

"Good afternoon, Richard," the Luthier greeted him.

"Good afternoon, Luthier," Richard replied with a smile, then shook his hand.

The Luthier wasted no time and he turned and gestured with his hand toward the bench against the wall where there was a violin case waiting.

It was dark-blue, trimmed with brown leather and it had sterling-silver latches and hinges. It was very similar to the light-blue case Cercie bought, only this one was much darker and had a style and flair of sophistication.

"How does it sound?" anxiously asked Richard. "Is it louder, fuller and sweeter?"

After a slight pause, he added, "Is it what I need?"

"I do not know how it sounds," replied the Luthier, "I have not played it."

Richard's jaw dropped. "Then how do you know it's ready?"

"Because you are ready, and it is what you need," answered the Luthier. Then he said, "You would always regret this day if I, or anyone else ever played upon this instrument before you, and before you open the case you must promise me that no one else will ever play this violin but you, for as long as you live."

Richard knew the story well. In 1802 Paganini was twenty years old and had an addiction to gambling. He had gambled away his fine Amati the afternoon of a concert and frantically inquired all over town, trying to borrow a fine violin for the evening.

Finally he found a businessman from Livorno who possessed a very fine Joseph Guarneri. Paganini was allowed to borrow it, but only on strict conditions: The owner would be given the front center seat during the concert, and after the concert the instrument was to be handed directly back to him, immediately after the last note was played.

Paganini agreed to the conditions and the concert went on that night with him playing upon the Guarneri.

It was said that no one had ever heard a performance with such life and expression before, that the audience was brought grovelling under his feet as he played upon the Guarneri.

When the concert was over, Paganini walked to the front of the stage and handed the violin back to its owner, who refused it and said, "Never shall any other hands defile this instrument! It is yours if you will promise that no other mortal shall ever play upon it."

Nicolo immediately promised that no one else would ever play upon the violin and the ownership of the instrument passed to him while he still stood on stage. It was Paganini's solo instrument from that night until his death and in his will he gave it to the city of his birth on the condition that it never be played again.

Richard did not understand the reason for the promise, but he felt he would as soon as he played upon this instrument in front of him.

"No one else will ever play upon this violin," Richard

promised. Then, without any more hesitation, he turned toward the violin case and opened it.

Richard's eyes immediately looked up into the lid. Imbedded in the top of the dark, Prussian-blue velvet interior were bright, shiny, buffalo nickels that looked like stars in the night sky. Richard could not help the tears from flowing down his cheeks as he stood and looked at them and thought of Michelle the night they gave each other everything they owned.

Cradled in the soft, dark-blue velvet, looking up at him and the nickels, was the most beautiful, golden-brown violin he had ever seen in his life.

The Luthier silently walked over and sat down on his chair and closed his eyes, leaving Richard standing there alone with the violin.

Richard's hands trembled as he lifted the violin out of its case and turned it over in his hands. Somehow he knew the flames in the maple would get narrower together at the waist. He looked at the curly maple back as he moved it back and forth under the lights. The colors of the flames changed just as her hair had from sunlight to moonlight.

He looked over to the Luthier sitting on his chair and said, "Thank you."

The Luthier looked up. A smile and a nod were his reply and he held out his hand as a gesture to play it. Then the Luthier closed his eyes again and listened.

Richard instinctively reached for the A string tuning peg to see if it was in tune before he began. As he touched the peg he felt Michelle's soft hand touch his. He flinched but he did not let go because her hand felt so soft and familiar to his touch.

"If this is a dream, I refuse to ever wake up," he told himself.

Then he picked up the bow. Engraved on each side of the frog was a tree. Richard no longer questioned anything; he believed. He closed his eyes and started to play.

As the first full, beautiful note rang out from the

instrument, Michelle stood before him with a smile, looking into his eyes. She was wearing the beautiful summer dress she had worn when they first kissed.

He kept his eyes closed, and as he continued to play, she walked slowly toward him and gave him a kiss. He could feel her soft lips touch his as he stood there.

He drew the bow lightly across the strings and he could feel her breath against his cheek. It had been so long! He kept playing the mellow passage, savoring each note as she kept moving her lips against his and kissed him that much more.

When the music began to move, she stepped back and danced and twirled in a way that made Richard realize that she was a mature woman now. As the tempo raced she threw out her arms and spun with her hair flying around her. She made a breeze that Richard could feel swirling around him from every direction.

He played the flying spiccato and she appeared in a Spanish dress and tapped her heels sharply on the floor, following his every note to perfection. On and on he played, knowing that every note that sang out from the violin now had something more than any other instrument he had ever played before.

He played a mournful song and tears of joy and happiness filled their eyes together as they experienced all their lonely memories of the past with each other, but now they were just memories.

He couldn't stop yet, he thought. There were so many other things to experience but one more thing would have to do for now. He brought the tempo up to moderato and the volume to mezzo piano and they talked.

"It has been so long."

"Yes," she answered. "I have missed you."

"Where have you been all these years?" Richard asked her, looking into her eyes.

"Waiting for you," was her reply.

"Will you be mine forever?" Richard asked.

"I always have been and always will be. You only needed to believe," she said. She kissed him good-bye as the song ended and he stopped playing.

Richard slowly opened his eyes and looked over to where the Luthier sat with his eyes closed.

"Master Luthier, I believe I know the last secret to becoming a Master Virtuoso," Richard said, as the Luthier opened his eyes and looked at him.

"Go on."

"True love," he replied.

The Luthier smiled and said, "Yes, it is and always will be."

A feeling of satisfaction and contentment seemed to fill Richard's soul as the Luthier confirmed what he already knew.

Richard now looked down at his instrument and started to wonder so many things. He was still thinking about the words Sheryl had spoken to him, that had given him so much hope, and now he wondered if the Luthier had any more answers for him.

Finally he asked the Luthier, "When I die?..."

"She will be there waiting for you," he answered.

"And until then?" Richard asked, still not sure if Michelle would be with him only this once, or if she would be there every time he played the violin.

"Never let her memory die," the Luthier answered with a smile. "It is now up to you."

Richard gently placed the violin back into its dark-blue case and looked at the small discoloration in the wood. It was still visible on the left side of the belly through the highly transparent varnish. It made him think of what had really just happened to him today and over the past six weeks.

He had seen and heard so many things that no one could be expected to believe, yet he believed them all. Richard knew it was time for him to leave and get on with his life, but he also knew that he could not leave until he had the answer to one more question.

He turned to the Luthier and asked, "Master Luthier, where did you get the two trees that this violin is made from?"

The Luthier nodded his head and smiled at Richard as he answered, "A very dear friend of mine called me when he heard they were going to chop two trees down in his small town to make room for a playground."

Richard started to cry.

"This friend had helped me search for violin wood in Canada a long time ago when I first started collecting wood for making violins. He called me and told me that these two trees were very special to him and that I 'had' to make a violin out of them someday.

"He met me at the park and even helped me cut and split the two trees himself, even though he was almost ninety years old at the time. He insisted that he 'had' to help because he was doing it for a very special friend of his that had died.

"He died also, the very next year, and the wood has been hanging from my ceiling ever since. That was over fifteen years ago."

"What was his name?" asked Richard, with tears streaming down his face.

The great Richard Gaspar who had learned to stifle and hide his feelings over the years had no desire to even try to hide his emotions now.

While he waited for the Luthier to reply, Richard closed his eyes and the picture of an old grey-haired man wearing a plaid shirt and green pants with suspenders appeared in his mind.

"His name was Veryl Edwards," replied the Luthier.

Richard now understood his dreams that had made no sense to him before. They were of an old man walking away from the park where the two trees had once stood. The dream ended with the old man leaning on an old twisty cane and looking back into the park with a smile on his face at where the two trees had once stood.

Richard fastened the latches on the case and pulled out his checkbook. He lifted his pen that he always signed his signatures with and he wrote down the date and signed his name.

"How much is the total?" Richard asked.

"Thirty-five thousand, as we agreed," replied the Luthier with a smile and a bow.

"I can never thank you enough," Richard said, as he finished filling in the check and set it on the table. Then he silently opened the door and walked out.

The Luthier didn't even look at the check as he reached down and picked it up. Instead, he looked up at the other pieces of wood that hung from the ceiling with a far away look in his eye. After a few minutes he walked over to the counter and placed it in his cash drawer.

Just before he slid the drawer shut he looked down at the check and a smile spread across his face.

It read:

Pay to the order of:

Jonathan Dewey Luthier $70,000.00
Seventy thousand dollars and no 'sense'.

$35,000.00 for violin + tip   Richard Gaspar

Chapter 28: Years Later

Carnegie Hall was packed. It was always packed when 'he' came to perform and this would be his final performance in the United States for over a year.

"Will you look at this crowd?!" Julia had to raise her voice and turn toward Janice just to be heard above the roar of the excited audience, even though they sat right next to each other.

"I hear they are scalping tickets outside for over seven hundred dollars!" Janice replied.

"Three chartered jets arrived from London this afternoon for the performance tonight," Julia commented.

"Unbelievable," Janice replied.

Julia looked down at her pen and notepad and commented, "His performances are so inspiring and enthralling, they are beyond description now.

"Each performance is more, the most, the most-est-est-est. I ran out of superlatives and adjectives and superlative-adjectives long ago. What will I write for tomorrow's edition, Janice? 'His performance last night was the very most, unbelievably, superlativest-est-est...?' What is a critic to do?"

Julia and Janice just laughed and smiled together.

"I remember when you used to use adjectives such as 'fitting', 'appropriate' and 'predictable'. Remember when you even told him to his face, '...lacking full expression. Technically perfect, but I've had better'?"

"Oh, oww, don't remind me. I wonder if he still remembers that? That 'was' before he acquired the violin he plays now, you know."

Then a woman sitting on Julia's right said, "I heard it's the perfect violin Stradivari kept on his wall all those years until he died, then it was handed down, sealed in its case until Richard bought it for an obscene amount of money from one of Stradivari's descendants who got desperate, and that is why it looks so beautiful and fresh and sounds the way it does."

A man sitting behind the woman chimed in, "I heard Richard Gaspar is really a descendant of Joseph Guarneri and that it was 'his' finest violin. Then it was handed down from generation to generation until one of his descendants was worthy enough to play it."

Janice turned and said, "It is a well known fact that Richard Gaspar has never released any information about the violin he plays on. We are from the Herald and we would know."

All the people around them went quiet for a minute, then a woman in front of them turned around and said, "It's also a well known fact that he never allows anyone else to see it except on stage. In fact, while he performs for the audience, there are two armed guards back stage protecting just the case!"

Most of the people around her gasped in amazement and looked to Julia and Janice for a reply. They both nodded their heads simultaneously.

The woman turned back around and asked, "And what does he say each time he pauses on stage, just before he kisses his violin and gives it 'that' look?"

Janice answered, "No one knows." Then she continued in a dreamy voice, "But I wish he would give 'me' that look."

All of the women within hearing distance blushed in agreement and they quieted down for a minute with a smile and a far away look in each of their eyes.

Janice finished reading her program, then she flipped it over and looked at the back page. For the past two years the back page of all of Richard Gaspar's programs were blank except for three small words in the center, "Thank you, Sam."

The woman on the right started talking again, "I hear he practices almost constantly when he is alone. Isn't it funny that Paganini never had to practice at all?"

A man directly behind Julia replied, "He doesn't practice. The last time he was here in New York I had the room right next to him all three days. He would never play the concert music. He only played love songs and happy tunes; he even played popular and rock and roll! And every note he played was even more passionate and beautiful than at his concerts. If I had made a recording I could be a wealthy man today."

The woman on his left added, "It's true. I hear he cannot get enough of the violin and he plays it constantly. He is either madly in love with it or possessed by it. I wonder if that's why he was in an asylum for all those years?"

A woman beside her added, "I hear the asylum is where he learned to play so well. After all, all great artists are a little crazy. I'm surprised he is as great as he is for as little time as he spent in..."

The lights flashed and the audience went silent. No one dared utter a word or make a sound. No one wanted to miss one moment as 'he' came out on stage.

Richard Gaspar slowly walked out on the concert stage carrying a dark-blue violin case, followed by two armed guards. They all stopped together, just off center stage, where Richard ceremoniously turned around and placed the case into the outstretched arms of the two guards. Each of the guards held one arm under the case and then grasped their respective end with their other hand, holding each of the handles there as securely as possible before offering it back to Richard for him to open.

The concert hall took on the feel of a crypt. Richard slowly and ceremoniously unfastened the solid silver latches one at a time, each snap sending a chill through the crowd. As the case opened, a rush of fresh air seemed to fill the hall and a gasp was heard from a woman in the audience.

He pulled out the engraved, silver rosin holder, that most

in the audience believed was owned by Paganini himself, and opened it. With only two perfect swipes of the bow across the rosin he set the silver container back into the case and turned to the violin. Every eye was focused on Richard in his long, old-fashioned, Italian tails that seemed to give him the distinguished look of a stately gentleman at one moment and that of a romantic knave the next.

An audible gasp was released from the entire audience as he quickly lifted the violin from its case and held it up in the lights. Its golden-brown stripes of color could be seen clear from the back of the hall.

The two guards ceremoniously closed the lid and marched backstage, where they would stand the entire concert, guarding it with their lives. Richard walked over to center stage, holding the violin like it was life itself.

It had not happened in more than a hundred years. Many women in the audience fainted just at the thought of what was going to happen next.

Richard gazed down at the violin with a look in his eye that was the envy of every woman in the concert hall. Many said it was the look of 'true love', that only a few women in the history of the world have ever experienced that look, and he gave it to his violin before each concert.

The audience hushed into silence while he whispered the words, those words that only his violin would ever hear…

"I, Richard Gaspar, truly love you, Michelle Ross, and I always will. I will live my life to make 'you' happy and will love no other."

Richard reached into his vest pocket and pulled out an old, silver ring, set with a large, oval-shaped ruby as he glanced up at the audience with a mischievous grin.

He slid the ring onto his wedding finger and looked back down at his violin with a passionate gleam in his eye.

"And I promise to be good."

Then he sealed it with a kiss.

Epilogue

There is another world within our own just waiting for us.

To order autographed copies of "Two Trees"

Please send $12.95 for each book, along with $2.50 postage and handling for the first copy and $1.50 postage and handling for each additional copy.

Example:
1 book = $12.95 + $2.50 shipping and handling = $15.45 total

2 books = $12.95 X 2 + $4.00 S+H = $29.90

3 books = $12.95 X 3 + $5.50 S+H = $44.35

add $14.45 for each additional book incl. shipping (up to 12)

All orders of 12 books or more are $12.95 (each book) and receive free shipping and handling.

Signature will appear on the title page unless otherwise specified.
For special inscriptions or dedications up to fifteen words, please add $3.00 per book and write neatly.

Please send check, money order, or credit card number (Mastercard, Visa, Discover, American Express) along with the card's expiration date.

No cash or C.O.D.'s will be accepted.
For quickest delivery, please use your credit card.

Expect delivery within 3-5 weeks, or sooner with credit card orders.

Kevin Lee Luthier and Lee Instruments reserve the right to change the price and availability at any time and for any reason. (Though things usually only get better with time at the violin shop.)

Or order from our website:

kevinleeluthier.com or leeinstruments.com

Comments about the books are welcome at: leeinst@infowest.com

Send orders and make all checks payable to:

Lee Instruments
P.O. Box 460999
Leeds, Ut. 84746-999

Name of book:_____ # of copies_____

Total amount, including shipping: $_____

Payment: Mastercard ___ Visa ___ Discover___

American Express ____ Check ____ Money Order ____

Credit card# _____

Expiration Date: _____

Signature (with credit card):_____

Name:_____

Address:_____

City:_____ State:_____

Zip code:_____

Special requests or
comments:_____

_____

_____
Large, color, trifold brochures for the violin shop are also
available for $5.00 ea (shipping incl).   # of brochures _____
(Just add dollar amount to that of books above).
Please realize that apprentice instruments are currently $5,000.00 -
$10,000.00 while master instruments with case and bow range from
$35,000.00 - $85,000.00 as of Spring 2001.

Authorization to copy 'this' page is granted without copyright
infringement for ordering purposes only.

...and please tell a friend.

Next in the Luthier's Diary Series:
Book 2

Choice of Loves

Even a beautiful woman can grow old, waiting for her dreams to come true.

Mary Anderson has 'saved herself' and waited most of her life, looking for the 'perfect man': a 'knight in shining armor', 'prince charming' and 'superman', all wrapped into one handsome package. She is still desperately clinging to her dream until the day she looks into the eyes of "...a drunk, sleazy guy in black leather..." and then must decide between her principles and her passionate 'love at first sight'.

Steve Miller is a lone, desperate man whose life would be considered a total waste by many people's standards. Neglected and abused as a child, he grew up to be one of the toughest Marines in Viet Nam. Now, haunted by his past, he decides to order a master violin from the Luthier while he searches for the greatest father in the world.

...the story of a man who finds himself.